Praise for

'*Nest* is a gently persuasive novel that leaves you richer for having seen with the eyes of a naturalist, entering an environment where the life force is palpable'
Australian Book Review

'a testament to her talent as a nature writer . . . [a] truly rich novel'
Sydney Morning Herald

'entrancing'
Adelaide Advertiser

'This gentle, introspective novel will delight . . . Inga Simpson writes wondrously.'
★★★★
Good Reading

'engaging'
Courier-Mail

'It's a joy to linger with Jen . . . life-affirming on its own terms.'
★★★★
Books+Publishing

'*Nest* is a delightful and uplifting read.'
Readings

'a thoroughly enjoyable, uplifting read from one of the most creative nature writers of our time.'
MiNDFOOD

INGA SIMPSON

Nest

hachette
AUSTRALIA

hachette
AUSTRALIA

First published in Australia and New Zealand in 2014
by Hachette Australia
(an imprint of Hachette Australia Pty Limited)
Level 17, 207 Kent Street, Sydney NSW 2000
www.hachette.com.au

This edition published in 2017

10 9 8 7 6 5 4 3 2 1

National Library of Australia
Cataloguing-in-Publication data:

Simpson, Inga.
Nest/Inga Simpson.

978 0 7336 3740 7 (paperback)

Missing children – Queensland – Fiction.

A823.4

Cover illustration by Emma Kelly
Cover image courtesy of Shutterstock
Cover design by Christabella Designs
Author photograph courtesy of Claire Plush
Typeset in Granjon LT Std by Bookhouse, Sydney
Printed and bound in Australia by McPherson's Printing Group

MIX
Paper from
responsible sources
FSC® C001695

The paper this book is printed on is certified against the
Forest Stewardship Council® Standards. McPherson's Printing
Group holds FSC® chain of custody certification SA-COC-005379.
FSC® promotes environmentally responsible, socially beneficial
and economically viable management of the world's forests.

For Nike

The character study of the bird is beyond the mazes of classification, beyond the counting of bones, out of the reach of the scalpel and the literature of the microscope.

Mabel Osgood Wright, *The Friendship of Nature*

Wing

Yellow

She was trying to capture the wild. The secret to what made it unique and other. She had been trying her whole life.

Today it was the eastern yellow robins bathing. Of all the birds, they were the most ridiculous, pitching chest-first into the water and shaking themselves into fluffy rounds until their eyes and legs disappeared. Even with the softest pencil, she couldn't achieve the same effect on the page.

The more brazen yellow of Singapore daisy – on the run at the edge of the lawn – occupied her peripheral vision, reminding her of all the things she should be doing now the weather had cooled.

She had forgotten, during the years she had been away, how much work a property was in this climate. There was always something needing her attention, which was fine with her most days; it wasn't as if there was anyone else to give it to.

'We get our hundred inches a year,' the agent had said, not realising she knew the majority of it came down over one or two months in summer, which, while keeping everything green and lush outside, also turned every formerly living thing inside – wood, leather, cane – green with mould. The sheer volume of water washed away driveways and vegetable beds, submerging roads and train lines. All the same, there was something satisfying about living in a place where you could still be cut off from the world. And autumn, winter and spring were close to perfect.

The trees gathered round, their trunks a steady grey-brown. Sometimes she suspected they shuffled closer during the night, just an inch or so, rearranging their roots around rocks and soil. In the morning sun, shafting down from the ridge, their new leaves were luminous, as if emitting a green light of their own. The robins made the most of it, their chests and rumps flashing a complementary yellow as they darted for insects.

Her tea had gone cold. Life's pace had slowed, living among trees again, and she had been happy to let it.

Missing

She heard the spray of gravel at the top of the driveway and the car door. Three-fifteen already. She left the pile of weeds where they lay, washed her hands under the garden tap, and made it inside in time to hear the thud of Henry's bag at the front door before he removed his shoes.

'Hey.' Red-rimmed eyes suggested he hadn't had a very good day.

'Hey,' she said. 'I've set us up out the back.' She put the kettle on and sliced two pieces of banana cake, sniffed at the neck of the milk carton. She didn't drink it herself and it never seemed to last long.

The boy's visit cut a notch in the week. Without it, without Henry, time tended to stretch to the point that she was no longer part of its passing. He anchored her to the world outside.

She carried out the tea and cake in two trips. 'You right to keep going with the movement piece?'

He shrugged. Set out his sketchbook and pencils.

'How was school?'

'Haven't you heard?'

'Heard what?'

He shook his head. 'You don't even listen to the radio?'

Sometime during her first year, she had stopped playing her steel-stringed rock albums and dropped back to folk and indie. By her second winter, she found that only classical music, which she had not often gone to the effort of playing before, didn't seem out of place. The birds moved in sympathy with cello and violin, and the trees dipped their leaves in time to piano. When she tired of all her CDs, she just left the radio on Classic FM, which included news at regular intervals, and interviews with artists and musicians that were sometimes interesting. But then the voices of the announcers, and the inevitable opera sessions, began to grate – and frightened off the birds. Now, into her fourth year, she preferred silence. Or, rather, the forest orchestra of bird, frog and cicada.

It was a hazard, though; nothing attracted greater scorn from children than not being up with things. You could lose all credibility in a moment. 'What's happened?'

'Caitlin Jones is missing,' he said. 'She walked home from school the day before yesterday but didn't make it.'

'Where does she live?'

'Annies Lane.'

'That's a bit far to walk.'

'She normally gets picked up. Her father had car trouble,' he said. 'Someone saw her near Tallowwood Drive but nothing after that.'

Jen blew steam off the dark surface of her tea. 'This was all on the news?'

'It is now. They told us at school this morning. The police were there when Mum dropped us off, keeping the reporters away. And they got a counsellor in.'

Jen held her cup against her chest. A treecreeper's claws scritched on a bloodwood, securing its hopping, vertical ascent.

'She's in your class?'

'Yeah.'

'That's awful,' she said. There were no longer any tallow-woods on Tallowwood Drive; council had made sure of that. Last summer, someone had taken the corner too fast and run their car into one of those old trees. The whole lot had been removed, thirty lives in exchange for one. It wasn't far from Slaughter Yard Road, which she had thought appropriate at the time. Now it didn't give her a good feeling. If the counsellor had been brought in, the police probably didn't have a good feeling about it either. 'Any other brothers or sisters?'

'A sister,' he said. 'In grade four. Briony.'

'I'm sorry.' What were you supposed to say? What was she supposed to say, the non-parent adult, the non-teacher? 'I hope they get to the bottom of it soon.'

The boy opened his sketchbook.

'C'mon,' she said. 'That cake's still warm from the oven. See if you can do it some justice.' She adjusted the wooden mannequin till it was sprinting, knees high, arms pumping. It was an antique she had picked up in a store down south, run by a mad Frenchman who felt obliged to comment on customers' poor taste and general ignorance if they were silly enough to ask for something he didn't have.

Henry lifted the wedge of cake to his mouth, disappearing almost half of it in one bite.

'Remember we're just going for impressions, getting that sense of movement.'

He took a gulp of his tea and selected a 2B pencil. Swallowed.

The afternoon light caught all the cobwebs she should remove from the deck railings. Snagged on leaves or floating free on the breeze, they were gossamer silver, part of the forest's magic. In the house, they were a damn pain. They appeared overnight, linking beams, rafters and lights. If you sat still long enough in autumn, you'd find yourself the corner post for a spider's lair. It drove her crazy if she looked too hard.

The boy's lines were good: no hesitation, not too much confidence. His technique was self-sown, with a few little habits that needed undoing. But he had a style of his own, and was interested. That's all that mattered at this point. He didn't look up, just drew and chewed.

He seemed all right, but you never knew what was going on beneath. She had been teaching him for three months and still didn't feel as if she had any sense of his hopes and dreams.

'That's good,' she said. 'Get some life in those legs.'

Henry wasn't quite nailing it. Her first teacher had always claimed he could judge her mood from her work. Perhaps there was something in that – and who could blame the boy today? 'What's the biggest muscle in the human body?'

His pencil paused. 'Thighs?'

'Well, there are two muscles there, the quadriceps and hamstrings. And together they are very powerful, and essential for running. But it's our buttocks, gluteus maximus, that are the biggest. That's where your runner's power is coming from – you need to think about the force of the movement, as well as the direction, to get your line of action.'

He didn't laugh, as grade seven boys mostly did at the mention of backsides, but looked again at the figure. She rifled through her folder, extracted a coloured sheet. 'Here, this shows every muscle in the human body – you can have that.' It had always unnerved her to see the human form represented by the red meat under the skin, but it was necessary to understand the biology of the body in order to draw it.

Henry leaned over, running his finger down the names. 'This is cool.' He clenched his fist and watched the flex of his forearm. 'Huh.' He returned to his running man with a little more enthusiasm.

'Maybe a softer pencil now, too. Strengthen some of those lines.'

'Why don't you draw people?'

'What do you mean?'

'All those drawings in there. There aren't any people. Just trees and birds.'

She smiled. 'Well, that says a lot about me, doesn't it? But I had to learn to draw people first. Spent years on the human figure,' she said. It had allowed her to see differently, develop an eye for shape and movement. Detail. 'Wait until you do life drawing.'

He pulled a face, probably aware that the classes featured naked adults and sitting for long periods of time.

She counted eight chirruping white-eyes on the branch shading the birdbaths, each smaller than a baby's fist, before they were sent packing by a family of Lewin's honeyeaters with their rattling machine-gun notes. The pecking order – or drinking order – played out right in front of her every day. From now until sunset it would be nonstop action. It just went to show, all you had to do was put out water and the birds would come. Sometimes, it reminded her of the classroom.

Maybe she should have kept Henry talking about the girl, but he would dwell on it enough in coming weeks. The whole town would be talking about nothing but poor Caitlin Jones.

'That's good,' she said. 'I can feel his athleticism.'

Henry leaned back to get a better look at his drawing.

'Is he you when you're grown-up?'

'I'm not much good at running,' he said.

'Who then?'

'An Olympian. Australian.'

'Short distance? Long?'

'Middle. Four hundred metres.'

'He has the right build,' she said. 'I can see him running the last leg of the relay.'

Henry looked up. 'Yeah,' he said. 'He needs to be holding that thing.'

'The baton?'

'Yeah.' He worked on the hands now, choosing to put the baton in the Olympian's rear hand rather than out in front.

Jen closed her eyes to listen to the birds' chatter. The splashing of water behind her. The afternoon breeze lifting. Things you just couldn't draw.

She tilted her head. A car had pulled up in the drive.

Henry packed his pencils back in their case, shut his sketchbook. 'Mum's going to pick me up from now on,' he said. 'Everyone's going ape.'

Henry lived less than a kilometre away and, until today, had walked home unless it was raining, and sometimes even if it was.

'I'm not surprised.'

'It's stupid.'

'Things will calm down.'

'You think?'

'I'm sure they'll find her.' The empty platitudes of adults. She followed him inside, sat the cups in the sink, picked up the envelope on the bench. 'This month's bill for your mum. And some homework for you.'

'Thanks.' He slouched his way to the door. Knelt to put on his shoes.

'Take it easy, Henry.'

She watched him walk up the steps to the driveway and waved at his mother, Kay, whose face she could not see for the late afternoon sun glinting on the windscreen. She should go up and say hello, have the expected discussion about what had happened. Kay would be worried, not so much about Henry as his little sister, Montana. The communal hysteria would have begun, all the parents working themselves up, not knowing what had happened to the girl or who was behind it, a nameless, faceless threat hanging over the town.

With it would come a renewed suspicion of outsiders or newcomers, although it was far more likely someone living among them the whole time would turn out to be the stranger.

She bent to pick up a narrow leaf on the path, from a spotted gum, still tree frog green. It had curled back on itself, forming a circle. There was some sort of reaching back happening out there, too. To a time she thought she had long left behind. She knew what else they would be saying – that it was happening all over again.

There was more than one hazard in returning to the town where you grew up.

Back

One of her father's most overused pieces of advice had been 'Don't look back'. As it turned out, it wasn't just his usual half-arsed attempt at wisdom, but a way of life.

Her friend Michael had always looked back. From his desk in front of hers, over his shoulder as he was marched off to the principal's office, or from the rear window of the car when picked up after school; he always dragged out his goodbyes. That afternoon, when they had parted ways at the end of the street running down to the oval, he had given her a salute, like a young soldier off to war. It was just football practice, but he wasn't the star he wanted to be, limited by his size. Some of the older boys had been picking on him, probably for hanging out with her.

She had kept walking up the road to home, as if it were any other day. The sun hung low, bathing the valley in golden light, and a string of black cockatoos flew overhead, their wings moving in slow time. Their cries had not sounded at all mournful, the way they did to her now. Wood smoke, from freshly lit fires, was sharp on the air. The whine of chainsaws, her father's among them, carried from just outside of town.

The hinterland had been different then, their part of it, anyway. Time had moved more slowly. People either lived there all their lives or just passed through on their way further north for their summer holidays. It was the land time forgot. There were no organic cafes, galleries or Asian restaurants. Just caravan parks, and the giant waterslide.

People struggled along, working a few jobs, selling their pineapples, strawberries and macadamias from roadside stalls, with honesty boxes that did not need bolting down. The biggest harvest then was still trees: food for the mills.

As she had learned since, the moments that most change your life, you never see coming. Your position, from deep within the movement – the shift itself – does not permit a clear view. It is just a feeling, a sense of the ground loosening beneath your feet. With hindsight, you see that you did know, somehow, that you had felt a profound unease, but something in your own mind prevented you from piecing it together. Perhaps to protect you for as long as possible.

Jen had dawdled, as usual, dragging a stick along the driveway. The chainsaws had stopped, leaving the valley quiet. She had kicked off her school shoes at the back door and thrown her bag into the laundry, done her chores with the minimum of effort. Lied and said she had no homework. She was supposed to be working on some stupid science project but didn't know where to start. When her father finally pulled in, she ran to hug him, his jeans pale with sawdust, his plaid shirt sharp with sap and sweat. He lifted her above his head, as if she was still small, although his great arms must have already been tired.

She had swallowed down her mother's casserole, scraping the sauce off the squares of meat and wrapping each one in mashed potato, so she would be allowed to watch *The Sullivans*. Afterwards, she had read under the covers with a torch long past lights out and fallen asleep with the untroubled mind of a child.

———

The second day Michael's wooden seat sat empty, her whole class was sent home from school. The principal edged into the room and made the announcement, his voice calm but sweat rings spreading out from under his arms. Their teacher, Miss Lander, handed out tissues, though she was in greatest need of them herself. Most of them had been together since prep and would have preferred to see out the rest of the day as one, but parents had been called.

Except hers, it seemed. There was no one waiting for her outside the school so she started up the road on foot. Mandy's mother pulled over and insisted on driving her. She couldn't remember if they spoke in the car. Sound had been muted out, and most of the colour.

Her father's red truck wasn't in the driveway, even though it was his day off. The dogs hadn't been fed. The breakfast dishes were still on the bench, black with ants. 'Mum?'

Her mother was sitting at the dining table, amid a strew of bills, crying.

Jen lifted the phone in the hall to find no dial tone.

'He's gone,' her mother said.

Jen blinked. Michael?

'He's left us, honey.'

There was a half-empty glass of wine on the table, in a pool of condensation. Her mother had forgotten all about Michael.

Something fell away, inside. Jen tried to catch it and jam it back, to stop the rush of realisation, the terrible clicking into place of all those images and pieces of information – but it was no good. Daddy wasn't coming home.

———

Jen knew better than to trust her memories. Not the details, anyway. The kernel of them, though, the emotion, was something to hold on to. Like dreams, they contained important truths.

Her father, teaching her to surf, pushing her out into a set she was not quite ready for. Whooping, for all to hear, when she popped up and cut right, floating along the face of the blue-green wave that spilled out and out in front of her. It was a feeling she carried with her still. As true and clear as a sunny day.

There were others. The last time Michael had stayed over, after they had seen *Rocky* at the drive-in to hype them up for the athletics carnival. Her stomach hurting from calling 'Rocky' to his 'Adrian' across the back seat on the way home. She had drunk too much Passiona, and had to get up to use the bathroom. On the way back to her room, she had stopped in the hallway, thinking she heard Michael crying.

'Michael?'

She had replayed it so many times it had become less clear, like an old VHS tape. He didn't answer. But the crying had stopped. Perhaps he had been asleep, just having a bad dream. She hesitated in the doorway, but didn't go in. Earlier that year her parents had sat her down for an uncomfortable talk, and made it a condition of Michael staying over that he no longer sleep in her spare bunk, and that they were not to go into each other's rooms at night or shut the door when playing. She had not quite understood at the time, but knew it was embarrassing.

Michael had rolled his eyes and said he had endured something similar. A conspiracy of parents.

Once back in bed she had tried to stay awake, listening, but there was only silence, and a dog barking far away. And then her father was up with the sun, for work, and whistling in the kitchen.

Something had stopped her asking Michael about it the next day; he had seemed the same as ever, singing 'Gonna Fly Now' out of tune, air-boxing like Rocky, wearing all his blue ribbons, and still managing to be encouraging about her third place in high jump. She had been happy to let it go, rolling shot-put balls down the grassy bank of the oval with him and Phil and Glen, until Miss Herford blew her whistle and made them stay back to pack up the whole school's sporting equipment. Now it was too late to ask.

Regrowth

The change of name had thrown people for a while but there was no hiding in a town this size. The woman at the post office was the daughter of an old schoolfriend and eventually a government letter came addressed to the real her – Jennifer Vogel – and they put it all together. It would be nice to think that you could rely on your sending and receiving of mail remaining private, as it was for people in the city – through sheer volume rather than any superior ethics – but it just wasn't the case. It was friendly, all right, but there was little privacy.

'Ah, you bought Mal's place,' the manager had said, the day she filled out the papers to rent a post office box. People were still saying it, three years on. More often, they'd say she was living in Mal's place, as if she was a boarder or some kind of squatter. He must have had some wild parties in his time. It seemed that everyone had been there over the years, able to describe exactly how the place was laid out and having some memory of this or that great night, with belly dancers and drums and fireworks – and likely a whole lot of hooch, judging by the smiles and shaking of heads.

Sometimes she made a point of mentioning something she had changed, her plans to rebuild or repaint – just to assert herself – but mostly she couldn't be bothered. She had spent a month filling a skip with junk she gathered up from around the place, and that didn't make for polite conversation. Bloody hippies. Campaigning to save the world, to stop injustice, and all the while burying rubbish in their own backyard because they were too tight to pay for the council service or go to the tip. She was still turning up bits of corrugated iron and plastic. Toy cars.

There were plenty of recycled materials in the house itself, like the old wooden windows and doors, which she appreciated, but there were times when short cuts had compromised the integrity of the building. The recycled screws in the roof were not galvanised, which might have saved fifty bucks at the time but meant that now the iron needed replacing. All the same, she wouldn't trade it for a standard house, or one of those black-roofed catalogue-order boxes spreading like lantana at the town's edge.

The house had a much quieter life now; she did not hold parties. She barely had any visitors, except Henry.

Although it was almost a week since she had checked her mail, there was nothing in the box but glass-windowed bills. She ripped them open while waiting to cross the road, as the mobile library laboured up the hill, holding back a string of traffic.

She made it into the cafe before the storm. The library bus brought everyone into town, fuelling up on books, coffee and muffins.

'Morning.'

'Morning,' she said, taking milk and yoghurt from the cafe's fridge, a loaf of fresh bread from the counter. 'Half a kilo of coffee, too, please.' All organic, all local. All unimaginable five years ago.

The chef and owner, Elena, was the real deal. She had trained in Paris, got into organics before it was trendy, and somehow ended up here. Jen figured the town would grow into it in a few more years, the cafe helping bring the mean age down from geriatric, and up from young families on the breadline.

Jen leaned on the counter. According to the local paper's front page, police were looking for the driver of a blue station wagon seen on Tallowwood Drive the afternoon Caitlin went missing.

'Terrible, isn't it?' Elena said.

Jen nodded. Against police advice, the family was offering a reward for any information.

———

Jen sat on the back step, in the sun, staring out at her trees. A king parrot called from somewhere high in the canopy, repeating one identical note over and over. Johnny one-note he might be, but what a note it was. And he always had his looks to fall back on.

She thought of it as her forest, but it was just regrowth – third or fourth generation – only forty or so years old. Brush box, tallowwood and bloodwoods all of a similar age, with a scattering of grey gums, ironbarks and flooded gums. In this climate, recovery was swift, and some of the young trees were starting to hit the thirty-centimetre diameter mark – old enough to harvest again.

The whole area had once been rainforest, thick and dark with ancient life, the great buttressed roots of cedars, bunya and hoop pines poking above the tree line. Canopy, middle storey and understorey, rich with stories that white folks had never bothered to learn. The carcasses of great cedars still rotted on her slopes, left behind because they were hollow inside, too large to haul out – or just forgotten.

The cedar-getters had ended up national heroes, opening up the area and mining a new country's riches. Bringing those big trees down and hauling them out was seen as a feat of strength, a test of manhood, of nationhood. In just ten years, they wiped the cedars from the landscape and came back for the rest, clearing the way for fruit and dairy production.

She had witnessed the last wave of clearing herself; it was her father who had done it. In those days, just about everyone had worked for the mills in one way or another. He had run a team, and was considered a gun with the chainsaw, so had brought down more than his share. At the time, she had thought them good men, and the work hard but honest. Dangerous, too. Before Michael, the dramas of the town had centred on a timberman's hand crushed by a log, or a limb severed by a saw. Whenever her father was late home, her mother would start pacing, afraid to go too far from the phone, although Jen would often be at the table doing her homework, and was, by then, quite capable of answering it. 'Hot chocolate?' her mother would say, in winter, or 'Cordial?' in summer, as if to give her some purpose in the kitchen.

In Jen's forest, only one original tree survived, a bloodwood, metres thick, and towering above the other trees. Their timber wasn't any good for building, riddled with veins of blood-like resin that oozed out when their trunks or limbs were cut or damaged. It was a shame all trees didn't bleed: there might be a few more left standing.

Cuckoo doves called from all sides; they had her surrounded. Her father had called them whoop whoop birds. For that was mostly all they said: whooop whooop. They were big, too, and slow, with tiny heads, so she thought of them as 'big whoop' birds. Her ear had attuned early to the heavy flap of their wings, her eye to slim boughs dipping under their weight. They had been plentiful in the early days, when whites first arrived, but they were easy targets, hunted for food and fun, until rare.

Here, they had grown back, with the trees. Like her, they favoured forest edges. Regrowth. If she were a bird, no doubt she would be brown and common, too. Not that cuckoo doves were really brown, more of a rufous to cinnamon, and the females quite auburn on the crown. 'Bloodnuts. Like your mother,' as her father used to say.

It was far from wilderness, but her forest was beautiful in its way. Remnant riparian sections clung to the creek, with palms, ferns and sedges spreading out beneath flooded gums. Rushing water roared over rocks in summer.

When she had realised, walking around the property the second time – while the agent took a call – that it was the right area, the trees of the right age, and that she had probably even been here with her father, she figured it was all meant to be. Something had drawn her back to look after the land he had cleared. To make amends.

Studio

It was the birds who saved her. They always did.

A yellow-tailed black cockatoo called from below the cottage, one lonely rising and falling note. It called again, this time answered by its mate, a little further off. It was the season for feasting on borer grubs in the acacias. One bird would rip the bark off the tree while the other screeched and squawked and chuffed from the ground or a nearby low branch.

When she had first heard the ruckus, she had thought the birds in distress, a young one fallen from the nest, perhaps, and made her way down the slope to see if they needed her help. The birds were fine, enjoying their ritual, and barely acknowledging her. Their dining practices pretty much destroyed the tree, exposing its hollow insides, but with that level of grub infestation, its life had already been on the wane.

While the robins were her favourite, she had come to see the cockatoos as her totem bird. They tended to appear whenever she asked for answers – and sometimes when she hadn't – giving some sort of sign. Hearing them fly overhead, or in the trees, was always a good omen. During the winter of her first year back, when her courage had failed her, only they had come to call her out of the darkness.

The morning she had been unable to get out of bed, still lying amid the white sheets in full sunlight, a dozen had turned up screeching and carrying on in the treetops. Their cries were somehow sympathetic.

Whether they sensed her plans for departure, or had taken in the unmown lawn strewn with sticks, the leaf-filled gutters, the junk mail poking out of the box, and thought her already gone, she was unsure. The cottage, after all, was not unlike a giant bird house.

One cockatoo had perched right outside the window, peering in. Despite herself, Jen hadn't been able to help smiling at its comical cocked head, the clown-like spots of yellow on its cheeks. Only when Jen got herself up and out of bed did the bird fly off, screeching, settling on a high branch with the others.

———

She opened all of the windows of her studio, pulling the screens from the frames and depositing them outside. The kookaburras were at it up on the ridge, chortling and cavorting for all to hear. It was difficult to imagine what they were communicating with such volume and gusto, and to fight the feeling that she was the butt of their jokes. Probably it was just a weather forecast. It was Percy Grainger who said that the soul of the climate and land could be heard in the song of native birds. It was in all of the other animals and plants, too, but only the birds had been given a singing voice.

The light had softened, filtering through the trees, and for a moment she was tempted to leave the studio in its own filth and go outside to keep on with the weeding. Weeding, however, was not on her list for today.

Jen sighed. Where to start? She stripped the daybed and put the linen on to wash, dragged the mattress out into the sun on the back deck and propped it against the rail, her nose upturned.

The old canvasses, too, had to come out, their top edges crusted with gecko poop and dust. She sniffed for mould. Perhaps they would be better burned than left to rot away. She carried them all outside, wiped down their exposed edges and set them apart to air, without looking at their fronts.

She emptied the room, her desk and cleared the sloped drawing table. Took down all of the pictures, removed each object and placed them on the dining table. Wheeled her chair out into the light, blinking and smarting in the sun like a wombat.

She extracted the vacuum cleaner from the hall cupboard and set it down in the middle of the room. Pulled its cord and plugged it in. 'Okay, here we go.' She vacuumed the ceiling, rafters and windows, knocking down a hornet's nest, sucking up webs and the spiders that fled them. Then the floor, pushing into every corner, and using the brush attachment to run along the skirting boards and window ledges. She sucked everything out from under her desk and the back of the cupboard.

'Ha.' She shut off the machine's noise. The room was beginning to look habitable. Or, more to the point, workable. Then she would be right out of excuses.

Jen set to cleaning the windows, inside first. The grime of summer came off black on the cloth. Fairy-wrens hopped from branch to branch in the lilli pillis outside, celebrating the beauty of their small lives – lives free of cleaning duties.

She gathered up all of the found objects Craig had given her, arranged on the windowsill in front of her drawing table. The fragment of a paper wasp's nest in a hexagonal shape, replicating each individual cell inside. The heart-shaped rock, a piece of pale green beach glass tumbled smooth – the colour of her eyes, he'd said – the pair of matching cowrie shells, and the leaf with a gall on one end so large it resembled a snail. It had dried and curled brown now, a husk of its original fresh green. She rearranged them each time she dusted, which wasn't very often, but they kept their places there, in her line of sight.

She had got rid of some of them over the years. Those rotting or decayed or the worse for wear. Some had disappeared, carried off by ants or mice. There had been so many at first; it had seemed an abundance. Even on a trip to the local shop to fetch milk, he would find some treasure, a butterfly's wing or an empty chrysalis, and bring it home as if trying to prove that even in the burbs nature survived. That there were forces at work visible only to him.

Now she had to hang on to the few she had left.

At her old place – the flat with the sad-eyed windows – her friend, Mary, one of the other teachers from school, had joked about her 'shrine to Craig'. Jen had smiled, and said nothing, but had not invited her over again.

Here, at least, there was no one to pester her.

Old Timer

Whenever she left the property, she could see the world in colour patches again. At home, and even in the studio, she couldn't stop honing in on the ever-changing detail. It helped to be in a moving vehicle, blurring things a little. At this time of year, the blue of the mountain came closer in tone to the green of the trees.

At the ridge she caught the glint of sun on sea, the river winding out to meet it. Her road had once been on the coach route to the goldfields. Now it was a road to nowhere, of interest only as a short cut for tradesmen, or weekenders shopping for real estate – Sunday drivers dreaming of a quiet life, and disrupting the quiet of others. Her road home.

On the edge of town, she slowed to allow a mother duck and her string of ducklings to cross the road near the lagoon, and drove on.

She shopped in the next town, only another five minutes by car. The supermarket was much better, part of the same chain but bigger and managed differently, and the fruit stall was on the way home – and there was less chance of seeing people who might know her.

Jen waited for a woman to reach the bank of the new pedestrian crossing, and reverse-angle-parked right out front of the store, which was a good start. She had remembered her shopping bags, too. Focused, for once, on the practicalities of the day. She had a list, her ATM card, and late morning was the least busy time.

She hurried past the headlines, locked in mesh outside the newsagent, screaming MANHUNT and STATE-WIDE SEARCH.

The store had the best parmesan for miles around; the manager of Italian origin, perhaps. She took her time choosing a piece, a thin wedge without too much rind.

'Excuse me, love?'

The man standing next to her was balding, sweaty, an aged KingGee shirt tight over his barrel of a belly. Surely she was too old to be called love, even by this senior citizen.

'You're Peter's daughter?'

She shut her eyes, just for a moment. Wished herself teleported home.

'Jenny.' He held out his hand. 'Sam Pels.'

His handshake was firm, as they all were round here. There weren't many concessions made for women. Not for her, anyway.

'That's me,' she said. 'I don't think I remember you, though. I'm sorry.'

'You were just a tiny thing. Riding around in that damned red truck,' he said. 'But I see that little girl's face in yours.'

She smelled sawdust, the oily cool of a shed. 'You ran the mill,' she said. 'Down by the creek.' The Pels mill had been the last to shut down, when she was sitting her final exams.

'That's it.'

She leaned on the trolley handle, slipped one foot out of her slide. She had been at the mill the Sunday before her father left, making a pyramid of wood shavings while the men talked. Her father had come out cranky, she remembered that. Didn't speak the whole way home. 'I'm sorry if he let you down,' she said.

Sam coughed. 'Your dad was a good man,' he said. 'I never bought into any of the talk.'

'Good men don't abandon their children,' she said. 'Or walk off and leave their wives with all their debt.'

'Fair enough. Must have put you and your mum through hell. I'm just saying I always figured he must have had a real good reason.'

That was exactly what she was afraid of. It would almost be better if there had been another woman. Another family. 'Guess we'll never know.'

Sam looked around, appraised a young mother filling a bag with Granny Smiths behind them. 'I know he loved you. Never shut up about you being a great artist one day. Getting out of here.'

She had failed on both counts. No surprise there. 'Well, I'm back now.'

'The mill's running again, too. We do a little business for the local woodworkers. Why don't you come down, have a look around?'

She counted seven different sorts of goat's cheese in the fridge, ranging in price from four ninety-nine to eleven dollars and twelve cents. 'Sure,' she said. 'I might just do that.'

———

Jen unpacked her groceries and put them away. Hung the shopping bags in the laundry. After all that she had come home without any bloody goat's cheese, which had been one of the main reasons for the trip. She examined the dairy compartment: a piece of old cheddar, the parmesan and some haloumi, which was close to its best-by date.

The sun had disappeared behind the mountain; it was cocktail hour at the birdbaths and she was missing out. Jen took a bottle of white wine from the fridge without looking at the label, opened it, and filled a glass. She carried it out to the back deck to join the birds. One rufous fantail, four Lewin's honeyeaters and three scrubwrens. The whole forest singing. A treecreeper hopped up the pole from underneath, made blind by the base of the bath.

The robins arrived last, splashing and fluffing, sending the other birds off. Their golden yellow was luminous at dusk, as if carrying the last gleams of the sun. Only now did they sing, with their sweet, piping whistle, and first thing in the morning. Their song was best suited to dusk and dawn – the in-between.

Her wineglass was empty. She could still make an omelette with the cheddar, but she'd had her heart set on goat's cheese and herbs. A little slice of toast.

The drinking frenzy was over, the ripples on the baths stilling, the light almost gone. Black cockatoos called overhead, late home.

Sam bloody Pels. What were the chances?

Weeds

Jen surveyed the pile of weeds she had ripped from the ground. Fishbone fern, Singapore daisy and velcro creeper – silver *Desmodium* – named for the way its seeds latched onto your trouser legs. Getting the weeds up to the rubbish pile was harder work than removing them – especially if she got carried away and worked until she was tired. This time she was determined to pace herself, and clean up as she went.

She piled up the barrow and pushed it uphill, stopping at the flash of a kingfisher over the vegetable patch to get her breath. She jogged up the last of the slope and upended her load.

The empty barrow dragged her downhill. She had a good look at the kingfisher this time, with his sleek yellow chest and flat-top hairdo, before he took off for somewhere less public. Full sun was blasting her solar panels, working while she worked.

She loaded the weeds straight into the barrow, making sure not to drop any of the nasty little baubles by which the ferns multiplied. Otherwise she'd be doing it all again next year. Lil, the doyenne of Landcare volunteers, said they spread downhill with water, and would take over the world if you let them.

Cobbler's pegs had been the big problem at her parents' place. Every year her mother had pulled them from the yard, in great angry handfuls, but always a little too late, so that the early pegs flew free or were walked about in their cuffs and socks, only extending the infestation. Aunt Sophie said that the year Jen was born, her mother had set fire to the little paddock behind their house, on purpose, to 'get rid of the weeds'. Her father had come home early – seeing the smoke and thinking it too close for comfort – and found the breeze whipping up a line of fire heading for the hills. He'd managed to put it out with the garden hose and a watering can.

Aunt Sophie said that should have been a warning flare to them all – though Jen hadn't understood what she meant at the time.

After seven loads, Jen stood back to admire the cleared patch. Bare, but weed-free. At Landcare, there would have been three or four volunteers working on an area that size, and tea and sandwiches afterwards. A bit of chat, too, which she was less keen on, but she was learning how to do things properly. Over the last year, they had restored the lagoon at the edge of town, removing all of the rubbish and invasive species and replanting the shoreline. It was a nice flat area to work on, unlike her own slippery slopes.

A team of kookaburras crowded around, surveying the cleared earth from low branches. Two swooped at the same time, crossing and snatching in formation, then whacking their grubs on a branch as if they were much more threatening prey.

Jen gathered up the last scraps of weed and dumped them into the barrow. She had cleared about a hundred square metres, and just about got rid of the daisy infestation. The fern would need more work.

Jen pushed the barrow up hill, taking her time. Yellow robins flitted alongside, from orchard tree to orchard tree, her constant companions. She tipped the last load of weeds atop the others, a great mound forming. Not bad for a few hours' work. She parked the barrow in the shed and washed her hands at the tap, wiped them on her shirt.

It didn't pay to think of how much more there was to be done. The only way to manage the enormity of it all was to focus on one small area at one time, as if working on a large canvas – while keeping a sense of the big picture at the back of your mind.

What Goes Around

Henry unpacked his pencils one at a time, lining them up above his sketchbook. 'Mum said that a boy went missing when you were at school, too.'

Taken. Like a village sacrifice. She usually enjoyed the questions of young people, but not when she was really having a conversation with their parents. 'She did?' Jen squeezed out her tea bag, dropped it in the compost bucket. She had thought Henry's mum twenty years younger and from somewhere down south.

'It's in the papers,' he said.

'Ah.' She managed two mugs and the plate in one trip, though she could have done with a quiet moment in the kitchen. 'Well, that's correct. His name was Michael.'

'Why didn't you tell me?'

She sipped her tea. 'I didn't want to worry you,' she said. 'And I don't really like to talk about it.'

The boy broke a chocolate biscuit in half, showering crumbs over the table. 'Was he your friend?'

Jen put her mug down. 'It's a long time ago now. But yes, he was my friend.'

Henry watched her face. 'So you know what it's like.'

'Yes, I do,' she said. 'Or what it was like for me, anyway.'

He chewed his biscuit. Washed it down with tea.

A yellow robin landed on the deck railing. Cocked its head. Its eye on biscuit crumbs, perhaps. She watched, waited.

He rubbed a tear away. Such luscious eyelashes were wasted on the boy; he was oblivious to them. Her own lashes were all but invisible and her eyes disappearing back into her head. Sometimes youth and beauty were painful to behold.

'The teachers don't get it. They think we should just go on as if nothing's happened.'

'Why do you say that?'

'They don't talk about it. They don't talk about Caitlin, it's like she never existed,' he said. 'It's weird.'

'I thought you were seeing the counsellor?'

'Yeah,' he said. 'He's cool.'

'You can talk to him?'

Henry shrugged. 'We talk more about other stuff.' The robin flew off, gripping onto the trunk of a tallowwood, scanning the lawn for grubs and insects. 'Mum says the cases might be connected.'

'Michael went missing nearly forty years ago, Henry,' she said, struggling to keep her voice even. 'Whoever is responsible would be quite old now.'

'And they never found him.'

'No.'

Henry chewed the rest of his biscuit. Scratched his leg.

'Something else bothering you?'

'Mum says your dad went away around the same time.'

Was that in the papers, too, or just the talk around town? Again. 'Took off' would be the phrase they would more likely use. Even in front of Henry. 'That's true, too.'

'Why?'

'I don't really know. I was only your age,' she said. 'There were some money problems, the usual things.' Jen tossed the rest of her tea over the railing, placed the empty mug on the table. 'The police looked into it back then and found no connection.' Except the timing, and Michael having stayed at their house, which was plenty.

A wet ring was spreading out from the base of her mug.

'Are you going to eat that?' He gestured to the last biscuit.

'It's yours. And enough chat for today – you're here to draw.'

———

She gathered up sticks and leaves from the back lawn and piled them into her kindling basket. The temperature was to drop down to eleven degrees overnight, cool enough for her first fire. The lawn needed a trim, too, and the old mower, with its broken blades, did a better job if there were no obstructions between it and the grass.

One big old grey ghost stood sentinel where the 'garden' ended and wilderness began. Although no longer living, it still had a presence – and must have witnessed some things in its day. Every time she passed, she placed her hands on its trunk, to try and hear what it would say.

The koels were at it again, singing up a ruckus. Her father had called them 'hysterical birds', for their rising *quow-ee quow-eel* calls, coming at quicker and quicker intervals during breeding season. The koel was a summer visitor from South-East Asia, a type of cuckoo. Another species that loved to inhabit the margins of the forest.

Its carry-on was something of a false drama; it was the other birds – those of a similar size that built open-cup nests – that had cause to be hysterical. The koels were a parasitic cuckoo, knocking the host birds' eggs out of the nest and laying their own in their place. The males were iridescent black, the females a duller speckled brown with pale fronts. Mostly they hid in leafy tree canopies, as if ashamed of giving up their young to be raised by another species. It was only during the mating season, when the males displayed themselves and chased the females, that she could get a good look.

Her father had once taken her to a site he was clearing to see a koel's eggs in a figbird's nest. He had helped her climb high up into one tree to peer across into another. She hadn't really understood what parasitic meant then, but she saw that the eggs were too large for the nest and that their not-parents were distressed.

Jen stretched for a clutch of dry leaves stuck in a lilli pilli at the edge of the lawn: a perfect fire starter. Once hatched, the host birds tended to raise the cuckoo chicks, although they were bigger and uglier than their own nestlings would be, even if it meant working full-time to feed the great things. Their parenting instincts outweighed the nightmare.

Her father had loved interesting nature facts like that. And passing them on. It was years later before she had realised that those trees would have all come down the following week, the nest and koel eggs with them. It was some comfort to think that the parent birds, at least, would have been freed up to try again with their own eggs.

Colour

She was up with the birds again, though it was a much more respectable hour now that the days were growing shorter.

Her mother had not been a morning person. No matter the time of year. When Jen's father was on a job, she had made an effort, making Jen toast and Milo to eat at the kitchen bench or, in summer, on the back steps. There would always be something placed in her lunch box: leftovers, or sandwiches, and a piece of fruit. But her mother did not speak until she was halfway through her first cup of coffee, and even then it was monosyllabic.

On her father's days off, her mother stayed in bed. He cooked eggs and bacon and tomatoes while Jen made the toast and tea. Or sometimes they made banana fritters together, Jen pouring in the batter and her father flipping them over with the wonky spatula. Its handle was all melted where Jen had left it leaning on the side of the pan.

After her father left, it was Jen who made her mother coffee, and breakfast, though her mother didn't often eat anything at that time of day. Jen hadn't bothered with lunches for a while, just taken an apple, or bought a punnet of strawberries from the stall on the way to school. When the neighbours realised what was going on at home, they refused her coins, and delivered a box of fruit and vegetables from their hothouse once a week.

Her mother had been grateful, and made an appearance the next time – in reasonable order – to thank them. She had been angry at Jen, though, assuming the neighbours' kindness was the result of some sort of complaint. 'It's nobody's business but ours,' she had said. 'Understand?'

Jen had not said a word to anyone, but people thought everyone else's business their own in those days – particularly around the welfare of children.

———

It was eluding her again: the essence of bird. The mystery of what held the tiny fairy-wren together, made it more than a spot of feathers on stick legs with a flitting tail. She could not seem to channel, even for a moment, wild bird, despite her well-trained arm.

'A good eye is more important than the hand,' her first drawing teacher had said, somewhat primly, in senior high school. Jen had trained her eye, and studied birds, but now it seemed the more she knew, the less effectively her hand was able to reproduce what she saw.

It had taken several years and several more teachers to help her realise that the most important thing was somewhere between the hand and the eye. Towards the end of her third year at art school, Mr Grieg had stood behind her, watching her work, which had been unnerving enough. She could sense he was nodding. With approval, she hoped. When he reached over her shoulder and placed his hand on her chest, she had nearly pissed her pants. The sudden wetness there was enough for her to think that perhaps she had.

'Good,' he said. 'Remember that you draw from here, Jennifer. An artist cannot afford to be afraid of her emotions.'

She had been more afraid of him, and the beautiful naked man arranged in front of the class, than her own feelings. She was not the first student Grieg had laid his elegant hands on, nor would she be the last. Still, it had led to something of a breakthrough in her work, though it was not the human form she was to excel at.

What she was most interested in was missing in people, except in brief moments of lust or rage – and these were not the faces they presented to the world, especially when posing for a portrait.

Not for the first time, she wondered if it wasn't a mistake to try to pin the bird to the page, to confine it to paper with her meagre scratches and marks. The pleasure of living among them should be enough.

Craig always said she should get out in the world instead of copying it, insisting on walking, climbing, kayaking, running, and abseiling flat-out past all the detail. It was true that she tended to inhabit a land of her own, somewhere between the work in progress and that which had inspired it, but in those days she had been in the world far too much.

As if to emphasise the point, the family of fairy-wrens flitted and flirted their long tails at the baths, the cobalt blue and russet of the males no less astounding for the frequency with which she saw it. It made them vain, though. She preferred the plainer females with their red eye masks and more subtle touches of blue in their tail feathers. Their cheerful chatter lacked the self-consciousness of the males, the need to perform. And she knew all too well what it was to be the plainer of a pair.

They landed on the railing so lightly, or on the edge of the birdbath, floating in and out of the water. How could she hope to draw such weightlessness, such grace, such joy.

A breeze shifted the palm fronds, scraping the roof. She got up from the table and stepped into the relative dark of the room. It was too early for lunch, just eleven, but she was hungry. She cut two pieces of bread, a couple of slices of cheese, and made a sandwich with a smear of mango chutney and the handful of fresh greens she had picked while watering after breakfast. She put the kettle on for tea.

She was too set in her ways, no doubt, but routine was what produced the headspace she needed. She sat on the back steps, to eat, in dappled sun.

Post Office

A slip in her post office box said she had a parcel to collect. The new birding book she had ordered, perhaps. It was peak hour – after-school pick-up – and there were seven people ahead of her; she hadn't timed it well at all.

It was dead quiet inside. Caitlin Jones's parents were at the counter with a great stack of letters; some sort of mail-out. They no longer bore much resemblance to the newspaper pictures, their features gaunt and somehow exaggerated; caricatures of their former selves. They stood close together, him with his hand on her lower back, but his eyes suggested he was far away. They would each deal with it in their own way, any cracks in their relationship magnified. They were aware, too, of standing centre stage, of having become the public property of the community.

Everyone in line stared, but averted their eyes the minute the couple turned, suddenly very interested in the Hallmark cards or true crime books. Jen stood her ground, determined to acknowledge them, and her sympathy for their grief, though she had never met them.

The father was Brenden Jones's son, and according to the paper, Caitlin's mother had lived here all her life. Without her maiden name it was hard to pick the family. She looked a bit like a Shorten, but Jen wasn't sure. She could find out easily enough, but the family had already lost enough of their privacy.

When Jen had first moved back, she had imagined getting a post office box at the unmanned office in the hamlet closer to her. She would walk down the hill every day, leaving the forest for the gentler slopes of the dairy farms, with their falling-down timber fences and iron sheds, cross the creek, admire the old stationmaster's house on its green banks, overhung with the great jacaranda dropping a purple carpet in spring, to check her deep square box in anonymity. But there were no boxes available, and a long waiting list, so she had been forced to take one in town.

She wasn't sure she would take the box if offered it now, having grown used to the exchange with the post office ladies when collecting her parcels and sending things off. It was how she kept up with the town and no doubt how the town kept up with her.

She still took envious note when driving through the hamlet of the characters who had come out of the hills, in from their farms and studios and sheds, parking outside and ducking in to collect their mail in dreadlocks and boots, without having to worry if they were properly dressed, or having to clear their throats to speak.

Their business done, the Joneses turned and faced the audience. The young woman directly behind them sloped to the counter, possibly the only person oblivious to who they were. Jen looked them each in the face, though what she saw there had her feeling bilious, and nodded as they walked past her and out the glass doors.

Normal conversation resumed, perhaps even a little more vigorous than usual, as soon as the parents were down the steps and into their white Pajero.

Jen took her parcel without looking at it and signed her name in the ledger. The Joneses' mail-out was still on the counter, in neat piles. Jen turned to hurry out into the fresh air.

Michael's parents had left town in the end. Separately. They divorced eighteen months after Michael went missing, and sold their house, with its pool and sunken garden full of adventures and memories. A childhood. Jen had liked Michael's mother, and staying over. Especially when she baked lasagne. His father had been a bit strict, and right into his football, yelling at the screen when his team – the maroon one – let him down. Jen hadn't minded him, except when he was mean to Michael.

The fact that he had a temper was enough for people to suspect him, to talk. Jen had thought that all rubbish, even at the time, but the police had him in more than once. In the end all that broke was their family. Michael's poor sister, Hannah, ended up living with a relative in the city.

Dreamland

Sometimes, especially when she first woke, she had trouble distinguishing between her dreams, her drawings, and reality. As if she had been set loose from her moorings to sail in other worlds. It happened more often as the weather grew cooler, the nights longer and her sleep deeper.

When working, she tried to inhabit that place as long as she could. To stay in a dreamy bubble. She had breakfast in her dressing-gown, left the phone unplugged. Tried to keep her toes deep down in her subconscious mud. Every now and then there was a touch of mystery, and it flowed into her work.

She kept a sketchbook on the deck table in summer, the kitchen bench in winter, in case of bird visitations, but also of inspiration. The book somehow gave her freedoms she didn't have sitting up at the drawing desk in her studio. Opening the door and stepping down into her place of work sometimes had the effect of driving ideas and dreams away. Like entering the classroom.

It took her weeks to recover from her first day on the job. She remembered only standing in front of their flesh-coloured faces, smoothing her navy skirt, and writing her name on the blackboard, her mind just as blank. All her clever ideas and plans had slipped out the window and across the oval into the blue gums. While the students seemed to manage to daydream just fine, she turned stern and plain. It became easier with time, but she finished each year a little more depleted.

Jen scratched at her scalp, her hair probably overdue for a wash. Her pyjamas, too. There was a tea-coloured splodge over one of the robin redbreasts on her front, and a bit of dried porridge stuck to her sleeve. She had ordered her robin pyjamas online, underwhelmed by the stripes and spots she found in stores. She should have ordered two pairs, or perhaps a set of the magpie ones, too, because she was always reluctant to give them up to the laundry basket.

The whipbirds were chuffing about in the lilli pillis. For the first few years, she had only ever heard a pair calling to each other, never catching sight of them. They were the opposite of what parents called for: heard but not seen. Now there was an extended family, and they had become braver – or her eye more accustomed, perhaps – and she sighted them regularly close by the house.

Where once she had thought the whip crack and the answering call the extent of their repertoire, she now appreciated the full range of their chat and fuss. They were highly strung birds, with their flat-crested heads and so much furtive, darting movement from one bit of cover to the next. It was a shame they couldn't relax a bit, feel safe; she was no predator.

At first it had been distracting to hear so many birds while drawing another, like trying to recall the tune of a song when something else was playing. Now, though, they all chattered away as one community, from the same songbook. From her forest. One would come to the centre of her attention for a while and the others flit back into the background.

The robin was always there, as if at the edge of her internal clearing, peering down from the side of a tree, defying gravity, in her consciousness just as they were in the real world, popping up wherever she looked. They were rarely still, however, which was why they were so damn hard to draw.

Sometimes pencil on paper was a magical thing – and birds flew out. Other times they were just marks, her hand an inadequate tool. Today was a good morning, she could tell by the sound of the lead across the page. Everything had aligned at last. A robin's eye looked back at her. Dark and inquisitive.

Station

'Thanks for coming in, Ms Vogel.'

'It's Anderson.' She swallowed a mouthful of water, which was, thankfully, refrigerated. The station house was not. It was only manned once a week, and most of that time they were out in the car, so she supposed proper air-conditioning was not considered a worthwhile investment. Or perhaps times had changed less than she liked to think in the state, and police still felt the need to make people sweat.

He frowned. 'You're unmarried. Is that correct?'

'Yes.' A crime of sorts, no doubt. A woman who could not hold a man.

'But you've changed your name.'

'I draw birds. *Vögel* means bird, in German,' she said. 'It seemed a bit much, you know?' Someone at art school had been generous enough to say something before the exhibition had opened. She'd had to run around to change it in time for the program printing and had chosen Anderson without much thought.

'Right,' he said. 'As you've probably heard, we're investigating the disappearance of Caitlin Jones.'

'Yes.'

'We're pursuing any possible connections to the disappearance of Michael Wade,' he said. 'It's all a long time ago now, but we wanted to ask you a few questions.'

It had happened before either of the policemen were born, which was going to make things tedious. Surely they could have wheeled out an old-timer who had some memory of the case and the times. Or at least a local cop. These two were from down on the coast, and one of them not long out of police college.

'Yes.'

'Michael was in your class at school?'

'Yes. Grade seven.'

'And it was June fourteen he went missing.'

'He went missing June twelve. June fourteen was when he was officially declared missing.'

'Right.'

She finished the water in her glass and waited while the younger fellow refilled it from the misted jug on the table between them.

'Thank you.'

'And your father went missing on that same day?'

Jen looked out the window. Shook her head. 'The fourteenth, yes.' At the time, Aunt Sophie had tried to reassure her, insisting there was no connection. But people thought it and said it, and that was more than enough for most of the kids at school. Most of the town. Half a lifetime later and here she was again, in the same damn place. What had made her think she could ever feel at home here?

'Where did he go, do you think?'

'I don't know,' she said. 'I was twelve.'

'What about your mother?'

'I don't think she knew anything.'

'Why do you say that?'

'There were a lot of bills. Loose ends,' she said. 'If she could have referred people to him, I think she would have.' In truth, her mother had been too heartbroken to do much about the bills, but she would have gone after him if there had been any sort of hope.

Jen kept her hands in her lap, channelling a stillness she didn't feel. There was blood around the cuticle of her right index finger. She placed her left hand over the right; it was never good to have blood on your hands in a police station. It was her own, but they didn't need to see it.

He cleared his throat. 'And he never tried to contact you.'

'No.' Outside, lorikeets fussed in the palms, dropping sticky seeds onto the roof of the police vehicle in the driveway with a satisfying thunk.

The officer took a long time to write three words: *no contact since.* 'Have you tried to find him at all, over the years?'

'The electoral roll, phone directory, Google, you name it.'

'No luck?'

'No.'

'When was that?'

'Started in the nineties,' she said. 'On and off till a few years ago.' More recently, she had been checking each state's death records, though without much enthusiasm.

He glanced at the other officer, still taking notes. 'Any reason why you stopped?'

'I figured that if he was alive, he didn't want to be found,' she said.

The officer chewed his pencil. From its mangled shape, the habit was not a new one. He picked a flake of paint from his lip.

'The police looked for him at the time,' she said. 'They didn't find him either.'

'Are you aware of any other names he might go by?'

'No.'

'Everyone called him Peter?'

'Yes.' They knew the answers to the questions; where was this going?

'But that was his middle name?'

'His first name was Mallory. He was teased as a child – people said it was a girl's name.' Perhaps if he had kept it, he might have had the courage to climb a few more mountains.

'And his mother's maiden name?'

'Dent.' She had searched using that name, too.

'And you've never received any gifts or money over the years?'

'No.'

'Not even a birthday present? When you were a child, perhaps?'

'Nothing.'

'How did your mother support the two of you?'

'A second mortgage on the house. Benefits. And my aunt helped out with my expenses.'

'No one else?'

'Not to my knowledge,' she said. Not until her mother had hooked up with the Brethren.

He tapped his pencil on his notebook. 'Do you think your father is still alive?'

'He'd be in his seventies,' she said. 'And it was a hard life – all the physical work, I mean.'

'Is that a no?'

She shrugged.

'So you last saw your father on the morning he left?'

Jen spilled a little water on her pants, leaving a dark spot. 'I said goodbye before I went to school.'

'Nothing out of the ordinary?'

'No.' His hands had been shaking and, looking back, his hug might have been a little longer than usual, but that could just be her turning a childhood memory into a sentimental film.

'And when you got home from school, how would you describe your mother's behaviour?'

'From what I remember,' Jen said, 'she was a mess.'

'Go on.'

'She was distressed, upset. Not coping. Her husband had left her, the phone had been cut off, and there were bills to pay.'

'She was clear that your father had left?'

'Yes.'

'Was there a note? Something for you?'

'Nothing.'

'Had they had a fight? How had things been between them?'

'I was not aware of anything out of the ordinary.' She swung her feet as if she were still twelve. Through the smeary window, Jen watched cloud sneaking in from the west; a thunderstorm tonight perhaps. It was a mild form of torture, shut in a small hot room in the middle of the afternoon, having all her deficiencies pointed out by a couple of men young enough to be her sons – and given enough water to push a middle-aged woman's bladder to its limits. It was worse than sitting in the shrink's office. Though he at least had air-con.

The water cooler gurgled as the sergeant refilled the jug. 'Do you need a break?' he asked. 'I know this isn't easy. We're just trying to get a sense of what happened back then.'

She crossed her legs. 'I'm fine,' she said.

'Were you aware your parents used drugs?'

Jen sat up straighter in her chair. There was an agenda here, despite what they said, and she needed to pay more attention. 'Not as a child. I learned later that they smoked marijuana recreationally,' she said. 'Like most of their generation around here.'

The corner of his mouth twitched. 'How did you become aware of that?'

'My Aunt Sophie,' she said.

'You went to live with her after your mother was . . . hospitalised . . .' He looked down at his notes.

'At the end of grade nine.'

'And you completed school down there?'

'Yes.'

'And your mother died three and a half years ago?'

'Yes.'

'There was a funeral?'

'Yes.'

'Was that here in town?'

She had to work harder now; too long in a hot, stuffy room answering questions designed to irritate. 'No,' she said. 'A service near the nursing home, in Canberra.'

'Anyone from your father's family there?'

Jen blinked. 'No.'

'We're nearly there,' he said. 'Would you like me to open a window?'

'That'd be good.'

The younger officer clicked his pen. 'This boy you tutor, Henry Green. You know his family?'

'His mother, Kay, answered an ad I put up on the notice-board in town.'

'In the co-op?'

'That's right.'

'So you hadn't met his parents previously.'

'No.'

'You don't have any other students?'

'I wouldn't have minded a few more.' By the time Kay had called, Jen had almost given up on the idea. It wasn't as if she had thought the phone would ring nonstop – but still.

'Okay, Ms Anderson,' he said. 'I think that's it. Thank you for coming in.'

The other one cleared his throat. 'If we do . . . track down your father, either way, would you like us to let you know?'

She tried to catch the feather of childish hope that had taken flight. Chances were the same as they had been this morning: slim to nothing.

'Sure. That would be good.'

Pub

She had walked into the wrong part of the pub; every head was turned. It was still that sort of town. She should have gone to the coffee shop, with all the other middle-aged women, but it was a beer she wanted. She could have tried harder, though, to find the entrance to the ladies' lounge or the beer garden or whatever they were calling the less pubby part of the establishment these days. For a moment, while she stood absorbing the collective stare, she considered backing up, going home. But she had been apologising for her own existence long enough.

She nodded, walked across the room to the bar. 'Schooner of Gold, thanks,' she said. She would have preferred a Tooheys New – or better still a Coopers ale – but in the local you had to make some concessions.

The barman placed her change on the towel runner, sat her dripping beer on a coaster, all without meeting her eye. She had a mind to perch on a bar stool, next to the old-timers, to discomfort them further, but in the end she would only discomfort herself.

She retreated to a table by the window, looking back out over the valley, and flipped through the local paper. The men of the town, or those free to drink midafternoon on a Tuesday, went back to whatever version of football was on the green screen that dominated the room.

She drank from the glass and breathed. Stilled her hands. Breathed again, from the stomach. Toughing it out was sometimes only a matter of moments and you were through to the other side.

That was not going to be the case for Caitlin's parents, on the front page again. They were raising money in some sort of appeal, putting up posters all over the coast. Jen couldn't help feeling sorry for the girl's sister, wondering if she was getting the support she would need. The whole town's attention was on the missing child rather than the one still at home dealing with it.

There hadn't been nearly as much fuss for Michael. Not that she had been aware of, anyway. They were expected to get on with it and, to a large extent, they had. It had only been after some lobbying by the school captains that they had even been allowed to include Michael in their grade seven graduation, projecting slides onto the wall when he was awarded best and fairest for football and most improved scholar. His sister collected the awards on his behalf, shaking the principal's hand.

When Jen's class each went up on stage to collect their certificates, they had to stop, face the audience, thank their parents for supporting them, and mumble about what school they were going to and what they wanted to be when they grew up. Glen and Phil had gone last and second last so that together they could read out Michael's plan to go on to the local state school and become a pro-footballer or a sports reporter.

The class had cheered Glen and Phil as much as Michael; they had volunteered to do what no one else could. Out of respect for their bravery, and in a somewhat misguided attempt at stoicism, the rest of them had managed, collectively, not to shed a tear. The same could not be said of the largely adult audience. The principal made a speech and presented a special award to the whole class, for citizenship, which had sent parents reaching for a tissue. Jen hadn't looked at her own mother. She didn't need to – she knew she would be blubbering.

That night, their class had been united – 'together forever' – before breaking for the holidays, scattering to six different high schools, and setting out on much more lonely paths through adolescence.

Jen sipped the beer. Ran her finger through the frost on the glass. Cars pulled in and out in front of the supermarket across the road, most shoppers leaving with a single plastic bag. She counted five young mothers pushing strollers up or down the street. Motherhood hadn't been part of many life plans in grade seven, but by grade ten it was a reality for some. More so these days, it seemed. But then who was she to judge. Perhaps they were happy, and just as likely to sneer at a barren old spinster.

Jen drained her glass. Noisy miners sang in the cotoneasters outside. Fellow interlopers, the pair of them.

Hinterland

The gallery was not yet open, though the lights were on and a radio playing. Jen crossed the courtyard to the lookout and leaned on the railing. It was too early for any midweek tourists; she had it all to herself. The air was clear, without the summer haze. She could make out the froth of foam at the water's edge, the white towers of the coastal centre, the river mouth spewing out to sea. Empty shipping containers churned back up the coast, sitting high on the blue.

The various textures of mangrove, rainforest and pasture flowed out from the river, handkerchiefs of mist lingering in the low-lying areas. She picked out the curve of Tallowwood Drive, school-hour traffic creeping along, as if Caitlin might reappear at any moment.

Jen's own plot was directly below, giving her a bird's-eye view. A rough rectangle on the outskirts of town, and on the high point of the ridge, between covered growing sheds and the main road, her house hidden beneath trees.

From above, it was easier to imagine it all as it had once been.

Before the best of it had been picked out and the rest mown down. The great trees, gone. The first people, gone.

The cedars, all but childless for several generations now, were a race persisting only in the forgotten damp, dark gullies. Forest kings who would soon pass into legend – too majestic for this world. Not that they would be alone.

She had sat through an artist dinner once, seated next to a shiny faced young scientist, the wife of a promising ceramicist. On the subject of the declining population of pandas, and the impact of the loss of their habitat, the scientist had declared herself a 'fan' of Darwin's theory of the survival of the fittest: a believer. 'They would have died out anyway,' she said. 'They have no sex drive, you know – you can't get them to mate. And on a diet of bamboo . . .' She had shrugged, as if to illustrate the hopelessness of it all.

Jen had felt hopeless, too, though for different reasons. Craig had too much marking to come along, leaving her to the mercies of such conversations. The ceramicist had tried to fire his wife a warning look over the table, but Ms Science was on a roll, spouting about the supreme human capacity for adaptation.

'Really?' Jen had said. 'We're the only species destroying our own habitat. That doesn't seem so clever to me.' She could have gone on, about being neither fit nor likely to survive, but had held her tongue. She had been distracted by a glimpse of what she suspected was a tawny frogmouth in the tree above the car park outside. Nonetheless, the woman had appeared startled, perhaps more by Jen's tone than the words that slipped from her lips. The ceramic couple left shortly after that, citing tiredness, and Jen had the end of the table to herself, and the rest of a bottle of very nice red from Margaret River.

She heard the bell of the gallery door behind her. 'Jen, darling. Is that you? Sorry. I'm running a bit late this morning.'

———

Each time she passed the asparagus fern by the front deck, she reminded herself that it needed watering. The hanging basket was half-embedded in the front garden, coming to rest on its side, like an amphora pot. She could see the fern's new growth shrivelling.

It had hung in the bathroom from the day she moved in, just about the only thing she had brought with her from her old place. All of the furniture she had placed out on the kerb had disappeared over the week; the books and clothes she had packed up and dropped at Vinnies. There didn't seem much point trying to make a new start with all of her old things. Her desk and drawing table, canvases, art books, camping gear and one suitcase of clothes had fit easily in the ute, the plant in the front seat. It was like the first rule of camping: only take what you can carry in.

At first the fern had luxuriated in the green, but in the longer and hotter dry period leading up to last summer, it had started to choke. The sun swung around to bake through the glass skylight in the afternoons and whatever steam she produced in the shower soon disappeared.

As soon as the rains set in, she had carried it outside and hung it over a palm branch, only to see the basket dip down, its pointy base resting on the ground among the gristle ferns. Her sleeve was already soaked, and water running down her arm onto her ribs, so she had left it. Over the summer, she had become used to the bathroom without the basket. The bath needed less cleaning without the plant's brown dripping, and the fern had done much better outside.

She stepped in and ripped the plant free from the grasp of the grabbing ferns. One tendril clung on to the basket's chain, circling in the breeze as if reluctant to let go of a cousin. She hooked the basket, upright, under the eaves.

Teacher

Jen topped up the birdbaths while she waited. She kept pouring until only surface tension held the water in: infinity pools, with dramatic forest views, for the birds.

The bottlebrush was in flower. She kept one eye out for the scarlet honeyeater she had spotted dining there yesterday, its head and throat the exact same flame red; nature had its own logic.

Henry's mother pulled out of the driveway, spraying gravel, and Henry clumped down to the front, dumped his bag. Jen put the water jug back in the fridge and lit the gas under the kettle.

'Hey.'

'How are you, Henry?'

He shrugged, dragged his chair out. Set himself up. She made tea, placed pieces of lemon slice on a plate. The first time she'd baked using her own lemons.

'How's school going?'

'Okay.'

She set his tea and the plate above his sketchpad. 'Did I hear right that Mr Barr is leaving?'

'Yeah. Moving back to the city.'

He'd been offered a job in the department, which was not necessarily a positive reflection on his teaching abilities. 'No word on a replacement?'

He swallowed his mouthful. 'You could do it.'

She smiled. 'I don't think they'd let me do primary, actually.'

'What grades did you teach?'

'Art right across all years, though just seniors in the end. And history for seven to ten,' she said. 'Grade sevens are in high school in New South Wales.'

'History?'

'There's no art without history,' she said. 'And we wouldn't know much about history without art.'

He almost gave his whatever face but stuffed another piece of slice into his mouth instead, his frown suggesting some attempt to digest her words.

'Why'd you stop teaching?'

'I'd been doing it a long time,' she said. 'Then I sold my mother's house when she died. I was able to retire early and buy this place.'

'Why didn't you just live in her house?'

There was enough backwards movement without returning to her actual childhood home.

'I wanted something further out of town, a little higher up,' she said. 'With more trees.' Not just their carcasses lying around on boggy paddocks.

'You're lucky,' he said. 'Not to have to work, I mean.'

That sounded like his mother talking again. Kay worked three jobs, including one as a teacher's aide at a high school twenty-five minutes away.

'I'd trade it all to still have my mother around,' she said.

He dropped his head.

'It's part of life,' she said. 'Though it doesn't make it any easier when it comes.'

'But you don't really need to teach anymore?'

The desire had left long before the need. 'I'm done with the classroom,' she said. 'My drawing is my work now, with a little teaching on the side. Instead of the other way around. But I enjoy teaching. You learn a lot that way.'

Henry did not look convinced.

'C'mon, let's get started.'

Henry flicked open his sketchbook, sending loose pages skidding across the table. She lifted the outer corner of one with her thumb and index finger. 'Is this Caitlin?'

A blush lit his cheekbones.

'It's very good,' she said. He had probably drawn it from the photograph they were using in the papers – it was from the same angle. It was better, though, because he brought his knowledge of the person to it. His feelings for her.

He held out his hand for the drawing.

'Have you thought of using this, for a poster? Or to give the police?'

He shook his head.

She placed it on the table between them. 'It's really good, Henry.' Perhaps portraits would be his thing.

He slipped it into the back of his book without looking at it.

'So, I want you to work on a still life,' she said, ignoring the slump of his shoulders. 'But I also want you to put it together. Do your own composition. From anything you can find out there.' She gestured to the bush surrounding them.

'Now?'

'Yep,' she said.

He came back with a lantana branch, heavy with pink and orange flowers, a piece of wood with a knot like the mouth from Munch's *The Scream*, and a large tawny feather so perfect it could have just fallen from the bird. She snatched it up.

'Hey!' Henry said.

'*Ninox strenua.*'

'Whatever.'

'It's from a powerful owl,' she said. 'I've never seen a feather before. And you find one in sixty seconds.'

He grinned.

'You would have heard them, they go *whoo whoo* in the evening, like a person impersonating an owl.' She got up to fetch her bird books.

'Like someone talking into a piece of poly pipe.'

'Exactly like that,' she said. 'They live in the hollows of big old trees.' She had always suspected the grey ghost at the foot of her garden as the likely nesting site for her pair.

Henry had already begun arranging the items in the centre of the table but looked over her arm at the pictures.

'It's our largest owl. They catch possums, and even koalas,' she said. 'And fly with them back to their roost.'

'I wish I could draw that,' he said, pointing to a male looking right into the camera, with lanterns for eyes, a possum swinging from alarming yellow claws.

'Maybe you can do a series,' she said. 'Starting with this feather.' She left the book open on the table.

He adjusted the arrangement and began sketching it all out.

'That's it, leave yourself plenty of space around them, too.' The corner of the Caitlin portrait was sticking out of his book. She was tempted to sneak it out for another look.

Lantana

She dragged lantana up the hill to the rubbish pile, leaning her head away from its prickly leaves and stems. It had a lemony smell, pleasant if you didn't know the damage it could do. More than any other plant, lantana had adapted to the subtropical environment. Far better than any of the human inhabitants. Nothing thrived in wet summers better than weeds, and no weeds thrived quite like lantana. She pulled it out by the roots when the soil was loose after rain, but it soon popped up again, swirling into thickets, and creeping closer and closer to the house.

It wasn't all bad, providing cover on the steep slopes and in the gullies that the shy wallabies loved. Butterflies and birds, too.

Her mother had cut lantana back with secateurs and then poisoned its stems. There had been a scrambling wall of it on their place, where the block backed onto forest. Every few years, her father would take to it all with the chainsaw. Both approaches had been more successful than her own. Her mother had said, more than once, that she remembered a time when there was no lantana, blaming the council for dumping rubbish on the roadsides and in easements, allowing it to spread throughout the district. Her father liked to say that he had arrived the same way, dropped at the side of the road by a truck driver, after hitching back from Darwin. He had met her mother when some sixties band played at the pub, and stayed. Marrying into the area, as it were.

Jen dragged another two lantana bushes up to the rubbish pile, taking care not to dislodge any seeds. Lil, at Landcare, said birds were the main culprits, eating the plant's fruit and spreading the seeds about. Something about their digestive process aided the seeds' chance of reproduction. But it wasn't the birds' fault. It was humans who had let it loose.

Thirty different insects had been introduced to control lantana, many of which now caused their own problems, and none of which had been particularly successful.

When clearing for Landcare, she cut back the lantana, sprayed it, and piled the canes up where they lay, like she was supposed to. But on her own place, she didn't like to leave mess about. Or use poison.

Lil didn't like using it either, holding the spray at arm's length, nose upturned, despite her pink gloves and long sleeves. Glyphosate was the lesser of two evils, its toxins disappearing from the soil before lantana ever would.

Sometimes Jen was tempted to let it all go. It was perverse, after all, to spend so much of her time fighting the natural world. There had to be a better way.

Lil never seemed to run out of energy, despite being twenty years older. She seemed to believe she could still make a difference. Perhaps that was her secret.

———

The asparagus fern was still hanging under the eaves, tips browning, neither inside nor outside, and denied any real benefit from the rain unless it were to come in sideways. There was a coating of cobwebs between the basket's canes, giving it a nest-like appearance.

Jen stopped. There *was* a nest. A nest within the nest. A kind of woven thatch dome against one fluted edge of the basket, with a round opening on the side. Jen peered in. It was lined with breast feathers, one a kind of mottled brown.

There was no one home. She had probably destroyed all of their broody plans when she ripped the basket out of the garden, where it had been better sheltered among the palm and ferns. She fetched a cup of water for the plant, taking care to pour it around the nest, just in case.

She scratched the gardeners' soap in the laundry so as to fill under her nails, scrubbed them out with the little brush, then did the back of her hands, and dried them on the handtowel. She should really shower, too, and get rid of all the lantana stink and spores, but the nest was at the front of her mind.

The gallery owner, May, had said she would be happy to have any pieces Jen had lying around, but she wanted to give her something new. To finish something new would be a start.

She blew on her hands and sat down at the drawing desk. Pencil, page, nest, breath. The weight of the pencil was just right, the texture of the page coaxed her hand to move, and her breath brought the outside in.

She had been searching for nests when she met Craig. She'd been up a tree in the Brindabellas, locked behind binoculars, looking for olive whistler nests, when he had come thundering along the path below. He had looked up, thinking her a large bird, though he had long sent every other animal scurrying or flying away with all his noise, and grinned a silly grin. Her bird's-eye view had afforded a glimpse of his energy, which she had mistaken for something wild.

It had probably been his dimples that called her down, the messy thatch of blond hair, and the promise of a cup of hot tea. She had grown quite cold sitting still so long. He was halfway through a great walk across the mountains, and could only stop for fifteen minutes.

When she ran into him on campus a few weeks later, it had seemed like destiny. He was a semester ahead in the same course, a DipEd, though she was half a decade older. They had tea again, in the coffee shop this time, and he took her number.

He had called three days later, and she had put down her pencil to answer, hoping it was him.

Chainsaw

Jen pull-started the chainsaw on the back lawn, eased off the choke, and made her way down the slope to the fallen brush box. Its centre had been dead for some time, dragging the rest down with it. She began slicing through that section, the saw protesting and sending out the occasional spark. Brush box wood was dense, and actually contained silicon, making the timber part stone, which was great for floorboards and building, but soon blunted a saw's chain.

She adjusted her stance on the slope, trying to bend her knees to reduce the strain on her lower back. She was into the main section of the trunk now, still green, and no good for burning for a couple of years yet, but she figured she might as well carve it all up while she was at it.

Where the tree touched the ground, she had to be careful not to cut right through. It had not been her father, as it should have been, who taught her to use a chainsaw – though she had seen him wield one plenty of times. She had been too young then to do much more than pour in the fuel and chain and bar oil.

It had been Craig, of all people, who had first given her the opportunity. He had carried a small chainsaw in the back of his four-wheel drive during holiday expeditions, in case of a fallen tree. She had thought it amusing but sure enough, on only their third or fourth trip, somewhere in the Grampians, they had rounded a bend and found a downed mountain ash, the white limbs of its crown shattered over the road.

Craig had started the chainsaw and cut up the tree with some pride, not realising that chainsawing an already fallen tree was unlikely to impress her. She would have taken more notice if he had not been able to do such things. To his credit, he had paused halfway through and gestured for her to come over. He handed her the saw, gave a few simple instructions, and stood by while she cut through the remaining sections. She had remembered her father's rules, imparted in the truck or when training new men, about relaxing your shoulders, cutting downwards and away from your body, using the tip of the blade and so on. In the end, she liked to think, it had been Craig who had been impressed.

Not long after she moved back, she had made a trip down to the large hardware store on the coast, with the intention of purchasing a saw for herself. The well-meaning fellow, both younger and shorter than her, had tried to sell her a kiddy Japanese saw, and gave dire warnings about severed limbs and the need for Kevlar pants, earmuffs, goggles, helmet and so on: a truckload of gear. She had listened politely but insisted on a McCulloch with a much longer bar and more powerful engine. She demonstrated that she could lift it and wield it, only relenting by purchasing a pair of bright green earmuffs. Most of the loggers, her father included, had been too proud to wear them, and were half deaf as a result. She intended to hear the birds as long as she lived.

The hardware man – Ted, or Tod, his badge had said – assumed she was clearing a block, that trees were her enemy, and she hadn't bothered to correct him. She came up against that a lot, people of a different mindset. It had frustrated her at first – assuming that because they had chosen the same place to live they must have plenty in common – but she had finally realised there was no point trying to bridge the gap.

Her art school friends would be shocked that she used a chainsaw at all, not realising that not to have one, living among trees like this, and in a subtropical climate, was to be vulnerable.

She started on the thickest section, near the base of the trunk. It would probably be the last she extracted from the saw, and herself for that matter. Her forearms were aching. Smoke chugged out of the machine; it was overheating.

She puffed, and stretched her hands. She wouldn't be able to do this forever, or climb the slope loaded up with wood. She had seen the tree cutters when they grew old, no longer able to wield a saw. Like shearers, their backs and knees were ruined. Their hands shook, too, from absorbing all that vibration. One fellow could no longer close his hands in any sort of grip, barely managing to lift a beer glass to his mouth at the pub, her father had said.

She baulked at buying wood, though – it was always cut too green and too small for her great fireplace. And they charged way too much. She stamped on the piece she had just cut to break the last wedge free, only to see it roll down the hill away from her, turning faster and faster until it went plop into the creek.

She was breaking her father's golden rule, 'never chainsaw alone', but she didn't have much choice. She could hardly call the neighbour over every time she needed wood or wanted to remove a tree, and it wouldn't be right to make Henry stand by. As soon as Kay got wind of it, that would be the end of his lessons. Though it wouldn't hurt him to learn how to do something practical, or to carry the logs up to the woodpile.

She did make sure she always had her mobile in her shirt pocket. When she was up on the roof, too. There'd be no use calling if she severed an artery, though; by the time the ambulance located the address and found her among the trees, she would have bled out.

She had been with her father, that last winter, when one of the men slipped and cut into his leg, just above the knee. She had steered the truck to the public hospital, and stood on the clutch, while her father changed the gears, holding an old towel against the man's leg. Her father had remained calm, and taken the time to praise her second attempt at driving, but the dark blood seeping into the seat and the pallor of her father's face left her in no doubt as to how serious it was.

Jen's concession was never to use the chainsaw in the rain, or if she was feeling unwell, and she tried to concentrate. She hung the earmuffs around her neck. The birds had started up again, celebrating the end of all the noise. She bent to lift a log with her right arm, loaded another on top of it, and carried them and the saw back up the slope to the house.

Mother

She tried Aunt Sophie again, imagining the old phone echoing up her wallpapered hallway. It was not unusual for her to be out midmorning – she was always busy with bridge or shopping for quilting supplies, or meeting friends. But it was the third time she had tried this week.

'Hello?'

'It's Jen,' she said. 'Everything all right?'

'Fine, love,' her aunt said. 'I've been enjoying this weather, getting out in the garden.'

'Planting?'

'Some more gardenias. Out the front.'

Jen smiled. Her aunt already had about a hundred gardenias. 'They'll get good sun there, in the morning.'

'I think so, yes,' Aunt Sophie said. 'Anyway. What about you?'

'Weeding, mainly and some replanting. I'm trying a native groundcover where I cleared fishbone fern. It has white flowers and edible fruit.'

'Midyim?'

'That's it.'

'Well, it's a good time of year for it. And the drawing?'

'A little. A local gallery wants a few pieces,' she said. 'You remember May?'

'Of course, I love her gallery. It's hard to know whether to look at the pictures inside or out, the view's so good.'

Jen laughed.

'I'm glad you're showing your work again. That's the best news I've had for ages.' Aunt Sophie hesitated, and Jen could hear the currawongs starting up out the back. 'I heard about that missing girl,' she said. 'Are you okay?'

'The police called me in. Asking about Dad.'

'After all this time?'

'I guess it's routine . . .'

'When was this?'

'Last week.'

'Oh, love,' she said. 'I knew I should've called.'

'It's fine.'

'It sounds awful,' her aunt said. 'Is there someone you can talk to?'

'I'm okay, Soph,' she said. 'They haven't called you?'

'No. Something to look forward to!'

Jen smiled at the humph in her voice. She could always rely on Aunt Sophie to be on her side.

———

Losing a parent at such a young age had not been easy. Nor had the not knowing. A lifetime of not knowing. She had always hoped – still did some of the time – that she might see him again. It was a child's hope. Whatever happened, he would always be her father. She had known him, which was more than some people had.

For her mother, though, his leaving had been the end of their relationship. The end of her. It wasn't until Jen's own relationship with Craig had ended that she had really understood what a deep hole that left.

There was the money stuff, too, which Jen had not been able to fully comprehend at the time. Bills and IOUs kept coming in for months. They had sold off all the timber lying around, and the machinery. Jen had taken the cash from the men who came, while her mother slept inside. After the last transaction, she had, on impulse, slipped a twenty-dollar note in her pocket.

In the long months that followed, whenever they could not afford milk or bread, she wanted to give it back, to retrieve it from inside the book Michael had lent her, inside her shoebox of Jen things, hidden behind a loose board in the wall of her room. But to do so would be to admit taking it, and by then even she had realised that there was only so far twenty dollars would go.

The shrink had asked if she had been planning some sort of escape, like her father, and Jen had laughed, but perhaps it had been the first expression of her desire for independence. For distance from the dark mess she found herself living in.

The first thing to go had been the private school enrolment. The Lutheran College offered a well-regarded arts program. Aunt Sophie had offered to pay, but for whatever reason, her mother had refused. And so Jen had started high school at the public school in the next town. She had not been at all gracious about it, throwing a rather teenage tantrum and screaming that her father had not wanted her to go to that stupid school. Her mother hadn't either; it was rough and ordinary. But it was free and she could catch the bus.

Probably, in the circumstances, and with her grades and acceptance into the arts program, she could have applied for some sort of scholarship, but it wasn't done then, to ask for help, no matter how much you needed it. And at the time, her mother had not been able to give much thought to the future.

Her mother had barely emerged from the bedroom for months, until Aunt Sophie came and took her to the doctor. She improved a little for a while after that – taking some sort of medication, perhaps – and was able to go through the motions of buying groceries and preparing meals most days.

People had called it a nervous breakdown. They had used that term to cover a lot of things then, especially of women. She couldn't recall a man ever having a nervous breakdown. Jen's shrink used the term 'breakdown', on its own, without the nervous part, more like an old car. He also talked about depression.

It had shamed her mother, being left like that, though it should only have reflected on her father. But perhaps it was always the woman shamed. When she and Craig had split, she had seen judgement on more than one of her own close friends' faces. That unspoken question: what did you do?

———

Glen and Phil ended up at the same high school; that had kept her going. For a while. When the principal suspended her, for the second time, in grade nine, and her mother declined to attend an interview at the school, Aunt Sophie finally intervened. She drove up and tried to talk to her mother. That night, or early the next morning, her mother tried to kill herself. With sleeping tablets – hardly original. Aunt Sophie called the ambulance, and signed the forms for her to be admitted.

By the end of the year Jen was living with her aunt and attending All Saints. At the time, she was relieved to get out of the house, the town, and the state, though she was ill with guilt at leaving her mother. 'You've got your own life to think about, Jenny,' Aunt Sophie would say. 'She's responsible for hers. Not you.'

As it turned out, it was the wake-up call her mother needed. Aunt Sophie had known her better than Jen could ever hope to. She had to turn to the Brethren to do it – they prayed for, and preyed on, people just like her – but it helped her out of the place she had been stuck in.

The Brethren were still hidden throughout the hills, their women barefoot and pregnant in the kitchen, just like the good old days. The biggest grossing cafe at the annual music festival – a replica prairie house – was Brethren-run. The women did all the work, while the men sat about watching the money being made; it was against their religion for men to handle food.

You could pick the women in town, occasionally, from their conservative dress code, but the men tended to blend in. As with hippies, hooch and politics, it didn't pay to mouth off in front of someone you didn't know well; you never could tell.

Heath

She found a shady spot for the Hilux in the car park out the back of the national park.

For her first walk of the season, Jen wasn't doing the mountain summit, which was tough going, but a circuit out through the heathland. It was flattish, with some steady elevation: good exercise and good training. Fewer walkers, too.

She pulled her pack from the back, slipped into the straps and put on a hat and sunscreen. It was still cool, and there were only a handful of other vehicles in the car park. Midweek during the school term was the best time to walk. The best time for everything, really.

It was one of the many advantages of not teaching anymore: no longer being locked into school holidays, setting up camp with hundreds of families. As if she hadn't seen and heard enough children during term. She and Craig had tried to go to more and more remote places, to avoid the crowds, but the days when you could just camp anywhere were gone. They had kitted out his four-wheel drive so they could sleep in the back, which gave them more freedom. She had only to say, 'What about here?'

when Craig pulled up somewhere nice, and he would nod and switch off the engine. That had been half the reason she had bought the Hilux, intending to set it up the same way.

She set out with the sun at her back, the path wide and well-worn at the start. She- and he-oaks whispered around her. She bent down to pick up a seed pod; its prickle, and the fissure of the tree's slim trunk against her hand, gave her the texture she had craved.

There was no sign of the inhabitants of the other cars, further ahead perhaps or doing the summit. It was her goal to climb the mountain again by the end of winter, and take some fresh photographs from the top. If her knees were up to it. There were always plants on top of volcanic peaks, and animals, too, that were unique to that environment.

The Castle, part of the Budawang Range down south, was the best example she had seen. Its flat, mesa-like top, when you finally scaled its walls, was a world all of its own, with Castle-specific pines and gums and banksias, glorious mosses and wildflowers, and a collection of wrens and robins. Camping there – in the holidays during her second year at art school – had been like inhabiting a fantasy story. So much so that she had had to force herself to return to earth, several days after she had run out of food.

The path dropped downhill and curved around, through a carpet of grass trees boasting tall spears from their green umbrella fronds. It was only forty minutes from her own forest, but a world apart. Drier and more open, despite getting a similar rainfall in summer. Another in-between place.

She began the climb up to the next lookout. Jen ran her hand through the cascading straps of a grass tree and watched her feet on the stone steps. She noted the geebungs thickening, and stepped over a cascade of pine cones. The last ten metres had her heart pumping, but she wasn't in such bad shape after all. She could thank the weeds, and her driveway, for that.

She leaned on the railing, looking out. To the west, she was surrounded by a moat of plantation pines, their dark green uniformity at odds with the native bushland. A mob of wallabies grazed on the slope below. She had a perfect shot, if she were inclined to eat meat, which she was not. She liked to think of herself as self-sufficient, but she did not think she could bear to kill an animal, even if she were starving. A fish maybe, or a crayfish. There were several hundred edible plants in this area; they would have to do. She wouldn't measure up against the woodsmen and women of the northern hemisphere she liked to read about, hunting elk and grouse. Living off the land was all very well, but she had to be able to live with herself.

Harming another person, let alone a child, was an even greater horror, and yet it festered in all of them: the capacity to hurt, and the fear of that capacity in themselves and in others.

Caitlin's parents were stuck. They all were. Waiting. No one could even say 'dead', although they all hoped she was, because the alternative was worse. Jen surveyed the land spreading out beneath her, running down to the creek, as if it could offer up the answers. For a moment, she thought she heard a whisper – the land speaking to her – but it was probably just the wind in the she-oaks.

She walked on, and down, quadriceps straining on the giant stone steps. At the bottom, a red-faced man leaned against the timber sign in singlet and shorts.

'Hi,' he said.

'Hello.'

'Worth it?' He pointed to the path she had just come down.

'Definitely,' she said.

'Righto,' he said. 'Thanks.'

He set off up the steps with a great deal of huffing and puffing. She should have offered him some water; he didn't seem to be carrying any. Hopefully he wouldn't give himself a heart attack.

Up and around the next bend, on a drier and narrower path, she dropped into a shallow mallee heath valley. The grass trees were bigger, and the geebung. The banksias, dwarfed and gnarly, were a sea of yellow candles, lighting the understorey. Fire came through here more often, seeding not only the banksias but the grass trees and wattles.

She had taken her mother on this walk, when she was still mobile. As a Mother's Day or birthday present. Packed a picnic lunch and carried it in. Chicken, potato salad, a French stick. Things Jen never usually ate. Her mother had eaten it all up, and gazed about. 'This is just lovely, Jenny.' She had even asked a Japanese tourist to take a photo in front of a stand of paperbarks, which was a turnabout. Jen still had it somewhere. She had been struck, when she saw it, by how much she looked like her mother, and how much her mother looked like someone else.

Jen took a drink from her water bottle. Fantails and honeyeaters flitted about as if she wasn't there, well accustomed to walkers and photographers.

There were pictures everywhere. The spiky zigzag leaf of the wattles she had seen only here – *Acacia hubbardiana* – as if they had been cut with pinking shears, or the flaking trunks of paperbarks, shedding stories. She had drawn from this scene many times and would draw it again. She lay back on a cushion of grass trees and held up her hands to reduce the frame.

It was impossible, though, to capture what it was like to be in the clearing, immersed in birdsong and soft floral scents, warm air. Not the work of one picture, but of many.

———

Jen scanned the undergrowth through binoculars. It was Gore Vidal who had suggested that ornithologists were tall, thin and bearded so as to imitate trees as they watched for birds. Not that she was a ornithologist. Or had a beard. Though a few unwelcome bristles had begun to appear – so who knew, given enough time. She couldn't imagine Vidal leaving his desk and seeing any ornithologists in action out in the wilds. Perhaps he had met one at a cocktail party. Vidal had probably never seen a banksia, either; they were rarely tall and thin.

Ha. There it was: the red-backed fairy-wren. This one's shawl was more orangey than usual but still striking against the black body, the intensity of colour impossible over such tiny bent sticks for legs. She watched him hop about on a limb, enjoying his time in the sun. He was the sun.

Jen imagined ornithologists becoming more and more bird-like, nesting in their hides in the trees. Beginning, over the years, to imitate the behaviours they observed.

Ornithology would have been her first choice when deciding to do further study, but it wasn't offered in Canberra and teaching had seemed the more sensible option. She had already gambled on her art, and failed. Teaching meant she wouldn't have to give up drawing altogether – or so she had thought.

———

The return journey looped through paperbarks and scribbly gums, the occasional blackbutt. For a time the path ran parallel to an access road. A gum had come down, now a great bench seat looking back to the mountain. Jen made her way around grass trees to sit on its trunk, and run her hands over the undeciphered messages on its skin: a full body tattoo.

She returned to the path, eyes skyward, to follow the progress of a goshawk watching for small mammals she might flush from the undergrowth. Jen crossed over a brackish creek on stone steps, listening to its trickle and tell. The banks were lined with bent she-oaks, their fallen needles forming an inviting brown carpet. It was always tempting to lie down in this whispering, burbling world, but it gave her the feeling she might never wake up.

Instead of crossing the access road, she continued along it, drawn by a smell. At the edge of the pine forest, she stopped and listened, gauged the slope and light. One of her earliest memories that she could be sure was her own, not born of Aunt Sophie's stories or augmented by photographs, was of entering a forest clearing, its sharp smell, the needles crunching beneath her feet. Her parents had set her down on a bright, chequered rug and returned to the truck for something – the rest of the picnic gear, perhaps. For a few moments she had been alone in that old grove, the breeze murmuring in its needles, the outside light shafting in soft lines, and she had not been afraid.

She had always wanted to know where that forest had been and why they had been inside it, when the sun shone so brightly outside. To be sure that it was really a memory, and not some dream harking back to old Europe. But that's what she got for not asking enough questions while her mother was still alive.

She had explored all of the pine forests for miles around, – even the plantations with their torn skylines so at odds with the soft curves of eucalypt forest – driving and on foot, and had not found the spot. Although it had felt extensive, she did not have the sense it had been a plantation; the trees had not been uniform or in rows. And yet she had walked miles of these forests, on forestry roads and trails, just in case. Of course, if it had been a plantation, it would have been cut down and consumed long ago.

This wasn't it: too low-set, too young. She walked inside all the same. The shushing above was somehow calming, like being by the ocean. Sometimes she thought there was no pine forest, no memory. Just a dream she had latched onto, a fairytale gone wrong. She envied people with firmer childhoods, their parents pulling down album after album of pictorial evidence of time shared, of happiness and solidity.

Melting Moments

She plated up her attempt at melting moments, which were all somewhat lopsided. The kettle squealed. She turned off the gas and flipped the lid, filled their mugs almost to the brim.

The deck was wet from the rain overnight, so she had set them up inside.

'What happened to your husband?'

Her tea scalded her tongue. His mother again. 'Who says I had a husband?'

'Partner, then.'

She smiled. He'd been pulled up on that one before. 'There was someone once. A man. We're not together now.'

'But Mum says your name is different.'

'I use my mother's maiden name. Not his.'

He gathered crumbs on a damp finger. 'But you like men, right?'

Was that the talk? 'I like men fine, Henry,' she said. 'I'm just happy on my own right now.'

He chewed on that, along with another biscuit.

People seemed to think she was missing out, and maybe she was. There were not the highs, it was true, but she was better off without the train wrecks. There had been enough of those. Great blanks of life.

Outside, a treecreeper perched on the edge of the birdbath threw its head back to let loose a string of loud notes in a rippling trill, exposing its clean white throat without self-consciousness or doubt.

'Jen?'

'Sorry?'

'What should I work on today? You said something about shading?'

She opened her folder. 'You can keep going on your still life, but I want you to experiment with some different shading techniques. You seem okay with crosshatching and tonal, but there are other options: accent, lines, smudging and so on.' She put the sheet down in front of him. 'Is that copy clear enough?'

'Yeah.'

'Would you like me to go through it? Or just have a play around?'

'I'm okay,' he said. 'I think I've done some of the lines before.'

'Great,' she said, watching his pencil movements. 'Been in the water lately?' Henry had been learning to surf – a rite of passage. She had been thinking of giving him her old board, but then there was always the idea of getting back out there herself.

'Dad's been too busy.'

'What's he do? For work?'

'Paints houses and stuff,' Henry said. 'But he's been doing more with the church. On weekends.'

A young male king parrot sat on the edge of the birdbath. She nudged Henry. He looked up, pencil paused. They watched the bird dip and swallow, one eye on them. A female called from a branch of the maple at the edge of the clearing, more cautious. When she flew off, he followed.

'They only ever drink,' Henry said. 'Not wash.'

'That's true,' she said. 'I hadn't thought of that. Perhaps if I had a deeper bath?'

Henry shrugged and returned to his drawing.

The cuckoo doves didn't bathe either. Except when it was raining. She had burned her toast the other morning, watching a female raise one wing and then the other as if washing her armpits in the shower.

'Do you go to church, too?'

He shook his head. 'Neither does Mum – it's Dad's thing.' He snapped a pencil lead, pushing too hard, and reached for another. 'Mum says when he did the painting job for them, they did a job on him.'

Jen covered her mouth and composed herself. 'Was that the pretty little church on the other side of town? Near the oval?'

'Yeah. And the hall. Took weeks.'

'It looks nice,' she said. It couldn't have been more than a few months since it was finished. Eggshell blue. Around the time Caitlin went missing, so perhaps Henry's dad's religion was just another passing phase. There was nothing like a tragedy close to home to focus your own fears.

Some of the boy's lines were a bit dark today. 'Keep your hand relaxed there, don't forget to breathe,' she said.

He shook out his wrist. Sighed.

'Sometimes it's not your drawing that's the problem, but your connection with the subject,' she said. 'There's a story there, you just have to find it.'

He blinked.

'I think of those objects as artefacts of the forest, but you might like to think of them as something else.'

'What's an artefact?'

'There's a dictionary on the shelf behind you.'

'You could just tell me.'

'I could,' she said. 'Or you could look it up for yourself.'

He sighed but fetched the dictionary, flipping the pages over more roughly than was required. He found the word, read through the meanings. 'But these things aren't man-made.'

'One definition is an object made or shaped by some agent of intelligence,' she said. 'Do you think we are the only creatures with intelligence?'

Henry looked at her for a moment, then stood to move the pieces.

'Good,' she said.

He stepped back, assessing the new arrangement through the frame of his hands, and sat once more, turning a fresh page.

———

She tossed another log on the fire and flicked stick ends from its edges to the centre. The lights dimmed and spluttered, but rather than switch over to the generator, she put down her book and lit some extra candles. The shorter days – and today had been a cloudy one – often meant shorter nights for reading as well.

Jen stretched out in front of the fire and watched the flames, the wood she had cut warming her once again. A train passed through the next valley, the familiar screech of metal on metal as it rounded the bends, the great shifting of air somehow comforting. Familiar. A gecko scuttled off into the rafters.

She had probably not been in a very good state of mind to

make decisions then, after Craig, after her mother's death. Aunt Sophie had suggested as much, in her gentle way.

Jen had come back looking for somewhere to call home, somewhere safe to recover. It was only now, here in her little house, that she sometimes felt something like contentment.

Still Life

She hurried her oats along with the wooden spoon, cut the flow of coffee into her mug, and set a bowl out on the counter next to the brown sugar and milk. A fantail flitted between birdbaths, only to be dislodged by a troop of white-naped honeyeaters. No robins.

Birds marked the seasons with greater accuracy than the shifting of the sun and the shortening and lengthening of days, or even the appearance of flowers, which were sensitive to the influences of rain and fluctuations in temperature. Every year, without fail, the robins disappeared for several weeks at the end of autumn, though she still didn't know where to, or why. The first year, she had been worried they had fallen prey to the owls she heard about her every night, or worse, had eaten the termites she'd had a man out to poison, and died. Without those flashes of yellow, she had become very glum indeed.

Then, in the first few weeks of winter, they had returned. Perhaps they had been off building nests or searching for mates. Now that she knew they always came back, she could get through those colourless times.

Jen sprinkled sugar over the oats and added milk, then put the saucepan in the sink, filled it with water and left it to soak. She wiped her hands on her pyjamas, took a sip of her coffee and carried her breakfast into the studio.

She turned a new page and sat for a while before picking up her pencil. Sometimes, when you looked at a thing too long, you stopped seeing it. Today she needed to focus on what had drawn her to the nest in the first place – its shape, and relationship to the larger nest, the promise of what might have been inside.

——

Jen knocked on the water tank at the top of the hill. Almost empty. She crouched to shut the valve down to the house, opened the other, and walked around the vegetable patch, down to the underground tank. Something slithered away into the gristle ferns.

She uncovered the pump and switched it on, sending water chugging back uphill. More epiphytes had made their home on the shady side of the tank, which was nice, although suggesting its leaks were getting worse. Pumping up was a pain, but the extra height gave her more water pressure.

While the top tank filled, she swept the path with the old broom she kept for outside jobs. Once left out in the rain, its millet head had swelled and mildewed, turning out on one side like an asymmetrical haircut. She paused mid-swish. In some magic of the light, her forest was aglow, like Mondriaan's *Wood with Beech Trees*.

Her trees were third or fourth generation survivors. There was some comfort in that – that the earth gave second chances. Brush box, with their rough, flaking trunks, flourished where others had once been, growing anywhere from open woodland to rainforest, and specialising in the transition areas between the two. Out in the open, they would spread out into a massive, broad tree. In the rich damp of the rainforest they grew fat and gnarly. Here, set close together, they were tall, thin and collegial, the heart of her wet sclerophyll forest.

Jen leaned on her broom. There was a picture everywhere she looked. She had given up trying to capture the place with the camera – it only broke things into parts. And the light was being tricksy.

The limbs of the brush box tended to horizontal, like a reaching arm, and their leaves were large and flattish. New shoots began as a pale green bud, emerging in early summer, vertically, like a flower, before opening up into a hand of leaves, giving the trees the look of a sculpted bonsai. Their real flowers were white stars, sticky with honey. For a time, the new shoots and flowers were all on display at once. As summer progressed, the leaves relaxed into a darker green, and their abundance enclosed her within the canopy. Coming into winter, the leaves dropped and thinned, allowing more sunlight in – and giving her a view out.

She resumed her sweeping, the job at hand, letting the green fall away into the background, and opening her peripheral vision – such that she was sweeping on a forest stage.

At the front deck, she changed directions with the broom, sending leaves flying over the edge into the garden bed. She stopped in front of the hanging basket. The fern was doing much better. But there was something else, someone in the nest: a scrubwren, her yellow eyes scowling beneath white eyebrow markings.

Jen backed away, and left the broom leaning on the wall. The top tank was overflowing, and she hurried down to switch off the pump.

While drawing her empty nest, she had imagined its lost inhabitants, trying to bring life and loss to the page. Somehow, she had drawn life to the nest instead.

Gorge

Jen headed home along the river. She tried to get down to the coast at least once a week. It was a chance to walk on the beach and swim. Today it had been too windy. Everyone was swimming inside the river mouth instead, crowded along the narrow strip of sand by the parkland.

It was also better to see specialists out of town, to avoid any gossip. Her mother, when Jen was small, refused to purchase even head lice treatments at the local chemist, but drove to one several towns away. 'I don't want to give them anything more to talk about,' she'd say. She had grown up in this town, too, so she would know.

Since coming back, Jen had heard them for herself, gossiping behind the counter, caught the raised eyebrow as someone came direct from the doctor's surgery next door with another script for Prozac or Viagra. Her doctor had referred her to the shrink as much for his location as his reputation.

Jen pulled over in a cul-de-sac by the river, beneath a straggle of paperbarks. There were flyers stapled to all the power poles, even down here. There was Caitlin, right in the middle of the windscreen. A heaviness trapped Jen in her seat. The girl was dead. All these pictures, all the fundraising in the world weren't going to change that. She had a sister – Briony. What of her childhood, her grief? Sometimes, you had to focus on the living.

Jen unclipped her seatbelt and opened the door. The breeze was stiff, she set off with it at her back. It was high tide, the water lapping right up beneath the mangroves. A new path had been laid, winding through native plantings, piled high with fresh mulch.

Upstream, the river widened and forked around mangrove-fringed islands. She kept meaning to hire a kayak, paddle out to them. They hid a different set of birds than she had at home. Egrets and gulls and herons. Once past the bridge, from this angle, there was little sign of humanity, just a couple of tinnies out fishing. A flotilla of pelicans drifted ahead of her, the wind ruffling the back of their proud white necks.

The session with the shrink had all her thoughts scrambled. Too many memories near the surface.

Her first river journey had been during her second year at college. Semester break. A friend of Craig's had driven along the old forestry roads, through spotted gums and cycads, to drop them, their kayaks and all their gear in a gorge at the back of the mountains, the source of the Deua. That river had been a world away from this one: cold, narrow and rushing over rocks. She had overturned on the second set of rapids, her kayak caught up against a log.

They stopped on a white beach by a rock pool, and Craig lit a fire to warm her. 'I should have warned you about logs,' he said. 'It's a bit of a trap. The water rushes underneath and generates suck. Like a plughole. If the boat gets up against the stationary object, the log, the force of the water is concentrated on one side of the hull.'

She had figured all that out while she was in an upside-down world of bubbles, her breath driven from her chest by the cold. Avoid logs. Deathtrap. She hadn't been able to right herself, as she had learned to from a roll, and the deck tarp hadn't held. The kayak filled with water and went under. If Craig hadn't been there to pull her out, she would have drowned.

'Don't let the river get you broadside,' he said. 'If you get into trouble, face it head on.' He rubbed her goosebumped flesh with his warm hands, dried her hair with a towel. And they made love there, while her clothes dried on the rocks, to the rush and swirl of white water.

The shrink said she had to let go of Craig. As if she were still hanging on by her fingertips and hadn't already plunged to the bottom of the gorge. He said it was time to let go of her grief, too. Jen had made a note in her diary, and dutifully reported on her progress each month. But she hung on all the same, nursing it like a blown egg, the fragile shell of what it had once been. It was what she had instead of him. Instead of love. It was all she had, and she had no intention of casting it out of the nest.

———

She took her foot off the accelerator as she approached the spot where Caitlin had last been seen. Probably everyone slowed down and stared, even though there was nothing to see. Humans, despite all their intellect and self-awareness, were as predictable as birds.

The spot had been turned into a shrine: plastic wreaths, flowers in jars, candles and notes. Jen had always thought such displays in poor taste: white crosses bearing bad spelling and faded plastic. The inappropriate public outpouring of emotion. The naive assumption that the person's spirit had departed from the point of impact, rather than in the ambulance or hospital.

Perhaps it was easier to see it for what it was – a simple expression of grief – when it was closer to home. It was the teddy bear that did it. Pink and fluffy, a little girl's toy, nailed through its neck to a tree. Jen pulled over into a driveway and leaned her head into her forearms, still on the wheel.

The Mill

'**M**orning, Missus,' Jen said.

The scrubwren didn't answer, but it was nice to have a neighbour. To wake up every day and know another creature was close by. Jen had been walking past as little as possible, half-expecting the wren to realise her nest was now in a public thoroughfare, but it seemed having invested in the building of the nest, she was going to stay. Perhaps she had even laid her eggs; she was on the roost more often than not.

Jen walked downhill beside the road, straining against the slope. It was land 'too steep for the plough', as they used to say, saving it from the fate of the more level country all around. Jen caught a flash of something iridescent in the undergrowth and stopped to peer through the fence. She jumped at the sound of a car horn, snagging her thumb on a barb. An arm hung out the window of the retreating van in a wave.

She sucked the wound on her thumb as she passed the old stationmaster's cottage, neat white on the bank of the creek, and continued down the track. A whipbird cracked from the tangle of lantana and bracken fern. The wooden gate was shut, a hand-painted Pels sign the only clue.

The Pels mill had once been right in the heart of cedar country. Down south, trees were sawn into planks with a pitsaw. Here, the pit would just fill with water, leaving the sawyer up to his thighs in mud, so the logs were rafted out. Where close to streams, the logs were rolled to the bank. If they were farther away, bullock teams had to 'snig' them to the water. It was these snigging tracks that had really opened up the country, giving travellers access through dense scrub and vines. The gravel track she was walking on had begun its life this way. Once the logs were in the water, the raftsmen had spiked them together with iron 'dogs' and floated them downstream.

A real dog announced her arrival, one part pig and three parts mystery by the look of it. Someone called it off and turned down the radio. 'Sam, Jenny's here.'

She stopped herself from wincing at that. Her schoolgirl self. By the time she shook his hand, she had recognised him. 'Glen. Good to see you again.' He had shot up early, in grade eight, but had more than grown into himself now.

'You look well,' he said, smiling the lopsided smile of the boy she had known. 'Never thought you'd come back here.'

Jen hadn't intended to visit the mill either, but here she was.

Sam emerged from the dark of the shed, concentrating on the three mugs in his two oversized hands. 'We were just about to have a cuppa.'

Glen produced an extra stool from behind a pile of logs – their ends still branded with the first letter of the owner's surname, as if it were a hundred years ago. Apart from the box of tea bags on the shelf, and the new white ute at the edge of the clearing, she could almost imagine it was.

Sam cleared his throat. 'I hear you bought Mal's old place?'

'I did.'

'Nice spot there. Tucked away.'

'It is.' She sipped her tea. Strong, milky and sweet. Just the way the timber-getters had probably liked it. Though they wouldn't have had tea bags. 'Sam said you've started up again?'

'Specialty stuff. For the local cabinet-makers and wood-workers. Sam trips around buying stuff up and we store it and cut it here.'

'There's still a market for solid timber.' Sam said. 'For quality. And if you know what you're doing, you can make some money. I got hold of a stack of wenge at twenty bucks a cubic metre. Bloke thought I was a total sucker. But now we're selling it for three times that.'

Glen watched her through the steam drifting upward from his cup. 'Do you have any kids?'

She shook her head. 'You?'

'Three.' He pulled a wallet from his back pocket, the surfie canvas style of a teenager. 'Aiden and Quinn – they're twins. We did IVF. And then little Sarah, she came later – a complete fluke,' he said. 'Boys have left home now. And Sarah's in grade twelve. Real smart, too.'

'They're all gorgeous.'

'Take after their mother,' he said. He slid out another picture, even older. 'Do you remember Karen Reynolds? From the grade below us.'

'Of course.' She had been good-looking even then, when the rest of them were bucktoothed and freckled, and went on to be school captain in senior high school.

White cockatoos were raucous in the pine trees up on the ridge, drunk on the fermenting kernels. There was something about sitting around with blokes out the front of a sawmill that felt completely normal, and plenty that didn't.

'Any other mills still going?' she said.

'Only Mannings, but they do large-scale mainstream stuff. Got the big machines,' Sam said. 'Which reminds me, I have something for you.' He stood and placed his mug on the corner of the bench. 'Just hang on.'

They waited while Sam lumbered back into the mouth of the shed. 'Do you ever hear from Phil?' Jen said.

'He visited a few years ago, and we had a good catch-up,' Glen said. 'Promised to keep in touch. One of us usually calls the other around Christmas.'

'He's still in Sydney?'

'Last I heard.' He gulped at his tea and looked off into the scrub. For a horrible moment, Jen was sure he was going to say something about Michael, but instead he coughed and made a mark in the dirt with his foot. 'Bloody awful about the Jones girl, isn't it?'

'Terrible.'

'I heard the police are interviewing someone local – their vehicle matches the description.'

'Oh?' she said.

'But they're probably interviewing a lot of people.'

'Probably,' she said.

'Got it.' Sam was out of breath. 'It's not much. Some old photos we had up here, payment slips and the like. But I thought you might like to have them.' He handed over a grimy, once-white envelope, like her father had used to take all his receipts to the accountant.

'Thanks.' She sat the envelope on the table beside her. 'I love this time of year,' she said, lifting her face to the sun.

'It's grand,' Sam said. 'Less tourists. No rain. Get a whole lot more work done, too.'

'Tourists make everyone money, Sam.'

A single black cockatoo passed overhead, beating its wings at such a leisurely pace it was a wonder it didn't fall out of the sky.

Jen put down her empty mug, stood and put her hand out. Sam pulled her in for a paternal hug. 'You come down again whenever you like, love,' he said. 'And if you need any help up there, just give us a call.'

'I'll do that. Thank you.'

Envelope

She had been in the woods again. How many times had she been there, in her dreams, and why did she keep going back? She shut her eyes, still in half-sleep, and could smell the needles, hear them crunch. She was sitting between her father and mother on the blanket. Someone was walking towards them, or was it away?

A shrike-thrush landed on the roof near the window, scratching with its claws. She should get up, but there was something pushing at the edge of the clearing that was her memory. There had been someone else there that day; why could she not remember? The thrush sang at full volume and then it was gone.

She pushed back the covers and climbed out of bed. The steps downstairs were cold on her bare feet.

She opened the front door a few inches. The scrubwren was out. Gathering breakfast, perhaps. Jen looked around, listened for any anxious *chew-wieps* in the undergrowth, and peered into the nest. There were eggs inside, speckled. Ha!

———

She had walked around Sam's envelope, still sitting on the kitchen bench, for several days, imagining what might be inside. It probably meant she was gutless or some sort of masochist. Just as when she was a teenager she had, for a time, taken pleasure in opening the fridge to assess all of the things that she could eat, only to close the door and walk away.

Aunt Sophie had managed it with her usual grace, cooking healthy meals, stocking the crisper with carrots and celery, and running on the beach with Jen most mornings. She had organised the house around Jen's study schedule and forked out for art materials she hadn't really been able to afford.

Jen made a pot of peppermint tea and sat down with the envelope and a letter opener at the table on the back deck. It was still cool, even in the sun.

The robins, she had to admit, were a little pushy. A bit larger than some of the other birds, and with the strength of numbers, they tended to dominate the birdbaths when they were around.

Today one sat on the deck railing, looking straight at her while she sipped her tea. They did that. She had been feeling a little low, and along comes a robin, irresistible in his grey and yellow suit, to remind her of all there was to live for. It was hard not to read intelligence into their dark eyes.

She paused, as motionless as a hunter. Or as if she were the subject of a still life.

You shouldn't want to tame a wild thing, and you couldn't. But sometimes she longed to have a robin as a companion, to sit on her shoulder or on her drawing desk, through the day, chirruping away. To be able to smooth its feathers, caress it. Just one. A creature that was just for her.

This one needed a little smoothing – the feathers on the back of his head were ruffled, as if he had just woken up, the line between body and wing all a jumble. She tried to concentrate, instead, on the detail of his claws, the mix of grey and yellow on his upper back, the touch of white on his wing.

She refilled her cup. Took a breath. She slit the envelope and spread the pieces out before her, one of the many puzzles of her life. The pictures had all been taken at the mill. Her father, Sam and two men she didn't know standing atop giant logs. Their eyes in the shade of their caps. A new truck. Neat stacks of lumber.

Sam had cut out a picture from the local paper back then, all yellow now. That gave her some names for the faces: John Coggil and Colin Yeeman. They were names she knew: men who had cut trees with her father. Colin had given it away after he put a saw through his thigh a second time. She remembered the blood on the floor of her father's truck and him getting home from the hospital as she was eating breakfast.

Her dad and Colin had some sort of falling out with John. Probably over money, or a job. He had provenance going right back to the first timber-getters, a third-generation sawyer, who probably didn't think much of a bloke cutting his own leg. But all she had were the gleanings of a child overhearing after-dinner adult conversation, most of which hadn't made much sense at the time, let alone years later.

She had a vague memory of an argument at the house, after she had gone to bed, brown longneck bottles strewn around the yard when she left for school. Her mother making her disapproval quite clear as she gathered them up. But that was the only time the men had visited the house while she was there.

A brown comb. A packet of Tally-Hos. An unopened pouch of Champion Ruby tobacco. Why hadn't someone taken that and smoked it? She sniffed – stale. But it still carried the image of her father with his brown forearm hanging out the window, the burned-down cigarette between his first and second fingers. She tucked the packet into her shirt pocket.

She sipped her tea. There was one of her old school photos, like the one he had kept clipped to the visor of the truck. Faded and creased. Grade six by the look of it. The uniformed girl in the photograph still had pigtails, her best friend and a father. No wonder she was grinning so foolishly.

It was because of their class photo, taken earlier. Michael had always pulled some stunt or another; it was a tradition. In grade one he rubbed his hair with a ruler until it was standing straight up at the back, and the photographer failed to notice. In grade two, he'd put his jumper on at the last minute – inside out. In grade three, he had an accomplice. He and Jason Ambley, on opposite ends of the second row, managed peace signs above the girls' heads. By fourth grade, the teachers were on to it. He had to content himself with one sock up and one down. He had been sick in year five. Whether on purpose or not, she didn't know, but that year's photo was nonetheless notable for his absence. Grade six had been the best yet, a classic. The grade sevens, due to line up first, had been milling about on the oval with them, in the care of a relief teacher while the real teachers had their group photo done. Michael had convinced the Owen brothers – only a year apart in school – to swap. Somehow, when their own teachers reappeared, they hadn't noticed. Both classes had managed not to crack up, though their smiles had an unusually uniform brilliance when the photos came back. The Owen boys reckoned their own parents didn't pick it until it was pointed out, and then – much to their relief – appreciated the joke.

There hadn't been many smiles in grade seven, and there were no jokes, because Michael wouldn't ever be in their photographs again.

There was an old Fourex coaster from the pub. She flipped it over. Stan Overton. A six-digit phone number. It didn't look like her father's writing. Probably some work contact, another tree-killer looking for work.

There was a stack of faded handwritten receipts for fuel. Never claimed. Today's were lucky to last out till tax time, especially in this climate. She often wondered what happened when people were audited and all their receipts had gone blank. If it wasn't, somehow, deliberate.

The pay slips, such as they were, didn't tell her a great deal. He hadn't earned much for hard work – but she had already known that from her lunch box contents. Some of the receipts were interesting: payments for loads of wood he had organised himself, perhaps. Those sums seemed larger, but then he would have had to pay his men, and maybe give Sam a cut. The date on one of them pulled her up; it was the day he disappeared. A larger sum than usual, too.

Feather

Coaster

Jen put on her boots at the front door. The scrubwren's eyes were less fierce in their little black mask. Jen would have liked to get a photograph, but that felt too rude, too intrusive.

She took advantage of the cool morning to walk to the village. It was always a pleasant journey down, but with a killer return. The council were doing something patchy to the side of the road, and one fellow gave her a wave. She waved back.

The dairy farm off towards the mountain was lush green, and the dams full, but the cattle were bellowing. It couldn't be for want of food or drink. Perhaps they had been separated from their calves. Jen's thighs were burning already, straining not to tumble downhill. A kingfisher sat on the powerline, surveying the scene. In the sun, his coat was indeed as resplendent as a king's.

It had all begun here – the 'opening up' of the area. The first white settler had lived just downstream, in a hut on the bank of the creek, accumulating runs until he controlled the land all around the river mouth. He had owned the abattoir on Slaughter Yard Road, too – quite a monopoly. He had grazed cattle, though not all that successfully – run off, in the end, by Gubbi Gubbi. It gave her some pleasure to know that the first people had been particularly 'troublesome' in the area. As if something in the country itself encouraged resilience.

This time the mill gate was open, as if expecting her.

'Hey, Sam,' she said.

'Hi, Jen,' he said. 'How are things?'

'Nice to get a bit of rain.'

'Reckon.'

She stepped inside the shed. It still smelled the same. Wood, of course, but all different notes, mixed with oil and metal and time. Old number plates covered one wall, dating back to the fifties.

'Coppers still haven't found that girl,' he said, holding up the local rag. 'Some big investigation unit set up in the city now.' Caitlin's parents, or the people who used to be her parents, were on the cover, pleading for public help.

'Someone must know something,' she said.

He looked over his glasses, which were in need of a good clean. 'Cuppa?'

'Sure,' she said.

She sat up at the workbench, scarred with chisel and saw marks, spills and chips, half-covered with old newspapers and scraps of paper scribbled with measurements and phone numbers.

'Sam?'

'Yeah, love?' He put her cup down in front of her, to the right, and flipped out a coaster to slip under it, as if the beach were still a more polished piece of furniture.

'These coasters,' she said. 'From the old pub. Where'd you get them?'

'Fred gave me a whole box, before the place was torn down. I pinched a couple of bricks, too, from the building. Nearly got myself arrested.'

It had divided the town, that demolition. Another of the Dean brothers' enterprises. It was the end of more than the pub when the wrecking ball started swinging. 'I remember that day.'

'Yeah?' he said. 'You would have been what, ten?'

'Eleven,' she said, and picked up the coaster. Her father had carried her on his shoulders so she could see over the crowd. When the police turned up they had slipped away, and weren't part of the fracas that followed.

'I know they're just coasters,' he said. 'But it reminds me of the old days. Old mates.'

'The stuff you gave me, of Dad's. There was a name. Stan Overton,' she said.

'Doesn't ring a bell,' he said.

'Wasn't one of your team?'

'No one I dealt with,' he said. 'And I knew most of the other blokes, too.'

'It doesn't matter. I was just curious.'

'They used these coasters for a long time,' Sam said. 'Fred got some deal, in 1977, I think, seventy-seven boxes or something. From Castlemaine. Didn't see what was coming.'

Jen nodded. She had noticed some dark timber half-dressed by the saw. 'What's that?'

'That's the wenge we were telling you about. Catches your eye, doesn't it?'

She stood up to take a closer look. Felt the weight.

'I've got some polished up somewhere,' he said. 'Hang on.'

Jen took the piece Sam offered. Black-brown and glossy with a partridge grain. 'I like that,' she said. 'Is it suitable for frames?'

'Perfect,' he said. 'A little expensive, but no more than you'd pay for lesser quality veneer from a framer.'

'You can do that here?'

'For you,' he said. 'Yes.'

'It would be perfect for some work I'm preparing now,' she said. 'Stand out a little.'

'It will that,' he said.

'It's not Australian, though?'

'African,' he said. 'From the Congo, I believe.'

Jen clucked her tongue. If it was a tropical timber, it probably hadn't been harvested ethically, and was possibly endangered.

'Hey,' he said. 'What did you say that bloke's name was?'

'Stan Overton.'

'A fella did come in here looking for your dad once. Said he was staying nearby for a while. I think maybe his name was Stan. Don't know if he gave me his surname.'

Jen sat up on her stool.

'Some artist from the city,' he said. 'Bit up himself, if you ask me.'

'When was this?'

Sam scratched his arm. 'Gee,' he said. 'I'm thinking it was a week or so before I last saw your dad. But I can't be sure.'

Jen turned at the call of a catbird and tried to pick it out from among the foliage. She didn't get those much. Only a kilometre away and a different world. 'That last Sunday. I remember Dad seemed angry when we left here,' she said.

'It was probably about his pay. I couldn't offer him the work I had been, things were pretty tough. It was cut everyone's hours, or cut some blokes off altogether, and I didn't want that. Most of them had families.'

'Right.'

'Your dad did some other work for me, on the side,' he said. 'He asked me for an advance, and I gave it to him – figured he must have been behind on the bills. Then I heard he'd left . . . felt pretty bad.'

'It's not your fault.'

Sam up-ended his mug. 'If you're worried about using a more sustainable local timber for your frames, we could do ironbark, or stain something if you want to go a bit darker,' he said. 'But this wenge was taken years ago. However you look at it, you'd be giving it a second life.'

'Let me have a think about it,' she said. 'Thanks for the cuppa.'

'You okay?'

'Fine,' she said.

Carcass

She had been clambering all over its body in her boots. The grey ghost at the end of her garden had come down with a crash in the night. There had been something of a storm, though without much rain.

It was more like a skeleton, after so many years dead, bleached hard, almost petrified. Like the remains of a great elephant. And here she was cutting off its limbs and carving it up.

She should really leave it as it lay – there was more life in a dead tree than a live one. It was so full of hollows it must have been a high-rise apartment building of the forest. Jen had peered inside, looking for inhabitants, but everyone had left – except the ants, cockroaches and other tiny critters.

Left alone, animals would return to the tree and everything would eventually rot back into the earth, as it should – but she had used up all the fallen timber she could easily access around the house. She sat down on the thickest part of the trunk. The timber was worn smooth, like a hide, and warm, as if somehow still living, still absorbing sunlight, still sentient. Still offering comfort. 'I'm sorry,' she said. She gave thanks and savoured the sun on her face. Listened. If she were truly a creature of the forest, she would make her home here herself. The hollow trunk, at its thickest, was big enough for her to sleep in, and there were several entrances and exits, storage places for food. Its centre had been eaten out by termites, leaving behind a strange, damp woodmud. Weakening it so much that the tree had eventually given way. The force of a lightning strike had knocked it over, its roots no longer gripping the soil.

A tree had fallen across the fence during her first year of high school. She and Phil had inspected the site and found the dislodged nest of a wompoo fruit-dove – with two eggs still intact – on the ground. They had transferred the nest onto a piece of wood pinched from the industrial arts workshop and set it up in the fork of a neighbouring tree. The eggs had probably long gone cold but it had seemed a noble project at the time.

Going out of bounds and being late to class that day had earned them detention, but when the deputy reviewed their files, while they squirmed on orange plastic chairs, he said something about them having a difficult transition to high school, and meaning well, and let them off with lunchtime litter duty.

Jen restarted the saw and carved off cross-sections. Many of the pieces fell apart, and what she had thought would be larger logs, suitable for burning overnight, split in half, or even quarters, as she cut.

With all the dirt inside, and the density of the timber, the saw was soon blunt. She stopped to sharpen it, sweating beneath her overshirt.

She and Phil had borne the litter duty punishment with pride, ridding the schoolyard of every straw, ring-pull and paddle-pop stick. Over the course of that one hour, they hatched plans to become naturalists and build bird shelters all over the world. If only life was as simple as it had seemed then.

———

She had abandoned her nest. The heart of the drawing had been its emptiness, and as it had turned out, it wasn't empty at all.

She had found a robin's nest instead – way out in a brush box where it should be, rather than hanging in a basket under the eaves – disguised by lichen and ribbons of bark. Two green eggs inside. For her new piece, Jen had torn strips from an irritating article on climate change, and pasted them over bark and straw, to achieve a similar effect on the page.

Now she worked on the robin mother, using watercolour and coloured pencils, which was all a bit of a hotchpotch, but she hoped it would come together somehow.

She couldn't help worrying about the mother scrubwren, though. Or, more correctly, her eggs. She seemed to be spending a lot of time off the roost. Such tiny eggs would surely cool, left unattended for so long. What if all of Jen's coming and going had disrupted the wren's mothering somehow? And where was the father?

Bunya

'What's this?'

She put four cupcakes on a plate. Chocolate. She only baked for the boy, but she had found her own sweet tooth returning as she grew older. Especially in winter. And most especially when she had been gardening, as she had today. 'It's a bunya nut,' she said. 'And a branch from the bunya tree. They used to grow all around here.'

Henry separated paper from cake and stuffed it whole into his mouth.

A captive audience; the perfect opportunity for a micro-lesson. 'The bunya is important to the first people around here, the Gubbi Gubbi – it was a major food source. Other groups used to travel from miles away every few years for a big bunya festival,' she said.

Henry sucked the last of the cake from the roof of his mouth. 'My aunt makes bunya nut pie,' he said. 'And bunya nut pesto.'

Just as well Jen had held back on her usual anti-hippie commentary. 'Any good?'

'Pie's all right. I don't really like pesto.'

Jen didn't either, garlic didn't agree with her at all. Or too many nuts. She broke a cupcake in half and took a bite.

Henry gulped his tea and pushed a second cupcake in behind it. He was beginning to shoot up, getting the lanky-legged look of a man on the make. Always hungry. He turned to a fresh page in his sketchpad, selected his pencils.

'The bunya goes right back to Jurassic times,' she said. 'Hasn't changed much since then.'

'They're about the right size for dinosaurs,' he said, mouth still half-full of cake.

She laughed. 'Megafruit for megafauna,' she said. 'Actually, it's not a pine tree at all, but a conifer. Like the Wollemi pine.'

'We learned about that in school,' he said. 'A guy found them growing in the Blue Mountains and kept it a secret.'

'That's it. They're related.'

She and Craig had climbed and walked all through what was now the Wollemi National Park. Craig had been miffed that they – perhaps more correctly he – hadn't made the discovery.

Finding bunyas on her own block had been the bigger discovery for Jen, eliciting a whoop for the whole district to hear. They were remnants of a distant past and, somehow, symbols of hope. None of the trees were old enough to produce nuts, though; she had picked this one up from a roadside.

Henry reached for the cupcake papers without looking up from the page and popped them into his mouth.

Jen raised an eyebrow. 'There are more inside.'

'It's okay,' he said, still chewing.

She had sucked the papers, too, when a girl, but had not attempted to digest them. Cupcakes had appeared more often at Aunt Sophie's than at home. She sighed, watching a pair of emerald doves on the back lawn, their iridescent wings catching the sun. Henry was doing a nice job of the texture of the nut – detail was his thing – but not so well on the branch itself. The leaf formation was challenging.

'Remember all your shading techniques,' she said. 'And try to get the overall shape first with those leaves. They're kind of triangular, I think.'

Jen cradled her cup to warm her hands. Black cockatoos called from the ridge, their voices drifting down over the house. One day, she would like to see them drinking at the birdbaths.

She smiled. Henry was taking great care with his shading, going for finer, more detailed movements. He hadn't put anything of the patty cake papers back on the plate; he must have swallowed them, which couldn't be good for his insides.

It was cooler today, a breeze getting up under the deck. She buttoned her cardigan and crossed her legs under the table.

Henry pushed his chair back. 'Bathroom,' he said.

A robin flashed across the clearing, into the dense foliage of the tamarind. She heard the toilet flush, and the sink tap. Good; he had remembered to wash his hands.

'Jen?' He had stopped at the dining table, where the two robin pieces were waiting to go down to Sam for framing.

She stood and went to him, blind for a moment in the womb of the house after staring at white pages in the sun.

'I haven't seen these ones before.'

'You're here for your work, not mine.'

He touched the one of three robins bathing. 'They look just like them!'

'Thank you.'

He leaned closer, examining her pencil work. 'I never noticed they had little whiskers there, above their beaks.'

'Cute, isn't it?'

'Did you do it from a photo, or real life?'

'I've been watching them for a while now.'

'Are they sold?'

'A friend of mine runs the little gallery up the mountain and asked for a couple of pieces.'

'Geez. I'll never be this good.'

'You don't know that, Henry; I've been doing this a long time,' she said. She placed her hands on his shoulders and turned him towards the deck. 'Back to work.'

Roadkill

A kookaburra swooped low across the road. Jen slammed on the brakes, reducing the impact, but the bird whacked right into the middle of the windscreen, leaving a greasy smear. The Tupperware container carrying leftover cupcakes flew off the front seat and onto the floor.

She pulled over and walked back, looking for the bird. Her whole life she had never seen or heard of a kookaburra doing that; they were too smart. Perhaps it had been sick, or young, or had a momentary lapse of judgement, too focused on some tasty morsel.

She couldn't find it. Not on the road or in the grass. The Hilux was blocking the road, cars ferrying children to school veering around, drivers frowning and beeping their horns. Perhaps the kookaburra had survived, flown off; they were tough. More likely it was lying in shock somewhere.

She walked back to her vehicle: the killer. Though, as the driver, she would be the one charged. She continued on into town, twenty kilometres under the speed limit, ignoring the string of drivers behind her. She had only ever hit a bird once before, a parakeet, when she was learning to drive in her father's truck, and had never forgotten the mush of bright feathers in the radiator.

She made the usual exchanges in the post office: a little banal conversation, a slip for a package, bright notes for a few items. Coin in her pocket. A smile. All the while thinking, I killed a bird.

In the cafe, she leaned over the newspaper. A father had abducted his own son after school, taking him interstate. With the hysteria around Caitlin's disappearance still fresh, parents were up in arms about the lack of teacher supervision at pick up. The election wasn't far away, either, so local politicians suddenly had a lot to say about child safety.

———

She parked the Hilux on the access road and carried the coffees on top of the Tupperware container down the hill to the worksite.

'Jen!' Lil removed her gloves and made her way up the slope. 'Coffee. You're a darling.'

'And cupcakes – though they took a tumble, I'm afraid,' Jen said.

Lil peeled back the lid with wrinkled hands. 'They're lovely. Let's sit for a bit. I need to get the taste of lantana out of my mouth.'

'Sorry I'm late,' Jen said. 'I hit a kookaburra.'

Lil brushed crumbs from her shirt. Her eyes were clear blue, with the sparkle of a much younger woman. 'Oh no,' she said. 'Are you okay?'

Jen nodded.

'And the kooka?'

'Couldn't find it.'

'I'm sure it's fine.' Lil grinned. 'They're tough old birds!'

'Like you,' Jen said.

'Yes.'

'How's your mother?'

'Bah,' Lil said. 'The meals-on-wheels lady went round on Wednesday, as usual, but there was no answer. She rang me, of course. So I tore over. And there Mum was doing a puzzle, curtains drawn, television on full bore. Dirty dishes in the sink.'

Jen smiled.

'I mean, I was glad she was all right . . .'

'Is she eating properly?'

'Subsisting on tea and biscuits from what I can gather,' Lil said. 'And refuses to drink water. Water! She's had to be hospitalised twice already just for dehydration.'

Jen offered another cupcake.

'We'd better save some for the boys.'

The 'boys', three men aged forty plus, had begun glancing up from behind the lantana. 'And we'd better get to work.'

'Yes. Wouldn't want to be thought useless women,' Lil said. 'Though I'd happily leave the lantana to them – they seem to enjoy hacking and slaying at it.'

Jen fetched her gloves from the seat of the ute, and walked downhill with Lil. 'Would you consider getting more help?'

'A carer? I guess I feel like I should do that myself,' Lil said.

Jen had felt the same guilt when her own mother reached that stage, though she had never seriously contemplated caring for her. And she'd had the excuse of working full-time. 'What about the aged-care facility in town? Or the one up the mountain.'

'Put her in a home?'

Jen stopped and put her hand on Lil's shoulder. 'I'd hate it, too. But my mother picked up once she went in. Enjoyed the company. And the attention.'

'At least they could put her on a drip if she refused to drink.'

Jen laughed. 'Exactly.'

Called

She took her time on the road down from the mountain. It was steep and winding, and the view out to the coast spectacular. There had been a rockfall since she came through earlier, partly blocking the other lane. Jen pulled over onto what verge there was and got out. Whipbirds cracked and chided. She stood for a moment, listening for traffic. It was just her and the birds, and a tractor doing some slashing in the valley below. She crossed the road and rolled the rocks off into the gutter, one by one. The largest of them was shaped like a giant toad, and would look good in her bromeliad garden.

Again she listened for traffic and, hearing nothing, bent her legs to heft the stone. She staggered across the road, holding it against her body, and just managed to lift it over the edge of the ute's tray.

She puffed to get her breath and leaned on the ute as a sports car sped past, throwing up what was left of the rockfall detritus.

Down the lane, a little ahead, black cockatoos started making a fuss in a big old grey gum. Dozens of them. They were squawking and carrying on – for what reason, it wasn't clear.

Jen bunched a tarp around the rock to try to stop it rolling about and climbed back into the cab.

The lane meandered off into the foothills. She nosed along, stopping close by the tree where the cockatoos were making such a ruckus. Jen lowered the window and raised her binoculars. The birds seemed to be getting grubs from high up in the tree – borers, most likely – which was generating a great deal of excitement. A celebration of abundance.

The sun was warm on her face, all the noise somehow cheering. Having finally delivered the pieces to the gallery, she did feel a little lighter. She was pleased with the wenge, in the end, setting off the robins' eyes. Only tourists ever went through the gallery, and they tended to buy up all of the local landscape painter's works – brightly coloured hills topped with mad houses – but the robins would at least get some sort of showing.

It was the best time of year. The air so clear. The colours so bright. The country steepened behind the old grey gum, and the lane disappeared around a corner into a patch of pine forest. The light was so soft, it was almost like a wash over the scene. *Pine forest?*

Jen stopped. Lifted her binoculars once again. The hair on her arms prickled. She started the Hilux and released the handbrake, leaving the cockatoos, who seemed to have settled down now, behind her. The road narrowed, dipped, then climbed again. The fence by the road was old and tumbling, disappearing into grassy tussocks. She held her breath as she rounded the bend.

———

The pines were over a ramp, on private property. Something about the row of mailboxes, battered old four-gallon drums, felt familiar. She stopped short of the entrance. Brown needles spilled out over the driveway. Her foot slipped off the clutch and the Hilux stalled.

It was more a feeling than any definite recognition or familiar feature; this was the place she had hung on to. She struggled with the doorhandle, dropping her sunglasses on the floor. The air was pungent with pine sap, persisting beyond memory, and distinct from the wet and dry sclerophyll of her more everyday experience.

It was barely a forest, an acre or two given over to pines. Probably planted in the early twentieth century. She stepped onto the narrow strip of dirt.

Jen slid off her shoes to walk on the pine needles. A crow called. She followed the path woven around fat trunks, their eighty or so years of growth more solid than her own, to the clearing within. Her vision spun loose, a blur of russet thatch and flaking trunks, interrupted light. It could be anywhere: any forest, any country, any time. And she was nowhere, stranded between her childhood and now.

Dry needles cut into her knees. A breath of wind had the trees whispering and shushing above her. Surely the memory would come freely here. Answers.

Nothing.

The movement was all around, only she was still. Half her life had gone by – like this.

She forced herself up and back down the path to the ute, driver's side door still open.

———

Jen passed a yurt and two A-frames, one of the many communal titles that gave away the area's hippie roots. The road's potholes sent the Hilux lurching. She loosened her grip on the wheel and dipped her head to see better, each bend promising something familiar, until she ran out of road.

She pulled up by an old carport, an original structure by the look of it, piled high with evenly cut wood. An old man emerged from between two coffee bushes.

She opened her door and placed her foot on the ground. As if that would steady her. 'Hello,' she said. 'I'm Jen. Jen Anderson.'

'Wayne.'

'I was Jenny Vogel,' she said. 'Your pine grove. I have this memory of having a picnic there when I was a child.'

'Picnic?'

She stood and leaned on the ute door. 'With my parents. Peter and Carol. I was only small.'

'Well, we had some great parties in there,' he said. 'But I don't think they would have brought you along.'

A brush turkey patrolled the edge of the lawn. Beyond, lantana and privet were taking hold.

'Place has got away from me a bit,' he said. 'Why don't you come inside. I was just going to have a cuppa.'

She followed him into a hexagonal room overlooking the forest.

'Might we have been visiting you?'

He busied himself with putting the kettle on and throwing some more wood on the fire. 'It was the seventies, yeah?'

'Yeah.'

'We were all hippies then, and young,' he said. 'Thought we were real alternative.'

Except, unlike the hippies she read about, they had cut down forests instead of saving them.

'Course, a lot of that's back in fashion now, just been rebadged. Slow living. Organic.'

Jen smiled.

'We all grew our own stuff back then. Swapped and bartered.'

The kettle whistled but Wayne didn't get up. He watched her, forehead wrinkled, waiting for something.

'Oh!' She laughed. 'They were scoring pot.'

'Sorry, love, didn't want to just come out with it. In case you're all evangelical or something. Coffee?'

'Yes, please.'

'I grew vegetables, too,' he said. 'But we had a little business on the side. Good stuff, and just for friends.' He filled the plunger with boiling water.

'And my father would drive up here to get it?'

'Sometimes,' he said. 'Didn't usually bring you or your mum, though.'

'Maybe he left us in the pine grove, came back,' she said. 'I remember a picnic rug.'

'Could be,' he said. 'He did take her there on a picnic when they were dating. Said there was a little magic to the place, that anything was possible. Course, a smoke or two helped.' He waited, then pushed down the plunger and filled two old mugs.

Jen rescued hers from Wayne's shaking hands before it spilled over the newspapers on the table. Her father had said once, a little tipsy, that he had asked her mother to marry him in a fairy grove. And her mother, after he had left, said that she had been a fool to marry a man always so far away with the fairies.

'Thank you.'

'Your dad and I were pretty good friends, for a time,' he said. 'Ever hear from him?'

Jen shook her head. 'You?'

'No, love.' He swallowed a mouthful of his tea. 'Would've

liked to. Never made much sense, him taking off,' he said. 'He really loved your mother.'

———

Jen slowed as she passed a schoolgirl walking home. She watched her in the rear-vision mirror until the car going the other way had disappeared over the hill. She was as bad as all the parents around town. Overcompensating. Trying to fix what could not be changed; they had let a child down.

And now they were letting them all down – to assuage their own guilt. It was one thing for the adults to be watchful, vigilant, as the papers suggested, but all their anxiety was absorbed by the children, at the very time in their lives when they should have no fears or worries. You had to prepare children for the realities of the world – she wasn't in favour of cottonwool – but she preferred to see their characters free to form within a bubble of endless possibility rather than limited by a world of horror and restrictions.

They had gone to Fraser Island once, when she was small. Just for the day. She remembered the feeling of swimming underwater in the blue lake, with the snorkel and mask they handed out. Flippers, too. She had not known then to walk backwards up the beach, and each time she came out to tell her parents about a turtle or fish, she had split the wide front end of the flippers – probably perished from the sun – and had to get a new pair. Neither the tour guide nor her parents had said anything, just let her go.

The memory of swimming in the blue lake was one of freedom, oblivious to anxiety, worry or the future. Before Michael. It was hard to imagine today's children knowing that feeling.

One for the Road

She paused with her cup halfway to her mouth. A pink robin had landed on the edge of the birdbath. She blinked. At least that's what she thought it was. A dusky pink breast and fat robin shape. On its own, it seemed. No mate. She set down her cup on the table rather than clatter the saucer and reached for her bird book. The robin section was well-thumbed, and thick with notes, but this was a first. 'Ha!' Rose robin. Uncommon.

It was peering at her now, but didn't take off. She opened her book and made note of the sighting, recorded the date and time, then began making some rough sketches. It was a little smaller than the yellows, more demure. She had a mind to dedicate her day to a study of the rose robin.

The scream of a chainsaw put an end to all that. The bird disappeared into the trees, and the morning was ripped apart.

Jen pulled a beanie on over crumpled hair, slid into her boots, and marched up the driveway. On the side of the road, the last threads of the trunk cracked and gave way, crashing down – in treefall – and shaking the ground. The smell of cut timber tickled her nose and throat. Bloodwood, probably; their

132

resin gave off a smell almost like flesh. Particles were caught in the light.

Three orange-shirted fellows encircled her mailbox, one with an axe resting on his shoulder.

Jen stopped just short. 'Can I help you?'

'This has to go. We're widening the road. Sealing it.'

She sneezed. 'I got the notice. But it said you were stopping at my boundary.'

'There's extra money now – we're going further.'

Jen noted the string of trees marked with fresh pink ribbon. 'Well, no one has talked to me about it. So perhaps you could initiate a conversation before taking to my property with an axe.'

'It's on council land.'

'The mailbox is on the side of the road, like everyone else's, so that the mail delivery person can pull over and put my mail in it,' she said. 'And I'm pretty sure it's on my land. As are the majority of those trees. Perhaps you would like to confirm where the boundary lies, and get me something in writing?' Which would give her a chance to object, on paper, rather than placing her body between them and the machines.

One of the fellows behind the axe-wielder smirked. The woman by the side of the road holding the sign spun it to slow and let a trickle of traffic through. Jen returned a wave from Alan, her neighbour from up the road. Great, caught standing on the side of the road still in her pyjama pants, for all to see. Tyres growled on the raw gravel. The mailbox, handmade from an old packing case, had been a gift. It was a bird house, the sense of humour of her found-artist friend, Geraldine, before she moved back to Western Australia. Jen was fond of its little rails and deck, and the circular hole, although it meant the postie had to roll up her mail to deposit it. It was in sympathy with the setting, and to scale with the landscape – unlike the standard little metal boxes.

The axeman examined the base of the pole it was resting on. 'We could shorten this. Reset the base.'

She breathed. 'If, in fact, it is on council land.'

'Right,' he said. 'And just move the box back.'

'Fine,' she said. And sneezed.

'I'll talk to head office and get back to you.'

'Righto.' She turned and headed back down to the house. The woodchipper roared, jaws hungry for freshly cut trunks.

———

Jen had tried working through the rumble of the grader and the *beep beep beep* of reversing machinery, without success. She took her sketchbook and an apple down to the far end of the block and lay against a log.

Her father had loved trees, in his way. He appreciated the physicality of them, the process of bringing them down, transporting them, and turning them from tree to lumber. He admired big trees, in particular, standing back, hands behind his head, to take in their height and girth. He would caress their trunks, assess the timber within, and gauge the best place to cut. After they came down, with a great crash that shook the earth on which he stood, throwing up a cloud of forest dust, he would admire the grain across their stump, breathe in the scent from their fresh-cut wounds. He loved them as he killed them.

He supported selective logging rather than total annihilation, and abhorred waste, bringing home scraps to burn in the fire or to build something from one day. He believed in using the whole tree, breaking it down as if it were an animal he had killed. And he knew no other work. He needed to put food on the table, and it was the job of the timberman to drive the forest from the country.

Jen put a hand on the log on which she leaned. She was a timber child, grown from fallen trees and sawdust. Standing on stumps before she knew them for carcasses and gravestones. She had counted centuries' worth of rings – a knowledge of fire and a rainforest world reaching back far beyond the arrival of the white ships – without any consciousness of loss.

As a child, Jen told her father that the trees spoke to her, and he had not seemed surprised. They spoke to her still. They gentled her, had allowed her to put down roots, and extend them – albeit tentatively – into the ground.

Turkey

Jen stepped out of the shower onto the bathmat. She reached for her towel, gathering it around her like a great cape, but her skin had already goosebumped. She padded out to the fire to dress. Although the sun was shining, the house, still in the shade of the trees, was cool; it was the time of year when it was often warmer out than in.

The log she had dragged inside burned red at one end and smoked from the other, like a fat cigar. She had just pulled on her jeans when she heard the scratching at the herb garden at the side of the house. She burst through the doors onto the deck and down the steps to catch the brush turkey red-necked, spraying mulch over the path and lawn.

'Piss off, you ugly buzzard!'

Just when she got a garden bed settled, along came a turkey and dug it all up.

It stepped down the lawn, head bobbing, crop swinging, but slowed after a few metres and looked about.

'Go on, or I'll eat you for dinner. Brainless fucking bird!'

She bent to pick up a stick fallen from the rose gum, long and straight. She lifted it above her shoulder and threw it like a javelin. What was left of her bare breasts slapped with the effort. The stick flew through the air and struck the bird in the rump, bouncing off into the lomandra. The bird ran on down the slope towards the neighbours', making the noise of an animal three times its size on dry leaves.

She was a little relieved she hadn't managed to spear the bird – she had never been much good at javelin, that had been Phil's area of athletic prowess. Her father had brought a turkey home – accidently killed on site – when she was a child. His rule had been that if you killed an animal you had to eat it. Or perhaps times were tougher then than she remembered. After her mother had prepared it for the oven, it did resemble a turkey bought from the supermarket or butcher. She had tried to approach the dinner table with an open mind, but the bird had been tough and gamey and she didn't fancy eating one again.

Some of the hippies hanging on in the area still had the same ideas. She had heard someone tell a story at the co-op, of eating the goanna they had killed to protect their hens' eggs, as if it made them self-sufficient. Since the goanna belonged and the chooks didn't, it would have been fairer, and tastier, just to eat the hens.

But who was she to talk, a middle-aged woman standing half-naked in the middle of the lawn. Henry was due soon and she was within clear sight of the driveway.

She scurried inside to finish dressing, hung up her towel, and combed the tangles out of her hair with her fingers. The woman in the mirror bore less and less resemblance to her imagined self. Neither young nor old, her hair more grey than brown; she was slipping into a hinterland all of her own, and mirrors were best avoided. She rubbed vitamin E cream into her cheeks and lips, dry from the cooler air and tending the fire.

She sat on the step to put on socks and boots. Soaked up the sun. A fantail in the birdbath splashed water over her shirtsleeve from above.

The lemon thyme was uprooted, splayed out on the path. She replanted it, gathered up mulch and patted it down around it. At this time of year, the brush turkeys came in looking for food, though she suspected they also enjoyed scratching loose soil and mulch around. Making a mess. They were the only native birds that she wished ill.

She filled her watering can and wet the herbs down, trying to settle them back in. When she heard Henry slam the car door, she went inside to wash her hands.

———

'Mrs Dunbar says I should enter the Regional Art Prize this year.'

Jen looked up. 'You should.'

'It's high school, too. And all the private schools.'

'Which piece were you thinking of?'

He shrugged. 'The owl feather one, maybe.'

'What about your portrait of Caitlin?'

'She didn't say anything about two entries.'

'Do you have the form with you?'

He extracted a crumpled piece of paper from his pencil case, flattened it out on the table.

Jen peered at it. 'There's the age category – they'll just do that based on your date of birth – and an overall prize. But there are also open categories for still life and portrait. I think you should enter both,' she said. 'Does it matter if you didn't do it at school?'

'Mrs Dunbar said we can enter anything, just to give it to her and she'll organise it.'

'You feel okay showing her the picture of Caitlin? No one else needs to see it, right?' Unless it placed, in which case it would be exhibited. But one step at a time.

He bit his lip. Fiddled with the crumbs of his muffin.

'I think it's really good, Henry. Enter it for me?'

'Okay.'

House, a Home

The male scrubwrens had appeared. At first she thought mother and male very busy indeed, but after watching for a while, she identified several different males bringing insects. It was all action outside the front door, chirruping and flitting about. One of the books said that female scrubwrens took several mates, and as they couldn't be sure which male was the father, they all contributed – taking the opposite approach to humans.

She walked down the path around to the back of the house, sweeping. She did not need to whistle as she worked; the king parrots were doing that for her, one on each side of her back lawn. She bent down to gather a few clutches of leaves and sticks of a good length for lighting the fire, and turned back to the house. There, climbing one of the corner poles of the back deck, was a terrible meandering trail, all the way to the roof. Termites!

She leaned the broom on the deck railing and placed the sticks and leaves on the top step. With her nail, she flicked off a section of crumbly tunnel. It was a white ant highway inside, some travelling up, some down, all to invisible road rules. She followed the trail along a crossbeam and into the soft timber above the back doors. 'Great.'

She dragged a chair over and climbed up to take a closer look, tapped the beam. They were all through the strip of oregon – it was nothing but a papery maze of tunnels, all leading inside. 'Far out.'

She followed the trail backwards, down and around the pole, to a section of rotting timber around the tap.

She could call the termite man, but that would cost a few hundred dollars, and he would pump the pole full of toxic chemicals and spray the deck timbers, fussing about identifying where the termites had come from. She had fallen for it at first, until she realised that there were nests and termite-addled trees all around. There was no getting rid of them, but there was plenty of tastier wood, out there, where they belonged. It was rotting timber that drew them in.

She dropped the sticks and leaves in the kindling basket, slipped out of her shoes and padded inside to put the kettle on. She could see the little train continuing inside now, climbing the beam up towards the peak of the ceiling. How had she missed all that? Daydreaming.

The kettle squealed. She turned off the gas, filled an infuser with leaves – a new herbal concoction promising calm – and sat on the back deck.

She sipped her tea. The robins came hopping about near the termite workings she had unveiled, pecking up the wriggling morsels, which gave her half an idea.

She fetched the vacuum cleaner from the laundry cupboard, plugged it into the power point on the deck and began sucking up the termites, workings and all. They showered down all over her, into her hair, biting her arms as they plummeted, confused.

She pushed the brush into the corners and dragged it along the beam, making her way down the pole until all sign of their trail was gone.

She went through the same process inside, wherever she could reach. After something of a wrestle, she managed to return the vacuum cleaner, full of dying termites, to the cupboard. She put on gloves to apply surface spray at the point where the timber munchers had entered the house, to the beam they had infested, and around the rotten timber by the tap.

She removed her gloves and washed her hands and arms, the flare of red marks evidence that termites were quite fierce in their own way. She sat down with her cold tea to watch the robins pecking up the last strays from the table and deck.

It didn't pay to relax her guard; the house needed her and she needed it.

Flight

She lay in bed listening to the birds. The sky was clear, sounds carrying clean and far in the cool, dry air. She frowned at the warbling of currawongs, close by, for the second morning in a row. Their song was pretty, but if they stayed, they would scare her small birds away. The canopy was thinning, giving predators a clearer view. Their range was spreading because of clearing and climate change.

She stretched out her limbs and back, yawned. Sunlight streamed in over her bed. 'Up, up, up.'

Something about the light, and breakfasting alone, had her thinking of her mother's house. Once her father had left, her mother had lost her centre. Perhaps she had never had one of her own, just the appearance of constancy through being anchored to her father. As it had turned out, he was not one to set your course by, but without him Jen's mother was buffeted this way and that by whatever the wind blew in.

Once the Brethren had set her back on her feet, there was the Bowen 'cleansing therapist' who ran a neat store in the old main street for a time, and for whom her mother had been a part-time receptionist. Her mother had a corresponding health kick, an overly organised home and a stack of expensive hardcover books from the States. She had taken Jen along for a colonic irrigation in hope it would cleanse her 'moods'. It hadn't. Though she had been pleased to weigh in several pounds lighter that night.

Then there was the community bank manager. Her mother's wardrobe went from rainbow to monotone, and their financial affairs were at least temporarily in order. Until he was transferred out west.

Her mother found some work at the co-op, which led to a revival of the flowing coloured clothes, a house stocked with vitamins, wheat shoots and carob, a tattoo on her ankle and a new library of soft-covered books on permaculture, organics and clean living.

It drove Jen crazy – albeit from a distance by then – and sometimes she had not been able to stop herself thinking that if that's who her mother really was, she understood why her father had slipped his mooring.

———

She shut the front door behind her and leaned on the wall to put on her boots. The scrubwrens had been chattering since sunrise, their feeding program struggling to keep up with their babies' growing appetites, despite the extra help. She stopped. A chick was out of the nest, all scrawn and skin, a single spiky feather protruding from its back. It was hanging from the basket by its neck, beak wide and gasping.

Scrubwrens were hopping about in the fern, and one flew close to the chick, landing briefly on the chain securing the pot and their nest, chittering and fussing all the while. But there wasn't much she could do without hands. One of the males returned with a worm. Jen peered into the nest. There was still at least one chick inside. They usually only had two or three. Had they tried to cast one out to focus on the other, intending it to land hard on the deck below? Was there something wrong with it? It seemed unlikely that it had crawled there itself. Its skin was transparent, revealing its insides – stomach, lungs and veins. Its slowing heart. It wouldn't live long out in the morning cold. Still, Jen hesitated. She shouldn't interfere.

She slipped her hand up inside her sleeve and lifted the chick free of the basket edge, placing it back at the entrance to the nest. Surely they hadn't meant for it to die. She forced herself up to the vegetable patch and began a half-hearted weed of one of the beds.

———

She slowed as she approached the front deck. The nestling was no longer in the opening of the nest, and for a moment she allowed herself a rescuer's smile. She had been worried that the parents would reject it. Or not be able to get it back inside.

Then she saw the bodies of both chicks on the boards beneath the hanging basket. She dropped down beside them. 'No.' The breeze fluttered the fluff on their little heads. One was dead, neck broken. The other was still breathing. A scrubwren flittered and chirped around Jen and the spilled chicks. Distressed. The mother, surely. Was it Jen's fault for interfering? Did they hold her responsible?

There was no saving them now; they were too young, too damaged. She should put the still gasping one out of its misery, but she couldn't. She couldn't make herself crush it or freeze it or break its neck or any of the things she should do; she just couldn't take a creature's life.

She slid out of her boots and retreated inside. It was a miserable day. She washed her hands and dried them on the towel then padded over to put on the kettle. Birds were fussing all around the house, the word of alarm or distress sounding far and wide. It was most unsettling. She could not get the image of those two little bodies out of her head.

Dry

Jen's skin had shrunk, like all of the timber in the house. It was a record dry spell: fifty-six days without rain. Her face was tight, hands flaky, her back itching, as if she was wintering down south, where she had always felt desiccated. Craig had rubbed moisturiser into her back through winter, his hands as soothing as the cream. Her own attempts to smear it onto those areas she could reach after her shower were just not the same.

The gesture had been, in part, an apology for keeping her in the cold and the dry. Although they had spoken about moving to northern New South Wales – to be closer to lush forests, rivers and the ocean – they were waiting for her to finish college, and then he had scored a job with one of the better state schools. He had rented a flat and she had moved in to save money. It all made perfect sense at the time, and perhaps it still did.

It was to be more than twenty years before she moved north again, but she had soon adapted, shifted back. Forgotten what had gone before. So much so that the cooler months now felt like a Canberra winter. The summers were so humid that late winter and spring felt dry, and they were. The screen doors no longer closed, retreating from their catches by a quarter of an inch. One of the kitchen cupboards had developed the same problem, swinging open with a creak whenever she walked past, or in the middle of the night.

She imagined the native mice – *Antechinus flavipes* – prising it open with their hands, and hosting midnight feasts of dry pasta, flour, oats and sugar. Or perhaps pushing their way out under the cover of darkness, having sneaked in while the door was open, only to have her close it on them. The colder weather, and the dry, always brought them in. They seemed to view her cottage as their cold store larder, or winter house, so a self-opening cupboard was not ideal. Not that doors necessarily kept them out; somehow the mice could flatten themselves to get through the tiniest of gaps. They dwelled in the spaces inside the walls, especially near the stove, where it was warm. They were cute creatures, with their dark eyes, long tails and jerky movements, and at first she didn't mind sharing her home. Hearing them hop down the stairs to the kitchen for breakfast was quite companionable, but they soon began to make a mess – and smell.

She had found a swarm of babies once, in a drawer of her desk, dozens of the little wretches in a messy nest – a mest – of receipts and leaves and, from goodness knows where, a gob of wool. She had pulled the whole drawer out, in disgust, and carted it outside. Several of the young, with more initiative than their siblings, had scampered away into the corners of the room, while their mother looked on from the rafters. The rest clung to home, too afraid to move, as they sailed outside into the world.

They were too young to release into the bush. She had found a plastic bag to tip the whole lot into, intending to put them to sleep in the freezer. But they had looked up at her with such imploring eyes, as if understanding that their lives were in her hands, and she had let them out beneath the trees, to give them a fighting chance. The mother had come and carried her pink babies away a few at a time, clinging to her thighs. Each of those mice had probably had a dozen families of their own by now, and soon she would be overrun.

She gathered sticks and leaves, filling the fireplace cavity and her basket by the back door. She had enough wood cut for another day or so and didn't feel like disturbing the stillness by starting the chainsaw.

Fairy-wrens flitted and flirted in the grevilleas, treecreepers sang their way up trunks. Jen filled her watering can and topped up the birdbaths.

It wasn't quite 'the dry' of the tropics, but by the end of winter, her forest was a different country. Moss and mould had disappeared, and the leaf cover thinned, allowing a view out to the valley. The colours paled, green to brown; the light softened. It was pleasant to work in the sun through the middle of the day. She lingered inside longer, ate breakfast and dinner in front of the fire. Vines and creepers died and fell back, and a coating of gravel dust built up on the leaves near the road. The place began to resemble bush. Dry sclerophyll rather than wet.

She cut a piece of rye bread and dropped it in the toaster, then sliced a piece of cheese to put on it.

Her father had worked flat-out all winter, when cutting timber was easy, he said. He also used to say it never went sixty days without rain, and the high cloud moving in suggested he was right.

———

She heard them before she saw them. Currawongs at the birdbaths. She ran through the house and out onto the back deck. 'Hey!'

They flew off – rather guiltily – and came to rest on a branch downhill. Still too close.

'I said *HEY!* You interlopers.'

They flew off a little farther, to the other side of the creek.

'That's better.' She looked around. Listened. It was too late; not a small bird in sight. Not a chirp.

She emptied and cleaned the birdbaths, soiled with regurgitated, seed-filled muck, and refilled them with cool, clean water. Henry had once spotted her trying to rescue a moth from the waiting tongue of a gecko, and said she shouldn't interfere with nature, and he was right, but she needed her birds around her. She had created a space they considered safe, and it was her job to keep it that way.

Break

She was halfway through rubbing butter into flour before she remembered it was school holidays. Henry would not be drawing today. She sighed. At least she had known what day it was.

She kept on with the scones, nonetheless; she could do with a treat. She had woken to the deep grunting of a male koala outside her window in the night, and the high-pitched scream of the female. Mating season had begun. Jen had smiled in the dark, knowing she wouldn't be getting much sleep, but relieved to know they were still out there – and breeding.

Her mixture now resembled breadcrumbs, as the recipe said it should. A pair of bar-shouldered doves roamed the lawn. They worked from one end towards the other, on opposite sides but coming closer together now and then. Cooing. She would have to look up what it was that they liked to eat, from among the grass in her little clearing, at this time of year.

Henry had said they were going to Stradbroke for a week, which wasn't far but a world away. Camping, he said. She had asked him for a drawing, which was probably a bit mean. He didn't need homework in the holidays, but going to new places meant seeing new things with fresh eyes, and that was good for his training.

She had never been on a family holiday. Except that week in Sydney with Aunt Sophie. Going on the Manly ferry and visiting Taronga Zoo were the highlights of her childhood.

———

She looked up at the sudden whack against the window above her desk: a bird trying to fly through. The trouble with so many windows and, possibly, keeping them so clean, was that the birds saw a path through the house. Or perhaps they didn't even see it as a house. She stood and leaned out, searching the ground below. A rufous fantail lay motionless among the leaves.

She raced to the door, slid into shoes and ran around the house. It was limp and still, its pretty tail spread. All she seemed to do lately was kill birds.

But she was not without hope. She had been caught out before, beginning to bury a female rosella only to have it return to life. This fantail, too, might just be in shock. She took off her shirt and gathered the bird up, carrying it inside – lest it become lunch for a kookaburra or currawong. She popped shirt and bird in a box and sat it inside the open front door.

When she had finished setting up her watercolours and brushes and changed the water in her jar, she checked on the bird. She found it blinking – as if waking from a deep sleep. She would have liked to believe he knew her as a friend and didn't blame her for hanging invisible glass weapons in his way. She opened the shirt up a little, resisting the urge to caress him, and backed away.

Sketching out the next robin piece was the most difficult part – committing pencil to paper.

The fantail was scrabbling against the cardboard, confusing the image in her head. Rufous over yellow. She focused on the lead trailing across the grain of the page, and the robins returned to the foreground, where they preferred to be.

When she got up to check again, the fantail was gone. It had flown the box. Jen smiled. She had not killed a bird today.

Gallery

The way in was a maze of roundabouts and canals, the signage unhelpful to the unfamiliar. Jen gave up on the map and followed her nose along the river. It was greener than at home, the lawns still lush. According to the map, the gallery was over the bridge on a little headland, near the library. Pelicans watched from the streetlights, and white boats celebrated the cobalt waters. Jen turned into the street she had written down, passed a brown heritage sign that probably said gallery, and parked the Hilux in the shade of a spreading fig. The road was closed for some sort of market, all white tents and rainbow clothing. A green-grassed park rolled down to the water's edge. A couple lay in the sun on a red blanket, next to two rather incongruous World War II shells.

She followed the winding path around, beneath Moreton Bay figs and tree ferns. The gallery's glass doors, looking out to the water, were closed. Jen peered in, past the shop counter, and noted some of David Paulson's later works occupying the main space. Her little pieces could not compete with their size and colour, their boldness. Or the photorealism of the Christopher

Page eagle in the foyer. A clock on the wall said she was ten minutes early.

She retraced her steps and browsed the tables of a second-hand bookstall at the edge of the market. A tattered first edition of Skemp's *My Birds* all but flew into her hand. At only eight dollars, she took it to the counter, sure it was worth three times that.

———

She nursed the cloth hardcover under her arm right through the meeting and tour. The curator, Maureen, was one of those eternally bubbly and optimistic women whose enthusiasm never seemed to flag. It was exhausting, but what was needed to persist in the art world, especially in this day and age.

'So, what do you think?'

'It's a lovely gallery,' Jen said. It was smallish, a series of rooms without any great space from which to stand back and appreciate larger works. But that would work quite well for most of her pieces. And the spot was tranquil, beneath trees and by the water, like some sort of hide – albeit open to the public. 'I'd welcome the opportunity to exhibit here.'

Maureen clapped her hands together. 'I'm so pleased. I absolutely love your work,' she said. 'As soon as I saw those robins, I just knew you were back.'

Jen smiled. Flattery, as uncomfortable as it felt, was always welcome.

'Wait just a minute.' Maureen flurried out of the room in a swish of silk.

Jen flicked through her book, scanning a paragraph to see if the bird descriptions were as good as she remembered. Maureen returned carrying one of Jen's early pieces, the second or third she had sold: black cockatoos feasting on a pine cone. Tearing it apart, really. Like lions at a carcass.

'I inherited this,' Maureen said. 'From my mother. I just love their faces.'

'That makes me feel a little old,' Jen said. 'It's from my graduation exhibition.' The exhibition, at the Drill Hall Gallery, had been politely received. A few sales, and some nice write-ups. But not glowing. With graduates producing shark skin 'heavy petting gloves' and enormous postmodern sculptures, she was all but invisible. A junior arts writer for the *Canberra Times* had given her the 'bird lady' tag that had stuck.

'I've been working on a list of galleries and private owners on record as having your works,' Maureen said. 'Perhaps I could email that to you, and if you have any you can add . . .'

Jen blinked. 'Sure.'

'We don't need all of them, obviously, but a good cross-section.'

Drier

The showers had freshened things up for a while, but three hot days had turned her world back to brown and crispy. Jen refilled the birdbaths, drunk dry already.

It was supposed to be hot again, thirty-three, with a late change and the chance of some rain. Despite all that technology and equipment, that was the best the bureau could come up with: 'the chance of a shower'. Even odds. Tossing a coin or glancing at the sky would be just as effective. The heat had to break but nothing about the bush suggested there was rain coming. The trees were dropping leaves flat-out and the birds kept to the shade, beaks open. Most telling of all, black ants swarmed the kitchen sink, encircling the plughole like miniature bison.

Lil said that getting hot like this, before the rain, was not a good sign. Except for lantana eradication.

Jen turned off the kitchen tap and stood still. There was a swamp wallaby at the bottom of the garden, ears twitching. He looked towards the house from behind his dark robber's mask. She memorised his stance, the lengths of his limbs. The ginger bases of his ears. She stepped out onto the deck, keeping behind a post. He sensed her, stood a little more alert.

She took another step, peering out from behind the post. He took off, downhill, each springy hop loud on the dry leaves. She refilled her glass with cold water from the fridge and retreated to her studio, beneath the shifting air of the fan.

———

She was still eating her breakfast when the phone rang. She looked up from the page, contemplated leaving it. But it was nearly seven, and a Henry Day. 'Hello?'

'Jen, it's Kay.'

'Hey.'

'Henry's not coming today. The counsellor, from school, he's had an accident.'

'What?'

'Fishing. Off the rocks. Washed out to sea. They found his body this morning.'

'Is Henry okay?'

'He's upset. They all are. He'd been seeing the counsellor every week.'

Jen swallowed.

'It's been good, I think. But it will make this even harder.'

'Yes.'

'Anyway, I'm sorry for the late notice. They only just found out.'

'It's fine, Kay,' she said. 'Take care.'

'You, too.'

Jen put the handset back in its cradle. Sighed. That class was having a bad year.

Driest

She hosed her lettuces and cherry tomatoes. Water trucks thundered up and down the road. Her tank was low, but it was only her, and if she was careful, she shouldn't have to buy any in. Surely it had to rain in the next few weeks.

Waiting for rain generated a certain tension, and endless opportunities for procrastination. Weeding would be easier when the ground was soft. There was no use planting – until it rained. It was better to leave the grass long. After almost two months, she had settled into a sort of malaise. She was spending more time in the studio, at least, and had an idea for a major new piece.

Of course, rain wasn't the only thing everyone was waiting for. There was no news of Caitlin, no clue. Not a word from the police for over a month. Even the media had moved on. It was sucking the life out of the town, just as the dry was browning the green.

Jen soaked her herbs, prone to drying out in their fat terracotta pots, to protect them from the thirty-degree day forecast to follow. The garbage truck tore up the hill, too fast, then locked up, its wheels braking in the loose gravel built up on the side of the road. A cloud of dust floated down over the orchard.

Her carry-on about the road – her mailbox and trees, at least – had been all too hard for council. They finished the tarring where they had first intended, just short of her property line.

She had loved the idea of a gravel road in the beginning, remote and inaccessible. The look of it, too: soft terracotta beneath a green tree arch. There was more traffic now, though, utes speeding through pulling rattling trailers, and she couldn't wait for it to be sealed. Council used to grade the road three times a year, taking several days to do the job. Now, it was once a year, and finished in a day. Within a few weeks it was full of potholes and corrugations, deepening to juddering pits, and she was sick of the dust.

Jen turned off the tap, picked a handful of rocket and lettuce for her lunch and returned to the cool of the house.

Her skin was dry and itchy, wanting to flake off like the bark of the spotted gums outside. Not that she was lucky enough to have a smooth new version of herself waiting underneath; she was stuck with the skin she had, stretching and wrinkling with each passing year.

When the rains came late, like this, it was easy to think, as Christmas and New Year approached, that this was summer. The way everyone else knew summer, with sunny days, clean surf and clear nights. The bright beach towel left on the line for next time, the outdoor furniture uncovered. Reminding her that holidays did not have to be as she remembered them as a child – stuck indoors with the mould while it rained and rained for a month. The last time the wet had come this late was 1996, Lil said, and it had held off until the very end of January. There was no escaping it, though. The annual rainfall had to come, and the later it came, the more condensed a period it would fall within – and the more damage it would do.

———

The rufous fantail who had hit the window – she was sure it was the same one – often fluttered about her studio now, as if remembering the encounter, flitting its tail this way and that to show off its span and fine russet tones, chirping and fussing. He was wasting his time, but it was the utmost flattery to be courted by a bird.

Why did birds sing? It was the gift of language, the birds' way of communicating with each other. But why so pretty? Perhaps to make up for the fragility of the singer, perched on hollow bones. Did it give them pleasure to perform their songs, as it did to hear them? There was no explaining beauty in nature. And there were horrors, too.

Only yesterday morning she had seen a butcherbird – horror enough – with something in its claws. Focusing her binoculars on the scene, she had found it was a yellow robin, flopped quite still and dead. She had chased the damned butcher away, but it was all too late. It was the way of things, and she should not interfere or sook, but she had been too upset to draw, cleaning out the laundry instead. All day she had tried not to think on it, pushing the image out of her mind. Red spilling over yellow.

She had given the robins a false sense of security, thinking that they were safe in this clearing. But with the trees dropping leaves and branches to survive the dry spell, the butcherbirds snuck in to spy little birds from the high branches, swooping to strike.

Moment

A cool change around midnight brought nothing but wind. She had fallen asleep amid a rain of sticks and gumnuts on the roof and the bending of trees, and awoke from turbulent dreams.

It was blown drier than ever, and the deck, lawn and drive were covered in mess. Still, the drop in temperature was a relief. She gathered up bits of branch from the lawn, some as thick as her arm. There would be less opportunity to burn them now. She had already filled her kindling basket, and the fireplace. Now she was filling the wheelbarrow, to push up to the rubbish pile. She set aside those sticks too thick to break under her boot to chainsaw later.

The birds warbled and sang, happier for the cool. A black cockatoo called from somewhere down in the gully. Everything was brown and crunchy, like down south in late summer. For the first time since she had moved back, fire was a worry. Someone had dropped a note in her mailbox – one of the neighbours wanting to discuss a fire plan. It was probably a good idea, but she was hanging on to the hope of it raining first.

The ants had come into the bathroom, drinking from the puddles of water left by her feet and climbing her toothbrush in its tall glass for whatever nutrients they found there. And she had almost trodden on a red-bellied black snake on the cool step of the studio.

She put on her boots to water the vegetables, which were limp and sulky. Even the herbs were burned off.

'Oh.' She had heard the crash in the night, of something coming down. There had been a brief silence afterwards, before the owls and bats and crickets started up again. Whether the silence had been surprise or a mark of respect, she wasn't sure. It was a brush box. Or half of one, at least. Grown top-heavy and then snapped off, leaving a splintery stump. The driveway was blocked. It was a problem; she had an appointment with the shrink in an hour.

She re-dressed: jeans and an old shirt. The shed, where she kept the saw and other tools, was cool. Her hands were clumsy pulling the cord; she had to relax her arm or the cord would jam and jar, wrenching her shoulder. The machine started without much protest and smoked until she shut off the choke.

It was the thin end of the tree, more bulk than weight. She trimmed each springy limb from the trunk before slicing it into lengths. It hurt a little, to cut a tree so fresh, although she had not brought it down herself. The leaves were still bright green, its heart sap-filled and rebellious, as if it did not yet know it was dead.

She took pleasure in the work, breaking down the tree, carving it up and hauling away the parts, the way she imagined a skilled hunter might cut up an animal out of need in the snow. She liked to think she now wielded the blade in a way her father would have been proud of, shadowing what she remembered of his own technique.

Craig had never really wanted her to be his equal in chainsawing. Or his equal in anything for that matter. It had amused him to let her play with his toys, under his guiding hand, to try the things he did, as long as she didn't surpass him. It had taken her a long time to see that. Those belief systems were so deeply ingrained in men, and women too, that they were replicated, consciously and unconsciously, all the way down the line.

When she had won a grant to work in the States and had the opportunity to walk the Sierras, she had just thought him jealous. He had always wanted to trace John Muir's footsteps but hadn't been able to take the time off work to come with her. It had been more than that, though; some kind of fear of her walking independently of him.

'What's the workshop, anyway?' he had asked.

'It's a retreat, with Kym Daniels, the wildlife artist,' she said. 'I didn't think I'd get in.' In those days she had still been trying to keep her art going on weekends and holidays, even harbouring ideas about working towards another exhibition. She had laboured over the application for weeks without telling him and sent her portfolio from work, as if it were a dream she had no right to have.

'What's so good about him?'

'*She* is the best in the field. I'll be working with ten other artists from all over the world. What we produce will be exhibited, and perhaps published in an artist's book. Part of it is about describing our practice, which I suck at.'

'But you'll have to take time off work,' he said. 'And we had the Bungonia trip planned.'

'Only a few days.' Teaching in a private school, she had an extra non-teaching week every term break, which had been burning him up for years. 'We can still do the trip, if we leave two days later than we planned.'

He had smiled and nodded, but she had felt him turn dark underneath.

The workshop, and the trip as a whole, had changed her life. The feedback process had been fierce – she spent more than one night in tears – but she produced some of her best work. She had been so focused on working with Kym at first that she had underestimated the value of working with the other students. A mature group of peers with such a similar focus, similar passions. Four years of art school had not even come close to that week.

Some of them had been postgraduate students from the school, and they organised a field trip. They had walked and taken photographs and sketched. She had seen her first wolf and lain beside its tracks in the snow. Somehow the new landscape had kicked off something in her. She was an artist. If not by profession, by way of life. By nature. On the flight home, several wines into the long dark haul over the Pacific, she had been determined never to let go of that feeling. To find a way to keep working, somehow.

Craig had not been at the airport to meet her. She arrived home, after a fifty-dollar taxi ride, to an empty apartment and a Post-it note on the fridge. He was walking the Bungonias – on schedule and without her.

Jen hadn't unpacked her bags, leaving them in the narrow hallway, as if she might leave again, still riding the great wave of inspiration. She had ordered takeaway and eaten it alone on the balcony with the bottle of Californian chenin blanc she had brought back to share with Craig. Made plans. For the first time, she had felt life to be full of possibilities.

Jen propped the end of the splintered trunk up off the cement with her boot to make the last cut. She misjudged it a little, slicing right through the timber and bringing the blade down on her boot. The log rolled down the drive. She turned off the saw. Her boot was steel-capped, stopping the blade, but there was an unsightly notch in the leather over the toe.

By the time Craig returned, she had washed her clothes, put all her gear away, and cooked his favourite – veal scaloppine – for a welcome-home dinner.

She had been a stupid woman. Weak. Still wanting to believe the best in him, that he would change. But people didn't really change and he never saw the need. Even as she watched Craig slice up the veal and eat it a little too fast, between stories about his walk, she knew she had made a mistake. He did not ask about her trip. She had told him anyway, shown him all of her pictures. But as she turned the album's pages, she felt all the magic slipping away.

The sun had lifted itself above the tree line, lighting up the leaves. She dragged brush box limbs off to one side of the driveway and threw the lengths of wood, with an exaggerated back swing, into a rough pile on the other. She would have to ferry it down to the shed later.

Koel birds were calling all around – drowning out any other song. There seemed to be more of them than ever, and knowing what the birds were really up to, their rising notes had her feeling anxious.

She dusted off her jeans and jogged down the driveway, put the saw in the carport and ran into the house, already peeling off clothes.

Chance of a Shower

The quail were at it again. Flecked brown, low to the ground. Chirping. A covey of at least twelve scuttling off into the undergrowth with a clumsy waddle, as if they couldn't fly. Only when she was a few feet away would they launch into the air and then plunge into cover again, watching her out of the corner of their red eyes.

They turned up in drier years, and not always then. She hadn't seen the pattern to it yet. Despite the dry, they looked out of place, their subtle browns showing that her world was still relatively green. It was easier to imagine them in dusty fields and dun-coloured grasses – open spaces. But the books said they also inhabited rainforest edges.

'Mmm, lunch,' her father would have said. Just to stir her up. And she would have resisted the urge to run after the birds to try to catch one. She'd had a child's affinity with all things small in those days.

'I don't eat quail,' she had told the birds, more than once. She did not eat birds or animals of any description. They saw her as a predator nonetheless. It was sad, their lack of trust in the human race – but understandable.

The Bureau were at it again: 'chance of a shower'. More than a dozen such forecasts within the last seventy-two days that had amounted to almost nothing. 'Bollocks.' Lil didn't believe it either, ringing early to cancel their current regeneration project. 'Even the wetlands aren't wet,' she said. 'We'll have to wait until it rains. And that could be some time.'

Jen had been a little relieved; she needed an extra day in the studio. But she would try to finish early to spend some time with her own trees instead, fertilising, remulching and watering the younger citrus in the orchard.

———

It hung over the town like a rainless cloud. The thing that no one was saying but everyone was thinking: it's been too long; she's gone and her body is buried somewhere. At the co-op, the post office, the servo, they had stopped talking about it. Waiting for whatever came next. Locking their doors and watching their children. Wanting answers – but beginning to realise they might never get them.

Parents would share a look, over dinner, during the news: their private thanks that it was not their child who had been taken. Remembering Caitlin's parents, living with it all, walking among them. Pretending to keep on living.

Gum blossom covered the path in a sweet carpet. Great streamers of bark lay about the flooded gums. A robin worked to flip one over to find what was hidden beneath.

After pumping up this morning, the underground tank was nearly empty. It was ridiculous to think that she might have to buy water in the subtropics. Her next windfall was going on an additional tank.

The only plant thriving was the sage, imagining it had been returned to the Mediterranean, with the lack of rain and higher than usual temperatures. If there was an upside, it was that the weeds weren't growing either.

Jen gathered a handful of salad leaves from the vegetable patch, already wilted despite a heavy watering last night and early this morning. Only the rocket was going to make it, the rest fried off before reaching maturity. She had planted the crop a little late, but had not anticipated the sudden heat and sustained lack of rain. The tomatoes were happy, though, ripening as she watched. That was a positive; mostly they mildewed on the vine.

Paint

'How dry is it?' Henry no longer knocked, figuring the car in the driveway and his stamping down the steps announcement enough.

'Tomorrow,' she said.

'What?'

'It will rain tomorrow.'

'Sunday, they reckon. Chance of showers.'

Jen grinned. 'I counted sixty iris out this morning; it will rain tonight.'

'Whoa,' he said, seeing the easel set up on the deck, cradling a small, home-stretched canvas.

'Yes,' she said. 'Today we're going to paint.'

'You mean I'm going to paint.'

'Exactly.'

He pushed up his shirtsleeves, a little ragged on the edges and spotted with stains in the way of boys' clothes.

'I don't want you drawing first, or worrying too much about shape or definition. Just prepare your pallette and focus on the colours.'

He forced some white out of the tube. 'How long since you used these?'

'A while,' she said. 'You can help me use them up.' Modern organic oils were too bright for realist landscapes. Even around here. She had spent all her Henry money on four new pots from a fellow who was making paint in the old style using the mineral pigments of the masters.

'Why?'

'Sorry?'

'Why leave it so long?'

'I wanted to focus on the drawing,' she said. 'And I lived in an apartment, for a time, which didn't help.'

Their life became geared up around the trips away. It was easier to pack a sketchpad. And she had wanted to shed the bird lady tag. Craig had latched onto that one, especially once she became thin and angular with all the walking and, in the beginning, making love all over the landscape. There was something about a rushing stream, mossy bank or freshly plumbed cave, that fired up the earthier part of the connection between them. That had been enough – more than enough – for a time.

Henry sorted his greens first, then brown and blue.

'Did you know that green is one of the hardest colours to create?'

'What do you mean?'

'Well, it's all around us, right? Natural. But the old masters had the hardest time making green paint. And all the successful ones were completely toxic.' Scheele's green was the best, and the worst – full of arsenic. It would have been easier to clean your teeth with your paints every morning than cut off an ear or shoot yourself.

Henry recoiled from the easel.

'These paints are fine,' she said. 'Organic.'

'Huh. Got a bigger brush?'

'In the studio,' she said. 'But from the green jar. Not the red.'

He wiped his hands on his school shorts and ducked inside.

'You've been painting, too,' he said.

She turned. 'That was covered for a reason!'

He stood in the doorway, as if scared to come out. 'Is it a man or a bird?'

'What do you think?'

He chewed the end of her paintbrush. 'A man turning into a bird.'

'Why do you say that?'

'I don't think you'd want a bird to turn into a man,' he said.

'True enough.'

———

She followed Henry up to the top of the driveway and paused at his mother's window. 'Hey, Kay.' She smiled at Montana in the back, who looked up only briefly from her computer game. Henry opened the front passenger door, placed his bag between his feet.

'Hi, Jen.'

'I'm having a little show, at a gallery down on the coast. If it's all right with you, I'd like to take Henry to help me hang the works,' she said. 'It will be a Sunday, in a month's time.'

Kay switched off the radio, turned to Henry. 'You're keen?'

He nodded.

Something was worrying her. Money, perhaps. Or sending her son off with the artsy daughter of a suspected murderer.

'I thought it might be interesting for him,' she said. 'And he'd be helping me. There are twenty-nine pictures to hang – I couldn't do it on my own.' One of the kookaburras swooped over the car, prised something from beneath the mango tree in the orchard. 'It's not a lesson,' she said. 'And I'll shout him lunch somewhere nearby. Have him back before dark.'

'Sure,' Kay said. 'He'll enjoy that. We don't get out much at the moment.'

———

It had turned dark and heavy outside, and the temperature had dropped ten degrees while she had been lost in her book of Margaret Olley's interiors. What a woman. Jen's favourite was one of her last: *Yellow Room, Afternoon*. No surprise there.

Jen sniffed the air. Almost. But no rain yet. She listened to the bush, waiting. There were fresh green tips on the bunya pine. 'Ha. It's coming.'

She sliced mushrooms for her omelette, blanched broad beans for the salad. They were on the small side, but she had grown them herself. The first spots almost didn't register. The smell of rain on thirsty earth and dry eucalyptus leaves made it real. It was raining. Properly raining.

She stood at the kitchen sink watching it come down, washing dust from the leaves, refreshing the lawn. Returning her forest to itself. She found herself breathing more easily, her own face and skin plumping up again. She no longer had to worry about running out of water, and all those jobs she had put off could begin. Tomorrow.

Gutter

She stepped off the ladder and onto the roof, taking care to place her boot on the screw line. The iron was almost rusted through and gave a little beneath her weight. Water had been getting in for some time, around the screws, rotting the timber beneath. That's what had brought the termites.

She threw off the larger sticks and brushed out the flashing around the chimney, swept all the leaves from the roof. It was hot already, on the iron, but she paused to look through the treetops to the mountain. Heat haze diluted blue and green, washing them together.

She squatted by the gutters to clear out the leaves and muck, flicking them onto the garden beds below. Despite her gloves, she managed to nick her wrist on the sharp edge of the iron. Blood oozed from the ragged line. She worked her way around the section of roof. A march fly had found her already – although it was not March – drawn by her sweaty scent, buzzing around her head. She swatted at it, nearly losing her balance.

A flock of lorikeets passed overhead, all noise, on their way to somewhere else.

She moved the ladder around to the side of the house. Here she had to stand on the very top of the ladder to reach, flipping leaves out over her shoulder. She climbed down again, moved along a few feet, and clambered back up. Everything was still damp in the corner, where the gutter hadn't been laid right, and her gloves were soon soaked through. She climbed back down and peeled them off.

She had intended to do the whole lot, but the sudden heat and humidity left her light-headed and shaky. It didn't pay to be shaky on roofs and ladders. She should have started earlier, instead of lingering over breakfast and the birds. Or waited until later in the afternoon.

She slid off her boots, shed her stinking clothes in the laundry and stepped into the shower. She ran mainly cold water, just bearable, to get her body temperature down. The pressure, gained from gravity from the tank at top of the hill, was weak. She had to scrub at her skin to get it clean. A plumber had suggested putting in a pump, incredulous that she should still be living in the dark ages, but gravity-fed systems were quiet, required less power, and meant she was not without water in a blackout.

Sometimes, coming into summer, she wondered what the hell she had done, moving back. She scrubbed under her nails and washed her hair, then shaved her legs and under her arms. If the weather held until midafternoon, she would get down into the water, walk along the beach. Swim.

She dressed under the fan: shorts and a singlet. Tied her hair, still dripping, back with a band and hung up her towel. She poured herself a tall glass of iced tea and set up at the table with her books. How anyone ever got any work done further north, in the real tropics, she didn't know.

A pair of red-browed finches chirruped about the pond, picking insects from grass stems and heads. The flashes of red over their brows and on their rumps were bright against the green, their world small but complete.

———

Jen took the paper from the bench and sat down at the counter in the window to wait for her coffee. The post office was already busy, cars backed up waiting for a park and blocking the street.

After-school care was in the headlines again. Legislation had been proposed to ensure that children were supervised until they had left school grounds, with no child left alone. Teachers were campaigning about the need for additional resources, and increasing demands on their time. One city principal had said on talk back radio that a school's role was to educate children, not parent them, enraging her community.

On the drive home, she slowed to get a better look at the paper sign taped to a bloodwood on the side of the road: MISSING PARROT. A male *Eclectus*. Two hundred dollar reward. Ha! If she was lucky enough to see him, she would not be ringing his captors. He would be vulnerable, if he were still alive, it was true – and lonesome – but at least he was free. He hadn't flown off because he was happy with his grain-fed life behind bars, that much was sure. He would be most welcome in her forest.

Backslide

She woke early, when the rain stopped. The frogs had sung all night, reconstituted as if by magic. She dressed and hurried out onto the back deck. The air was washed clean. Green had returned to the land, moss refreshed, birds out hunting. Even the lettuces were sitting up in a way they never did after hand-watering.

Mist drifted up the valley, enclosing the cottage and orchard with a moist caress. The bark of the spotted gums had turned orange with the rain, as if the trees had laid it all out to be wet. Or perhaps they had wanted to be bare-trunked when the rain finally came. To have an unencumbered wash. The weather bureau would do better looking at the trees and flowers and birds than all their charts and satellite images.

The orchard had greened up, the ragtag of weeds at varying lengths she had let go now an irritant.

———

She slid the ride-on into low gear and released the brake. Still the back wheel spun, midair. She had lost concentration while reversing, hitting the non-functioning brake rather than putting it in a forward gear, sending her flying back into the gutter the other side of the steep driveway.

She hopped off, hands shaky. If it hadn't been for the tree against which the machine was now wedged, she would have continued right down the slope. She collected sticks and half an old brick, to give the wheel some traction.

She started the mower, released the handbrake. What the thing needed, at times like this, was a throttle. Still the wheel spun. A pair of kookaburras laughed from their position in the twin-trunked bloodwood. Jen pulled her hat down over her eyes. It was warm, humid, and more rain was coming. She needed to finish the lawn before it arrived.

She put the machine into neutral and hopped off again. From behind, she leaned forward to release the handbrake. A little weight shifted back onto her, but it stayed as it was, anchored by the tree. She took a long breath and pushed forward with all her strength. Something popped in her shoulder and she had to strain beyond all she had, but she got the back wheels out of the gutter and onto the sealed driveway.

Of course, now all the mower wanted to do was roll back, full force, and she was the only thing standing between it and the creek. She could not quite reach the handbrake, not without shifting her weight. She turned the steering wheel, trying to direct the machine across rather than against the slope. She strained again, one more big push, but lost more ground than she gained.

She was doing damage in her back now; she could feel it. She turned herself around, so as to push backwards, in the hope that using different muscles would give her enough leverage.

The birds had gone quiet. What breeze there was had stilled. 'One, two, *three*.'

She was superhuman, roaring with strength, inching the mower – all five hundred kilograms – up and across the slope. And then her boot slipped on a spray of gravel and all that weight came back at her. She rolled out of the way and watched the mower crash back into the gutter, out the other side and down the slope, crunching into a log.

'Fuck!'

She lay on the ground, staring up at the sky through the leaves of the bloodwood. She had all sorts of tricks, to turn the world into patterns and shapes and shades. A type of seeing that required a relaxing of focus, forgetting what you knew. In this case, forgetting about the damn mower and the pain that was coming when she stood up.

The birds hopped and sang and flitted in the leaf light, oblivious to her 'epic fail,' as Henry would call it. Light in the canopy had been one of her favourite subjects for a time, seeking to see what the birds saw, a world of dappled shades and whispering breezes, a bounty of insect life.

For all her years of striving to see like a bird, be like a bird, in the end she was only a lumpy human. And not an especially gifted one at that. She was barely coping on the ground, let alone going to fly, and there was nothing as sad as a bird without wings.

Help

Glen knocked while she was still having breakfast. She hobbled to the door, tying her bathrobe more securely about her.

'Morning.'

'Hey.'

'Saw the mower,' he said. 'You're lucky you didn't kill yourself!'

'I'll just get dressed.'

'Righto. See you up there.'

She tipped out her tea, put the plate and cup in the sink and picked up her work clothes from the laundry. They were rather ripe, after resting in sweat and petrol fumes overnight.

It hurt to bend, to put her arm through her shirtsleeve, and she struggled to do up her buttons. Everything hurt – particularly her pride. She leaned on the front door to slide on her boots. This was what it must feel like to be *really* old.

She walked up the steps and the driveway, to where Glen was standing.

'You all right?' he said. 'Did you come off it?'

She shook her head.

'Brakes not much use on a slope like that.'

'No.'

'Gotta keep across the grain,' he said. 'Opposite to wood.'

She smiled.

'Righto. I've hooked up the tow rope. I think the ute will manage. I'll go nice and easy – you right to steer the beast?'

'Sure.'

'Don't hop on, mind. Just kinda walk beside it. Okay?'

'Okay.'

'I'm going to pull it right up to the top of the drive, then you can drive it across, back onto the lawn.'

'Sounds good.'

She slid more than walked down the slope, wet after last night's rain, and waited by the wretched machine till the rope went taut. For a moment it looked as if there was no shifting it, then it was crawling back the way it had come. She adjusted the wheel, took note of the plants snapped off en route.

When it came to the ditch, it needed an extra push from her to get through. She used her body rather than her arms, which were without any strength at all.

At the top of the drive Glen stopped, leaned out the open window. 'Righto. On you get. Just whack it in low and drive across there.'

Jen swallowed. Breathed. The kookaburras were watching from the bloodwood. Five of them this time. Word of human entertainment had got out. They had the decorum to be quiet at least. She put on the handbrake, turned the key. Gave it some choke. It started, with a great chug of smoke. She put the thing into low gear and released the handbrake, reassuring herself she could not roll backwards while secured to Glen by the rope.

Forward it went. Eagerly even, as if it had not done everything it could to go in the other direction only yesterday. She parked it under the orange tree and cut the engine.

Glen's knot wasn't hard to untie, so at least she could hand him the end of the rope by the time he strolled down, winding it over his arm. 'Piece of piss,' he said.

'Thank you.'

'Must have given you a bit of a fright.'

'You could say that,' she said. 'Thought it was going to end up in the creek.'

He bent to look at the guard surrounding the blades, smashed in from its cross-country travels. 'Might have to bang this out,' he said. 'I've got some tools with me. Could give it a go if you like?'

'It's okay,' she said. 'You've done enough.'

'Won't take a minute,' he said, already on his way back to the ute.

That was another trait of the men of the place, they didn't take no for an answer. Not always a bad thing.

He banged and twisted, sending the kookaburras further afield to seek their laughs, or morning tea, perhaps. 'That should do it,' he said. 'But your blades might be a bit the worse for wear.'

'It's due a service soon anyway.'

'Where do you take it?'

'The dealership come out.'

'Bloke in town, the mower repair place, is probably cheaper. They'll come and get it. Or I could take it in for you. Got a ramp – just drive it onto the back of the ute. Not a big deal at all.'

She didn't fancy driving it up onto the ute, but he was being very sweet. 'Thank you.'

They stood with their faces up to the sun. 'Things have gone awful quiet about the Jones girl,' he said.

'It's not a good feeling.' Not a good feeling to have again. 'Can I make you a cup of tea?'

'Wouldn't say no.' He smiled. 'I'll just put all this back in the ute and get my phone. Me and Sam have a job on this morning, if it's not too wet.'

He took off his boots at the door – the difference between the last generation and this one. 'Nice place,' he said.

'Thanks.'

'These all yours?'

She nodded.

'Geez, Jen. They're real good.' He peered at one of her tree series. Probably a bit abstract for his liking. 'Love this quandong,' he said. 'They do kind of reach for the sky like that. And their red leaves could be on fire.'

Jen smiled, turned to tap the old tea-leaves into the compost bucket. 'So what's this job you and Sam are hoping will be on today?'

'Not one you'd like. Taking out some trees for the power company. Too close to the lines, they reckon. Pile of crap, but they're going to pay someone to do it. And we get some good timber that way.'

'How is it working for Sam?'

'The old man's all right.' He stirred two sugars into his tea. 'I gather he was more of a hard case in his younger days. He was competing with two other mills then.'

'He seemed a little scary, but I was only small.'

He laughed. 'He was fond of you. And your dad. Helped your mother out, too, when your dad . . .'

'Took off?'

'Yeah.'

She offered him a biscuit, shortbreads left over from Henry's last visit. 'What do you mean helped out?'

'Financially,' he said. 'And popped down to check on her from time to time. Fix things. Said he owed it to her.'

Jen sipped her tea. A little too strong, the tannin biting her teeth. 'What do you mean?'

'Don't know. I gather he didn't pay those blokes any more than he needed to. And they never had super or insurance or anything in those days.'

'True.'

'Your mum didn't mention it?'

'No. But there were a lot of things we didn't talk about.' Probably she had been protecting Jen when she was a child and, later, protecting herself.

Glen's phone rang, his ringtone a tinny rendition of a familiar seventies tune. 'Yep. On my way.'

'Job's on?'

He swallowed a mouthful of his tea. 'Job's on.'

First

Jen recognised it from its call, a grating chuffing – like a bird playing a comb – and looked up from her planting to confirm. A spectacled monarch, egg-yellow chest, dark face mask, its smaller mate answering its call.

The last of the native frangipanis were in, and she was almost out of lomandra. She had gone a bit overboard at the nursery, leaving herself short for groceries, but the slope down from the house was going to look fantastic. A vast improvement on her old view of lantana.

She heard a car door open and slam, then running footsteps down to the house.

'Jen?'

'I'm out the back, Henry.' She washed her hands under the garden tap.

He was inside before he could possibly have removed his shoes properly, and the spectacled monarchs fled the scene.

'I won!'

'The art prize?'

'FIRST in my age group,' he said. 'And highly commended in the open section.'

Jen dried her hands on her shirt. 'For Caitlin's portrait?'

'Yeah.'

'Well done!' she said. 'Told you it was good.' She patted him on the shoulder. 'Lucky I made chocolate cake. Must have had a feeling.'

Henry grinned and began spreading his gear all over the table. And so an artist was made.

Jen fired up the gas and cut cake. 'Tea?'

'Yes, please.'

Shame he was too young for champagne; she had a bottle in the fridge that had been waiting some time for something to celebrate.

'What happened to your mixmaster?'

She had left it outside to soak. 'I was mixing paint in it.'

'How'd you make the cake?'

'I have beaters for that,' she said.

'You want me to finish the forest painting?'

'That's why it's there.'

He sighed. A comedown from prize-winning, no doubt.

She carried out his tea and cake, spilling over the sides of the little plate.

Henry was splotching on the paint a little too casually.

'You know, I met some people once who spent their whole careers, their lives, really, studying forest canopies.'

Henry gave her his sceptical look and filled his mouth with cake.

'What percentage of species would you guess is located in the treetops?'

'Twenty,' he said, spraying crumbs.

'Fifty,' she said.

That earned her a raised eyebrow, a pause of the brush. 'What, like animals?'

'Plants and animals. That includes rainforests. There's a lot going on upstairs there. Insects and reptiles and mosses and fungi and epiphytes.'

'And birds,' he said.

She smiled. 'Yes, and birds.'

'Why are jungle birds so bright?'

'Is this a joke you heard?' She didn't do jokes, especially about birds.

'I'm serious,' he said. 'Why are tropical birds so big and colourful? With big beaks?'

'Like toucans and macaws?'

'Like Long John Silver has.'

'Well, I guess there's a lot of competition in the jungle, all that colour and life. And the male birds have to work harder to get the females' attention. Our tropical parrots are bright, too, if you think about it.'

'Not blue, with striped beaks.'

She smiled. It was nice to have someone to talk to about birds.

Aunt

It was time to ask some questions of Aunt Sophie. Jen was overdue a visit anyway, and a long drive was just what she needed to clear her head.

Her aunt had never seemed as sympathetic as everyone else towards her mother, perhaps because she had been the one who had to pick up the pieces. Whenever her mother had let her down – a visit had fallen through, or money for something – her aunt had shaken her head and looked unimpressed. Also unsurprised. Perhaps it began earlier, in their childhoods. Jen couldn't pretend to understand what it was to be a sister.

At the time, she would have preferred an explanation, something spoken out loud, spelled out. She had thought herself mature enough to be treated like an adult, to handle any information. She appreciated now, having worked with children herself, that Aunt Sophie thought she had enough to deal with. She had put Jen's interests before her own, which was what parents were supposed to do, and more than either of hers had managed.

Aunt Sophie seemed more frail, smaller in her house. Jen had put off coming for too long. 'You still walking?'

'Every morning,' Aunt Sophie said. 'And swimming. Though not without a hat. Doctor's orders.'

Aunt Sophie had had many skin cancers burned off her face and arms, the legacy of a life spent in the water. 'Good,' Jen said. 'I'm glad you're listening for a change.'

'Well, it's all too late now,' her aunt said. 'For the wrinkles, too.'

Jen smiled. 'Better late than never,' she said. 'You always made me cover up. It didn't escape my notice that you weren't adhering to your own advice.'

'Most damage is done when you're young,' Aunt Sophie said.

'That's very true.'

'So tell me how you've been.'

'I'm well,' Jen said. 'I've got a little show coming up.'

'That's great,' Aunt Sophie said. 'Where?'

'Just on the coast, but it's a retrospective.'

'Oooh,' she said. 'They'll love you. And the teaching?'

'Tutoring. Just one boy,' she said. 'But I quite like that.'

Her aunt spooned tea into a pot. 'When's the show? Maybe I can come.'

'Next month – but it's a long way.'

'You're the only family I have left, girl,' Aunt Sophie said. 'I can drive a few hours.'

Jen smiled. 'You're all I've got, too,' she said.

'Have you caught up with any of your school friends?'

'Glen,' she said.

'What about Phil?'

'He's still in Sydney, apparently.'

Her aunt chewed on her cheek. 'You know, I was thinking. It's not too late for children. If that's what you want,' she said. 'You could adopt. I was only talking to someone the other day who—'

Corellas were making a racket in the palms outside. 'I'm having one last shot at looking for Dad,' Jen said.

'I see.'

'Well, the police are. Around this new child,' she said.

Aunt Sophie stepped to fetch the cupcakes from the sideboard. 'That's just ridiculous. It was ridiculous then. I mean, I hope they find him, but . . .'

'I guess they need to follow everything up,' Jen said. 'I've been talking to Dad's old boss, Sam Pels. Still runs that mill, you know.'

'Still?'

'Did you know he helped Mum out?'

'She didn't mention it.'

Jen frowned and scratched a mosquito bite on her arm. 'Did you ever hear Mum or Dad talk about a Stan Overton?'

Aunt Sophie dropped the plate, which clattered and broke into three pieces, sending cupcakes rolling about the tiled floor.

Jen squatted down to gather up the cakes. 'These will be fine,' she said. 'Your floor's always clean enough to eat off.' She pulled a plain plate from the shelf above and set the iced cakes out in a circular gathering.

Her aunt picked up pieces of crockery – a handmade plate with a green glaze. She started to cry.

'I'm sorry about the plate,' Jen said. Perhaps it had been a gift.

'It's fine,' she said. 'My fault.'

The kettle burbled and steamed, then switched itself off. Jen poured hot water into the pot. She stepped around Aunt Sophie, busy with the dustpan, to fetch milk from the fridge. 'You okay?'

Her aunt nodded. She stood, stepped on the pedal bin's lever and dumped what had been a plate, and crumbs, inside. 'I think,' she said, 'I'd better find the brandy.'

Jen turned the teapot and tried to keep her eyebrows where they belonged. It was ten-thirty in the morning.

Aunt Sophie disappeared into the pantry. There was a clanking of bottles. Had she become an alcoholic?

'Even better,' she said. 'Calvados.'

Jen placed the pot, cups and plate of cakes on the table. Waited.

Aunt Sophie plonked the bottle and two liqueur glasses between them. 'I bought this to bake some flash dessert,' she said. 'It's made from apples. Quite a nice one, apparently.'

Jen's stomach lurched. 'Is everything okay?'

'No,' her aunt said. 'I've made a terrible mistake.' She filled the glasses with pale browny liquid. Her hand was shaking. 'I really wanted to look after you. Do the right thing,' she said. 'When your mother couldn't.'

'But you have. You did.'

'No. I didn't.' She slugged back the calvados.

Jen sipped at hers, hoping it would settle her stomach. And the drumbeat in her ear.

'Stan Overton was, for a time, my lover.'

'You've never mentioned him.'

'It was before you were born.'

'Mum never mentioned it either,' she said.

'No,' her aunt said. 'I don't imagine she did.'

'I thought . . .'

'You thought what?'

Jen filled their cups with steaming tea, trying to restore some order to the morning. 'I've never known you to have a partner,' she said. 'I thought maybe you and Maeve . . .'

Aunt Sophie snorted. 'Well, she'd be a better prospect than any of the fellas I've chosen, but no. We're good friends is all.'

'So what happened with Stan?' That required calvados midmorning on a Tuesday.

Her aunt refilled her glass and topped up Jen's. 'He had an affair.'

'But why would he . . .' Jen lifted the glass, felt its weight, and sculled it. She was in one of those moments, again. She could feel it all around her, pressing in. The pieces grinding together with the magnitude of tectonic plates. The drink was strong and sweet. Her skin prickled. She slid her glass out to the middle of the table. 'With Mum.'

'Yes.'

'I'm not . . .'

'I think so,' her aunt said. 'Your mother was pretty sure.'

Jen watched her refill the little glass.

'Stan was in the area – I forget why. He saw you with your mum down on the coast. And figured.'

Jen blinked.

'Carol wouldn't see him. She was scared, I suppose. So he asked around. Must have gone looking for Peter.'

'And that's why Dad left?' Because he wasn't her father at all.

'It was the dishonesty of it, love. He said he felt tricked.' This time her aunt sipped at the liqueur. 'He was angry. But I thought he was going to stay. And I managed to convince Stan to leave you all alone. I'm sorry,' she said. 'I know Peter loved you.'

'And no one ever felt the need to tell me any of this?'

'Carol said she would. And I thought, when she was better . . .'

But she never really got better. The second slug of calvados had a whole lot more flavour. The warmth it gave Jen's otherwise cold body was welcome.

'I'm sorry my mother did that to you,' she said. 'And left you to clean up the mess.'

'Oh, Jen,' her aunt said. 'I offered to take you. I wanted to have you. You were never a burden.'

'I need to go,' Jen said. 'I need to get home.'

'Please don't rush off so upset.'

Jen stood.

'Jenny,' her aunt said. 'Should you be driving right now?'

'I'm fine.' She took her keys from the hall table and let the screen door slam behind her.

Away

Jen parked in the driveway. She slammed the door of the Hilux and went straight to the shed. She scooped up her tent and her pack – ready to go, with swag, cooking gear and survival kit. She threw it all in the back of the ute and stomped down to the house.

She used the bathroom, snatched up her toothbrush and paste. Filled her water bottle, and the spare. Gathered together what food she had: apples, rice, a tin of tuna, half a loaf of bread, a chunk of cheddar cheese, tea and a box of fruit and nut bars. A slab of leftover cake. Stale but sweet.

The keys were in the back of the cutlery drawer. She held them up to the light to remember which was which, and locked the house behind her. Last, she dropped everything in the box on the back of the ute and secured the cover.

She headed up the mountain, taking the corners a little faster than she should. Tree trunks rushed by, mailboxes marking hidden driveways. At the top, the tree cover gave way and the road turned to follow the ridge. She glanced out, when she could, at the ocean sparkling below. At all that bright and busy life.

Something rattled around in the back, something not secured. A water bottle perhaps.

She turned inland, towards the old hippie town that still had its working heart, tolerating the tourists rather than deigning to rely on them. She passed through without stopping, veering around a senior citizen attempting a reverse angle park.

Once out the other side, there were more houses than there used to be, an estate where there had just been pasture, ficus groves and forest – all the tree-changers bringing suburbia to the country.

The road wound deeper inland, down and around, narrowing to enter forest groves. She passed cottages in the hills, smoke clouding out their chimneys and hanging over the valleys. The air had cooled, and her blood calmed a little.

She turned off the main road and crossed a creek, the Hilux's cabin pitching and lurching, and accelerated up the pitted gravel slope. She pulled up in the car park with a screech. Ignored all the council signs, gathered up her pack and gear and loaded herself up like a snail. A penitent headed into exile. She took the less used path, heading out the back of the falls. She walked, one boot in front of the other, further into the forest, until she could breathe.

It was a weekday, and school was in, so she figured she was most likely alone. She climbed up onto a rock beside the path and roared until the gully was filled with her rage.

———

She woke by the river, pink light brightening behind the trees. The kookaburras began their telegraph chorus, passing their gossip and joy along the line until Jen could no longer hear it. This was the cue for the rest to start, the whipbirds and cuckoos, wrens and robins. The fire she should not have lit was almost out. She sat up in her swag, pushed sticks and leaves into the coals, leaned in and blew until there was a flame.

It had been too long since she had done this. She had made all sorts of excuses: her drawing, the exhibition, the boy, the birds, the house. Of course she had been afraid of going without Craig. Not afraid of being out here alone – but of feeling the terrible space he had left. She had reached the point where the pain was manageable, just so long as she didn't disturb anything.

Jen unzipped the bag and extricated herself. A breeze tickled her bare skin. She padded naked over the sand to the river's edge to fill her billy, then fanned the fire's flames and rigged up the rack to boil the water.

She watched a kingfisher swoop from overhead, sharp-beaked and craning forward, to snap something up from the water's surface.

'You're right,' she said. 'It's perfect.' Mist hung over the slow-moving water. She ran down the beach and threw herself in, gasping as the water gripped her ribs. She splashed out to the middle like a child, in a rough dog paddle, then back-stroked upstream, into the dawn sky, pinky-orange giving way to pale blue.

The kingfisher darted from tree to tree along the bank, as if following her progress. Her skin was yellow under the river water, muted. Far from pretty. She breaststroked back, watching her arms. An idea began to form for a picture. She had stayed at a bed and breakfast in Copenhagen once, where the host – something of a celebrity and a member of local government – had a life-size full-length nude portrait hanging in the foyer, in full view of the breakfast table. Jen had never understood Scandinavians, though she was fond of their part of the world.

Something shifted under her foot, a turtle perhaps. She felt like fresh fish for breakfast, cooked over coals. A decade-old hunger. The effect of fresh air, running water and sleeping outside. Without a proper line and hook, though, there wasn't much chance of a catch, and she was too hungry to wait. Toast and tea would have to do.

She walked from the water, dripping. A full complement of birds were up and about now, singing in the day. The water gave their voices a resonance, the backing track for their vocals. She plucked a leaf from the low-hanging branch of a flooded gum and held it in her teeth while she squeezed out her hair and wiped herself down with her squidgy towel. She threw a handful of tea into the billy, and the gumleaf.

She sliced bread for toast and flicked it onto the grill, wiped out her mug. Kept her thoughts on what her hands were doing. Everything was better in the open air.

———

She prepared for her walk American style: water and food for forty-eight hours, fleece-jacket and a light bedroll. The first time she had hiked alone in the States, in the Sierras, she had set out on a nine-hour return trip above the snowline with a pocket water bottle and an apple, attracting a few looks along the way. Those she passed on the trail all carried full packs, bear spray, spare clothes, EPIRB, tent – the lot. She had thought them ridiculous. Stupid Americans. As she realised later, after she had passed the mangled haunch of a deer beside the trail, and plunged thigh-deep into snow, leaving her wet and cold, they had rightly thought her a naive tourist. She had assumed she could drink from the river, or suck on snow, but there had been signs about bacteria, so she didn't take the risk. On the return trip, a snowstorm had come in – light flakes swirling around her and dusting the branches as if in a fairytale – giving her energy just when she had been beginning to flag, but if she had been higher up it could have ended differently.

There were no predators in these mountains, and there would be no snowstorm, or even rain, but she had come to enjoy being prepared for anything. Knowing she was self-sufficient for a few days allowed a freedom that was not a feature of everyday life.

———

The sun was dropping low in the sky. She had been walking all day, a little above her usual pace. It had seemed important to keep moving. Her feet were sore but her body otherwise bearing up well. She judged she was in about the middle of the national park – though she wasn't sure exactly where – deep in a gorge, surrounded by remnant forest. It was a good feeling.

She made for higher ground, looking for one good tree. Wisps of hair had worked themselves free of her hat, and her face needed a wash.

A golden whistler flew in front of her, darting from branch to branch just above her eye line. She let him lead her away from the path, taking his bright yellow chest as a sign. She stepped between a grass tree and a black wattle without taking her hands from her pockets, letting its tips brush her face. The bird alighted on the low branch of a tallowwood, then flew up into its higher branches to sing an encouraging song, his white face banded by black.

'Really?' she said, looking up. 'This one?' She could just reach the solid lower limb, but it was a stretch to the next and the trunk without footholds.

Before her time in the Sierra, before they had finished their DipEds, she and Craig had travelled together, climbing some of the world's tallest trees – Californian redwoods. He had made contact with a team of post-grads who were documenting the heights of trees within remote groves and organised for them to go along and document the botanical finds. A friend of a uni friend, he said. Craig had done forestry as his first degree – about as practical as art. There weren't many jobs, but there was research funding available. Somehow it ended up that they were among a handful of people in the world who knew the location of the Giant Grove and had seen the worlds within their crowns. Fanatics were kinder to fellow fanatics than artists were to fellow artists, as it turned out.

Jen had been unimpressed with the nerdy looking fellows at first, with their crapped-out car and college clothes. She had been less comfortable leaving the ground in those days, too, and didn't like all the fuss and gear, let alone being trussed up like a rack of lamb. But once up in the mist, among salamanders and lichens and liverworts barely seen by another human being, she had found her tree legs. There were bonsai species growing in the clouds, redwoods within redwoods, and whole other genera sending their roots into rotting timber. The seeds had been dropped by animals and birds, though apart from the occasional osprey, there weren't many birds up there – the only disappointment.

The ropes and gear – a 'spider rig' – allowed them to 'skywalk'. The science fellows called themselves Skywalker One and so on, imagining themselves in outer space. Or a movie. Stepping lightly along a branch, birdlike, and peering into a whole ecosystem within the tree's crown was indeed an otherworldly experience. She had finally been able to imagine what it was to fly.

Jen had stopped to sketch what she saw while the boys mucked about with tapes and protractors and ropes. The search for the world's tallest tree had them always gazing off around them, to the next tree, one perhaps a little higher, but for her there was more than enough right there in each crown: burned-out caves, fern forests, lost citadels of dead redwood spikes, hanging gardens of lichen, all dripping with mist. To think she had almost not gone along. She had worked with a fever she hadn't known at home, nibbling on ripe huckleberries from a bush beside her, trying to capture on the page and in photographs what few had seen.

On the last night, they had slept suspended from the branches of the freshly 'discovered' world's tallest tree, the base of its trunk larger than most houses. Their coloured sleeping bags were nestled within treeboats: nylon hammocks rigged from the tree's upper branches, like brightly spun cocoons. An anchor rope connected each of them to the tree itself, in case a branch failed or they rolled out in their sleep. It was a feeling she had never forgotten, swinging free in the tree's lemony scent, rocked to sleep by creaks and groans and the *shhhh* of the wind in its needles.

When they got home, and began to unpack, heavy with the lag of flying and sudden descent to reality, she found that Craig had bought them each an olive green treeboat. From then on, they sought out places where they could sleep swinging from the trees. Sometimes, when they could not get away for the weekend, they would settle for hanging them from the one tree in Craig's courtyard for a night. The neighbours probably had a giggle, but she and Craig had been oblivious. Making love in a treeboat – although something of a challenge – was perfection, every movement, sensation and emotion magnified by the weightlessness under the stars, as if defying gravity. Craig would climb down to her, and she would unzip her sleeping bag, and herself. But it was not safe for him to stay there overnight, unsecured, in case he toppled off, so he would climb back to his own rig, leaving her a little empty. It had been worth all the fuss, though, for the rush of their love meeting air and leaf and sap.

Now she was just a husk of a woman. Orphaned. Childless. Little more than bone and sinew and skin. Without feathers to hide beneath or a song to sing.

The light was hurrying away. She took a running step, heaved herself up, and shifted from a crouch to standing full height. Gripped the branch above backhand and attempted a chin-up. She managed to lift herself and the pack easily enough, but could no longer force her chest above her arms and onto the branch. She hung there for a moment, then dropped back onto the broad branch below. Even from there, she could see out over the whole valley, the river glinting below, and the roar of the three-basin falls echoing up to her.

She slipped her pack off her shoulders and unclipped the front flap to remove the treeboat. She swung the ropes over the branch above, ran them back through the little pulleys. It wasn't spider rope, like they had used in Giant Grove, but it would do. Craig said they were trialling rope for the special forces, to use on black ops. Perhaps he was teasing, perhaps not, but she had always wondered how geeks with the backside hanging out of their pants could have got their hands on such high-end gear.

Jen spread her sleeping bag out into the hammock, ready to climb into. The tree was hardly a giant, and her position a little lame – only eight or nine feet off the ground – so she needn't anchor herself, but it was a nice spot and she was too tired to search for another.

She climbed into her nest while it rested on her porch branch, then raised herself, hand over hand, with the little pulleys. She secured them so that she was close enough to touch the rail branch but free to swing. Evening air bit at her lungs, just enough to let her know she was outside, and alive after all.

The first stars twinkled through the branches above, and birds settled into their roosts around her. She smiled into the dark, snuggled further into the bag and folded her arms over her chest, stuck her knees out, like a frog.

A powerful owl *whoo whooed* nearby but received no answer.

'Whoo,' she said. 'It's okay. It's going to be okay.'

———

She lay snug in her nest, watching the sun come up. Light flowed into the valley, revealing layer upon layer of colour and texture. Finches and wrens chattered around her, and a breeze ran up, tickling her face and rattling the leaves. It was Thoreau who said that in wildness lay the preservation of the world: one of his more optimistic remarks. She knew that she could not save the world by drawing it. There was nothing, it seemed, that could shift or slow the human compulsion to consume the planet – but she could still save herself.

The shrink said she should relish her freedom, the possibility of the unknown, and out here it didn't seem as difficult. She unzipped her bag and wriggled out, lowering herself to the branch below. She released the harness, dropped it on the ground, and climbed down to pack it all away.

———

She hopped from rock to rock, relying on her boots to grip, her balance and judgement to hold. Water roared all around. Craig had loved rock-hopping, though he often left her far behind with his goat legs. Sometimes he was impatient to see what was around the next corner, and sometimes it was to prepare a surprise upstream, like the day he proposed. By the time she had caught up, the sparkling wine was chilled, a picnic laid – and Craig washed clean and lying on a rock in his shorts as if he had never hurried.

She had been happy that day in the gorge, shouting out 'YES' for all the world to hear – and thought her life secured. They had made love on the rocks, with the water rushing and falling about them, drunk on bubbles and love.

———

Jen lay full stretch on the sand watching a stony creek frog – *Litoria wilcoxii*. Only the black spots down her lower sides had given the female away, her back the same smooth brown as the coppery stones over which clear water flowed. She swam with her nostrils just above the water, leaving a trail behind her. A male called from the water's edge, his soft purring intended to elicit a particular type of attention.

They had been at a barbecue when Craig said it. At one of the other teachers' new townhouse. It had been hot and they had all drunk too much while the host was preparing the meal. Someone was about to go off on maternity leave, and there must have been a conversation about children. Jen had been focused on the food, worried about what she would eat from the mountain of meat burning on the hotplate.

She soon tuned in, though, at the home ec teacher's question about their choice not to have children. Jen was thirty-eight by then, though she looked younger, especially when with Craig. People no doubt wondered, though the more obvious question might have been why they were still engaged. They kept spending their savings on trips away, and then Craig broke his leg rock climbing. He was stuck inside, for months, and it took some time after his physical recovery for him to return to anything like himself. She had figured they would talk about children once they were married and told herself they still had time – but things had drifted.

She hadn't quite caught Craig's answer, at the barbecue – there was something about 'our lifestyle' and perhaps he had shaken his head.

Miss Hanaford, her name had been. 'Was that something you and Jen decided early on?'

Craig shrugged. 'I guess if it had been important, it would have come up.'

Bone

Bushed

By the time she emerged from the trees, the sun was dropping from the sky and there was a council officer reclining in her chair at the campsite. 'Hey, there,' he said, from behind dark aviator glasses. For a moment she thought she was back in the States and he might add 'little lady'.

'Can I help you?'

'Yes, you can, as a matter of fact,' he said. 'Do you have a permit?'

'A permit for . . . ?'

'To camp here, Ms Anderson.'

She slipped out of her pack and dropped it on the ground between them, a strap flicking his boot. He knew perfectly well she didn't have a permit; he had already run her rego number and checked back with council. Officious little prick.

'I thought this was a public camping area?'

'The public camping area is by the car park, as the signs indicate. Or further along, at Tallowwood. And to camp there, you still need a permit.'

'I didn't realise. Sorry,' she said. 'It was a last-minute thing, not very well planned.'

He made a point of looking over her gear and rather immaculate camp. 'It's a hundred and fifty dollar on-the-spot fine for camping without a permit,' he said.

'Ah.'

'Out of interest, where did you sleep the last few nights?'

Jen crossed her arms.

'I was here until dark yesterday afternoon,' he said.

How dedicated, for him to come all the way back out here today to check on her. 'I slept rough,' she said. 'Up in the gorge. I got a bit lost and left it too late to make it back to camp.'

He looked over her pack again, but his face remained blank. 'When were you planning on heading out?'

'Now,' she said. The serenity had been spoiled by this snoop in uniform.

'In that case, I'll leave you to pack up,' he said, extracting himself from her chair. 'You can apply for a permit online,' he said. 'Takes five minutes.'

'Thanks.'

Bio

She unpacked the Hilux, hanging the tent, sleeping bag and treeboat over the line to air. Another cloudless sky – warm day and cool night, just the way she liked it.

She undressed, put on a load of washing and ran a shower. As much as she had enjoyed bathing in the river, hot water and soap were delightful. She shampooed and conditioned her hair, washing the last of the camping smells down the drain. The windows of the bathroom fogged with steam. Though not before she caught sight of a koala's bottom in the grey gum overhead.

There was a message from the gallery owner, chasing her bio for some promotional material. The machine said it was Tuesday when she had called. But when was Tuesday?

She opened up the laptop. Waited. Friday, the calendar said. There was an email from Aunt Sophie. Hoping she was okay. Apologising. Four days ago. Jen scrolled down. Nothing else worth looking at.

She opened the bio she had spent days fiddling with, all those careful sentences detailing her professional achievements and family connection to the area. She selected the text and pressed backspace – on purpose for once. She stared at the blank page. She had a great deal in common with that page. Jen Blank.

She tapped her fingers on the desk. Looked out the window at the warm brown trunks. Imagined herself swinging from a branch again. Free as a bird. Finally, she typed a sentence: *Jen Anderson is a local artist with a particular interest in birds.* She copied and pasted her major achievements from her résumé. That would have to do.

———

The birds were making such a fuss off the deck it could only mean one thing. Snake. Jen leaned out over the railing. The Lewins and white-naped honeyeaters were flying about, dipping and calling. A baby python wound its way up a tree, thinking itself well-camouflaged and obscured by vines, but the birds were sounding an early warning for all to hear. 'Snake, snake!' Other species understood the snake alarm, and frogs and bandicoots and so on would have already tuned in and taken off to make their families safe. She felt a little sorry for the snake, with his specially designed camouflage, who thought himself a master of stealth; how did he ever manage to catch a feed?

She poured a glass of wine and sat out on the deck with the birds. It was the shrug that made her wild. Craig had been quite cheerful on the way home from the barbecue, droning on about some new abseiling gear Ken had shown him, and ideas for their next big trip. If he noticed she was quiet, he chose not to acknowledge it, or perhaps that was why he was so chatty. She had forgotten she'd said she would drive, and having had several too many wines, was also keeping her eye out for police.

He was right. They hadn't discussed it. Not since early days, and none of that had been very realistic. Still, she fumed. That shrug. As if it was nothing. That he would presume to speak for her in front of their mutual friends. It was always the woman people judged when a couple decided not to have children; she was the one going against biology. Against nature.

It was as if a door had been opened and a light had come on. She saw his arrogance after that, all that she had been blind to. He probably wondered at her new-found prickliness – insisting he do more of the housework, or snapping whenever he made a sexist remark or put some tedious triathlon on the television without asking – but she had just been trying to find spaces to assert herself in.

Shrink

'Sorry about last time,' she said.

He looked over his glasses, typing straight into his tablet, or whatever he called it. Prescribing her a tablet might be more productive. 'Everything all right?'

'Fine,' she said. 'I went camping. Just lost track.'

'How long were you away?'

'A few days.'

He wrote that down. 'And how was that?'

'Camping?'

'Yes.'

'Good. It was good to get away.'

'How long had it been?'

'A few years,' she said.

His hands paused.

'Seven,' she said. Though it was closer to ten.

'The first time on your own?'

Since Craig. 'Yes.'

He typed. Left one of his little pauses. 'And how did your trip to see your aunt go?'

Jen frowned at the artwork opposite the clock. A bright abstract print. Just what you'd expect in a shrink's office. 'Okay,' she said. 'She's getting old.'

'How does that make you feel?'

'Old.'

He had stopped typing. It was encouraging, really. She had always suspected he was actually emailing his lover, not listening at all to her whining. 'Did you stay with her?'

'No,' she said. 'Just tea and cupcakes.' The bowl of green apples in the middle of the side table was the best thing about the room. What would he do if she walked over and picked one out to eat? 'And calvados.'

He smiled. 'Calvados?'

'The apple liqueur.'

'I know the stuff,' he said. 'It's quite a long drive just for tea and cupcakes, isn't it? Even with calvados.'

She picked at a thread sticking out from the seam of her pants. 'I asked some questions,' she said. 'Something I'd come across. It turns out that my father is not my father.'

He typed. More quickly – or so it seemed.

'My mother had an affair with her sister's boyfriend. My aunt's boyfriend.'

'Your aunt told you this?'

She nodded.

'Do you think your father knew?'

'He found out,' she said. 'The man – my real father – came to town.' Stan the man.

His fingers moved over the screen but made no sound. 'And where does this leave you, Jen?'

'I guess it explains a few things,' she said.

'Such as?'

'Why my father left.'

'And how do you feel about that now?'

She swung her legs, in the hot seat. The man was just too damn neat and controlled, always pushing at her. 'It's better than not knowing,' she said.

'What about when your aunt told you – how did you feel?'

'Angry.'

'Tell me about that,' he said. 'Angry at who?'

'Everyone! My aunt. My mother. My father. The other man.' Her real father.

'Why your mother?'

'She lied,' she said. 'I felt *sorry* for her. They all lied, for years and years. My whole life was a lie.' She was a damn cuckoo, raised by others out of some weird sense of obligation.

'All of it?'

'Yes.'

'You have strong memories of your time with your father. Does this change any of that?'

Jen began to sniffle and reached for a tissue from the box in front of her.

'Does knowing this change that?'

She blew her nose. 'Yes! He's not even my father.'

'Isn't he? He raised you. Loved you,' he said. 'You loved him.'

Great. Now tears were streaming down her cheeks. And he just sat there in his neat fucking silence. 'He still left me. Changed his mind when he realised I wasn't blood.'

'It sounds like he left the relationship with your mother. I imagine it would have been difficult for him.'

'And never contacted me again.'

The shrink put down his tablet. 'We don't know what happened,' he said.

She shrugged.

'What about your biological father?' he said. 'What's his name?'

'Stan Overton.'

'Do you want to get in touch with him?'

Jen shook her head.

'Why is that?'

'He didn't try particularly hard, either,' she said. 'Having split everything apart. I'm done chasing after people.'

He paused, lowered his voice. 'It's pretty tough for you to find this out now.'

Jen felt more sorry for the little girl she had been. So trusting. So stupid.

'It's a lot to process. But I'm pleased you went camping,' he said. 'I think that was important.'

She wiped her nose.

'How are things going for the exhibition?'

'Okay,' she said. 'I've been working on another new piece. A painting.'

'That's great,' he said. 'Especially with all this going on. Tell me about it?'

'It's a self-portrait,' she said. 'Of sorts.'

'Have you done anything like that before?'

'No,' she said.

'Interesting.'

His smile didn't reveal exactly what was interesting, but a smile was as good as it got in this room.

'When do you think you'll finish?'

'This week,' she said. 'If it stays fine.'

'I'm impressed,' he said. And then the pause. 'Is that an okay place to end up for today?'

Jen shoved her tissue in her pocket and stood. He held the door open in a way that meant she had to pass close by his arm, in a without-touching hug. 'Take care,' he said.

She paid, and took two red frogs from the white bowl on the way out. At the rate he was charging, he could afford to give away a few lollies, the sugar hit no doubt intended to counter the trauma of the session.

She chewed. Sucked the last of them out of her teeth. When they were children, she and Michael had dissected red frogs at the kitchen bench, giggling, even though they weren't meant to touch his mother's knives.

Michael had never had to grow up and do the real thing, in high school, laying out poor frogs on the lab bench and making their legs twitch.

He'd never had to grow up at all.

Portfolio

'I have to put together a portfolio. For my application to the creative arts program,' Henry said.

'Okay.'

'Mum said you might be able to help me,' he said. 'Like what should go in it and stuff.'

'It's really just a selection of your work,' she said. 'But I can show you mine, if you like.'

'Okay.'

'Well, it's in my studio, leaning against the other side of the drawing desk. Black.'

She sipped her tea, cold now. Somewhere above them a catbird called, *heeear-I-aaam*. Jen searched the treetops for the telltale patch of green, usually perched on a horizontal branch.

The boy returned with the portfolio and placed it on the table with more reverence than was warranted. She wiped off gecko poop and a layer of dust and insect crud.

'How long since you've used it?'

'A while.'

He unzipped it, spread it open like a book and stayed standing to turn the pages. He frowned at her résumé. 'You won all these things? The Dobell Prize, the Wildlife —'

'They were mainly just short-listings,' she said. 'You only need to do one page. Put your details, your prize. Your class with me, I suppose.'

'What happened here?'

'What?'

'There's all this stuff and then a big gap between 1990 and 1995, and then from 2003 until now.'

She moved their cups and plates out of the way. 'I was teaching full-time,' she said.

He turned the page. Examined each drawing. 'Where can I get a folder like this?'

'Yours wouldn't need to be very big for now,' she said. 'We could even make one, if you like. I think I have the materials.'

He had stopped at the thumbnails from her first solo exhibition and bent over to examine them.

'These are cool.'

'Thank you.'

She had been told not to read the reviews but of course she had. The work had been a little naive, she had only been twenty-three, after all. Not long out of art school. It was expected that young artists have something to say, a little more anger, edginess. She'd had plenty of anger – she had just put her mother in yet another institution, albeit a nursing home this time – but she didn't see that she needed to pour all that onto the page.

She had been trying to capture what, to her, was the most mysterious thing, the essence of animals and plants. It was, after all, the essence of them all – though buried deep in most cases. She was pigeonholed as a wildlife artist then, which there wasn't much of a market for. Unless you went for that big photographic style; people seemed to snap that up.

'I'll get us some materials,' she said. 'We should get started.'

He had stopped again, frowning at one of the pieces she had done in the States: an aspen grove in a sea of leaves.

'You don't like it?'

'It's different from everything else.'

'It's more abstract. I worked with someone who encouraged me to explore a little,' she said. 'Groves like that are all one tree, one organism.'

'Cool.'

She took a few breaths in the studio, gathered the things together and returned. 'You can have another look later, but we should start on this.' She plonked down the cardboard, Stanley knife and cutting board.

'I don't have enough to put in mine.'

'No?'

'There's the one I won the prize for, the feather, the first still life, the bunya cone, and the running man.'

'What about your animation?'

'Oh, yeah.'

'What else did you do in art?'

'Pottery.'

'Anything worth keeping?'

'I gave a raku vase to mum. She puts flowers in it.'

'You could take a picture of it,' she said. 'If you email it to me, I can print it for next time.'

He nodded and placed the A3 sheet of paper on the cardboard.

'Okay. So you want it a bit bigger than that. Maybe a ruler-width wider on all sides.'

He picked up her old wooden ruler, whacking it down for effect, and began marking out the border in soft pencil. 'Did they still give the cane? When you were teaching.'

'I'm not that old!'

'Dad says he got the cane when he was at school.'

'Did he?' Queensland had been one of the last to ban it from public schools. Now you couldn't even touch the students at all. Sometimes all a kid needed was a pat on the back. It was sad.

'So I just cut it?'

'Yep. Make sure you keep it on the board, though. And cut away from your fingers,' she said. 'That's right.'

The king parrots had varied their song, adding in a kind of chirrup. 'Now we just need to put a hinge at the back. Two sets of two holes.' She marked the spots with his pencils.

He picked up the hole punch, hesitated.

'As far in as you can, that's the way,' she said. 'And just one on the front.'

'Ha!'

'Now, do you want ribbon or metal rings for the hinges?'

'Metal rings at the back and ribbon to tie it at the front.'

'Good.'

'What about the pages?'

'We can do plain paper and attach the pictures from behind, or clear plastic sleeves.'

He looked again at hers and frowned. 'Sleeves?'

'I think so, too,' she said. 'Easier to work with.' She watched him line the sleeves up with the holes in the card and feed the ring through. 'Good. Do you want to put something on the cover?'

'Like what?'

'Your name,' she said. 'And what about a single frame from your animation?'

His mother tooted the horn in the driveway.

'I forgot. I have to go a bit early today.'

'Okay.'

He packed up his things in a hurry, struggling with all of the folder's parts.

'When's it due?' she said.

'Not till the end of the month.'

'You could leave it here if you like,' she said. 'I'll pack up.'

'Thanks.'

Jen held the door open and watched him jam his feet into the front of his still-laced school shoes, squashing the backs down. Not for the first time, judging from their crackled finish. It was going to be a tight race between destroying them and growing out of them.

She smiled. 'Don't forget about Sunday.'

'What?'

'The installation,' she said. 'I'll pick you up about eight?'

'Oh, yeah,' he said. 'Cool.'

Heat

It was too hot to draw. Her hand kept sticking to the page, even with the fan on flat-out, and the paint still hadn't dried on her portrait – she was running out of time to apply the final touches.

She refilled her glass with iced tea from the jug and sat out the back on the deck, hoping for some movement. The tops of the trees were shifting every now and then, suggesting something was coming. Usually she could rely on the cool sea breeze by early afternoon, but this weather was proving to be not only unusual but stubborn.

A tail hung down from the gutter. Jen peered up. 'Hello?' A young female king parrot flew down to the birdbath. The first female progeny, her green feathers lush and her red pantaloons circus-bright. She bobbed up and down to some tune of her own and peered at Jen, curious but not afraid.

Jen reached for her sketchbook and pulled a pencil from her hair, knotted up at the back. Two or three other king parrots called from nearby. They had synchronised themselves, or dropped out of sync, perhaps, to sound three slightly different notes – a family song.

———

She put off going to bed until after ten but the change still hadn't come through. The cloud cover was only keeping the heat in; the stillness was oppressive. She left all the doors and windows wide open, cut the lights and lit a mosquito coil to set up in her bedroom. It was possible something larger might wander in through the night but hopefully it would soon wander out again.

Opened up, it was no longer a house, but a shelter. A bed in the forest. Even a year ago the feeling would have bothered her, left her feeling vulnerable or worried about her things, at least. Now she lay under the sheet listening to the night's music – frogs and toads and crickets and bats and owls – quite at peace. More so, if anything.

———

The change had finally come; she'd had to pull the doona up from the bottom of the bed in the early morning. She didn't bother to close up the house after breakfast, leaving everything open to catch as much fresh cool air as possible. To breathe, while she headed out to walk and breathe herself.

She followed the ridgeline, to keep the sea breeze in her face, and then cut down to the riparian zone along the creek. It was like dipping into another world, another time. Cool, dark and quiet. She climbed up onto an old stump, wider than she was high, though now hollow inside, and coated in green moss. It was well preserved, more like stone than timber, almost petrified. Cedar, surely.

She perched, eyes closed, listening. Whipbirds cracked along the creek bed, a powerful owl *who-whooed*. Sound stayed inside the forest, like a secret.

A stillness had fallen, whether it was her mood, or the forest overhearing her thoughts. She watched the play of light dappling the trunks around her. The earth was damp, the memory of those trees that had already lived and died and fallen rich in the humus.

There was a fresh beer bottle inside the stump's missing core, which burst her bubble.

She climbed down and lay on her back, staring up at the canopy. The rustling and chirruping and gentle shift of the leaves smoothed her, until she was breathing with the forest. She was forest.

———

She laboured up the steep slope back to the road, carrying the beer bottle. Fourex, of course. Red-browed finches danced from shrub to shrub all about her. They were such chirpy birds that she couldn't help but smile.

A car roared past on the road. Jen crouched down and waited until it was quiet again to climb onto the verge and cross over. She cleared the advertising out of her mailbox and dumped it in the recycling bin with the bottle. The robins were flitting about the orchard, darting down to snap up insects.

She slid out of her boots and stepped inside the shade of the house, then stopped. It had cooled down nicely, a breeze running through, but that wasn't it. There was someone inside. 'Hello?'

She padded through to the lounge and stopped again. There were five wompoo fruit-doves resting in the rafters, their great white heads bobbing over violet breasts. For a moment, she felt herself in the wrong place. A stranger.

The doves were fond of the red berries on the palms just by the high windows – but there were no berries inside.

'*Wom-poo*,' said a dove.

'Hello,' she said.

They took flight, in one ringing uplift, and exited via the open bay windows as weirdly as they had come. No sign of distress, or having flown in the wrong door to the wrong place, or fled the coop. As if her home really was just a bird house, another tree.

'I still live here, you know,' she said, to no one. 'I wasn't gone that long.'

She hung her hat in the laundry, poured a glass of water and sat on the back steps to drink it. Thoreau wrote that a house should be as open as a bird's nest, delaying caulking the walls of his own cabin in the woods as long as he could to enjoy the breeze running through. He soon sealed it up when winter came, though, and hadn't lasted long out there on his own.

The idea of a house was interesting to think about, if you could set yourself apart from it. The cottage had been someone else's home before it was hers. A family's. Before that there was no house, no clearing – just trees. Home to birds, possums, koalas, wallabies, bandicoots and goodness knows what. And for so long before that, home to the first people, who did not need to own or destroy to live in a place, or belong. Everything had been clear-felled for her benefit, however she looked at it.

Jen already shared the house with the geckos and native mice, the occasional snake. The final act of the character in *My Birds* had been to bequeath his property to the birds – his will stipulating that the house be torn down and the block let run wild. It was an idea that appealed, especially with no one to leave her 'assets' to. Not that her house would need tearing down in this climate – it would soon rot and fall and begin its own journey back into the forest.

Hanging

'They're not as heavy as they look,' Henry said.

'No, just awkward.'

They had decided to unpack all of the pieces from the ute first, to get them inside. There were showers forecast. Although the approach of the exhibition had kept her awake every night, she had no real plan for how to hang the works.

The two larger pieces went last, requiring four arms to transport them. Henry flipped the final one over, exposing her to the world.

'Whoa,' he said.

They manoeuvred around the reception desk and leaned it against the foyer wall.

'Is it you?'

'What do you think?' Jen said.

'It kinda reminds me of you,' he said.

'Oh?'

'What's it called?'

'*Flightless Bird*.'

He frowned.

Had he not noticed the stumps of wings, the feathers around her mouth? The old, claw-like feet. Of course, she was not only flightless but childless and mateless.

'Would that be your superpower?'

'Sorry?'

'To fly,' he said. 'If I could have one superpower, it'd be to swim underwater without needing to breathe. Like a fish. Or surf through the air like the Silver Surfer.' He crouched, goofy-footed.

'That would be good, too.'

'Are you going to hang them both here?'

The paintings were the same size, and the foyer was probably the best place for them, allowing for a long view on approach. 'Let's prop them here for the moment and think about it.'

There were canvases everywhere, pieces she had long forgotten. Henry ran around turning them all outwards, like some sort of alarming TV game show: *This Was Your Life* or *This Was Your Art*.

———

The gallery's rooms were now full of birds, which was a vast improvement on the guns and penises displayed on her previous visit. More appropriate for her young assistant, too. She and Henry had decided to arrange her pieces chronologically, showing her development, such as it was. Regression, really. It was all rather revealing.

She had put Henry in charge of hanging the smaller pieces and talking with the lighting fellow to get them right. He was being a good sport, showing Henry how the tracks were adjusted and how to set a piece off perfectly, even accounting for all the variations of natural light. She needn't have worried about Henry handling the works – he was more careful than she was. The piece they were hanging, a rosella beside its dead mate on the side of the road, was getting more attention than it deserved. It had come from Phil, apparently, requiring considerable sweet-talking from Maureen. Or so she said.

Looking at it now, she wasn't sure if it was the best choice for the exhibition, or to get Henry to focus on. She placed her hands on either side of the ladder, as much to steady herself as the boy.

'Dad says she's dead.'

'He said that to you?'

'I heard him say it to Mum.'

'He's home, then?'

Henry nodded. 'For five days.'

The boy, like all children, had big ears, but the man could have been a little more careful. He had taken work in the mines, which had eased their financial problems but not improved his parenting skills. 'None of us really know what's happened yet,' she said.

'How long did you think Michael might come back?'

She gripped the ladder a little tighter. 'I don't know. For a long time. That's what's hard, yeah?'

He leaned back to inspect his work. 'Is it straight?'

'Perfect,' she said. 'Now come down and let's go get some lunch. Do you like burgers?'

———

To hang the last two pieces they had to work together. Henry had taken to calling them *Bird Man* and *Bird Woman*, which reminded her of a silly event they used to run in Canberra during summer: the Birdman Rally. Men, and even some

women, jumped off a bizarre temporary tower set up in Lake
Burley Griffin to launch various homemade contraptions into
the air with the intent of flying. The distance travelled – usually
a disappointing downward arc into the water – was measured,
and a winner awarded. There had been a consolation prize for
best outfit, which was usually the most birdlike.

'You okay with that?' Best not to send the boy home with
a wrenched shoulder.

'All good,' he said. 'You've found the hook?'

'Got it.'

He dusted off his hands and stood back, nodding: already an
expert. The lighting fellow was waiting up the ladder. Together
they fiddled about trying to set the pictures off for maximum
impact on entrance.

Maureen was floating around in her silks with a serene
smile, sticking the notes for each picture on the walls. 'Lovely!'
she said, at every painting.

Jen winked at Henry.

He rolled his eyes.

A white ibis fossicked through the garden bed outside. The
light was getting away.

'I just love these two,' Maureen said. 'A match made in
heaven.'

Henry smirked.

'Are you pleased?' Maureen asked. 'It's going to be such a
great show.'

'It's come together well. Thank you.'

'And Henry, what a great job you've done!' Maureen said.
'First time, too, I hear? I would never have guessed.'

'Thanks,' Henry said.

'We should probably head home soon,' Jen said. 'If you don't need us anymore?'

'Of course, of course,' Maureen said. 'Now, I have your list here, Jen, but will you just go around for me and check what's for sale and what's not? I'd hate to get that wrong.'

'Sure,' Jen said.

'Back in a sec,' Henry said.

Jen needed to visit the bathroom herself, but took the opportunity to take one last walk around on her own.

Opening

Jen had hoped to get there before the crowd but the traffic had been worse than she expected. It was already difficult to find a park. She eventually found a spot between a truck and a van, almost down to the main street, which didn't help her stay in the calm space she had carried from home.

People milled about the gallery entrance in a clump, forcing her to approach side on. She should be pleased; there could be no launch without people, and she hadn't really invited anyone except Henry. Aunt Sophie had been too ill to travel, in the end. Jen suspected it was less about the unsightly scabs on her face from the latest skin cancer treatments and more about the unsightly subject that had arisen between them.

She collected a glass of sparkling on her way past the reception desk and wandered the rooms, trying to see her work as others did. It was difficult to avoid overhearing the comments, even standing back, as if long-sighted.

'There you are,' Maureen said, and took hold of Jen's elbow, as if she might take flight at any moment. 'Come and meet the mayor; he's launching you.'

Jen let Maureen lead her through the crowd.

'His mistress and his wife are here,' Maureen said. 'So he's sweating already.'

'Where will I stand?' Jen said.

'I thought in front of *Flightless Bird*,' she said. 'Everyone loves it, and it's big enough to get picked up in the photos.'

Henry was in the foyer, with Kay and Montana, smart in his new graduation suit jacket. He gave her a thumbs up.

Jen managed a weak wave.

'Mayor Jardine,' Maureen said, 'may I introduce you to Jen Anderson.'

'Congratulations,' he said. 'It's a wonderful exhibition.' His handshake was warm and soft.

She attempted a smile.

'Everyone just loves your work, Jen,' he said. 'And one of our own returning to the coast is a good news story and a half.' He sipped his mineral water. 'We need all the good news we can get at the moment,' he said. 'I have my eye on a few pieces for the meeting room of the new council chambers.'

His eye was actually fixed on a young blonde, but he was welcome to buy up as much as he liked.

'You right to start in a few minutes, Jen?' Maureen said.

Jen nodded through the blood roaring in her ears. While Maureen handed the mayor his speech and set him up at the lectern, Jen slipped a beta-blocker under her tongue.

She had no speech prepared and few to thank. Just Maureen and Henry, the council for their sponsorship. The little anecdote about yellow robins and colour she had composed on the drive up seemed silly now, among all these suits.

She could tell the story about her first exhibition, as a student, which had the right level of self-deprecation and humour. And appropriate, perhaps, given that some of those works were hung here today. The Canberra twitchers' association had been her biggest fans, turning up late on the Sunday, still with binoculars around their necks. One reviewer had quipped that that was just as well, given how small some of the pieces were, and suggested it was work that would please the enthusiasts despite its 'lack of artistic mastery'.

Not many art school graduates demonstrated mastery, except perhaps at eking out a living and throwing a party on a shoestring. The words had stung nonetheless.

Or she could tell the story of her last exhibition, when she had drunk too much champagne. The former National Gallery Director had done a lovely job of the launch, but Jen had stumbled through her speech, put off by Craig's late arrival. She had thanked him for his support, nonetheless, hoping he would grow into the role.

The crowd was clapping and Maureen was waving her up, the mayor grinning. He had said something about a life's work, which grabbed her attention. It *was* her life's work – and there was no one to tell her it shouldn't be. She downed the rest of her bubbles, a little warm and flat now, and took a deep breath.

Swinging

She had dreamt that the roof blew off the house and the rain poured in, filling it up to the windows before spilling out over the sills in great cascades. She had not been in the place when it went, but looking down from above, as if it were an architect's model. At the point at which she woke, she had decided to hand the wreck of the place over to the birds, only to see it break loose and float off downhill, like a houseboat.

For a moment, it seemed real enough – her face and pillow were wet, and she felt herself adrift. But it was just a mist blown in from the windows behind the bed that she hadn't bothered to shut, despite the forecast.

She sat up, groggy. She hadn't been able to wind down after all the hoo-ha of the opening and had taken a sleeping tablet that was still hanging over her eyes like a heavy fog. The shrink disapproved of the sleeping tablets, but sometimes her mind wound itself up so tight that Sleepytime Tea didn't have a hope of fetching it back.

The roof was still on, though again littered with branches and sticks. The back lawn, too, was a mess, hidden by a green throw of leaves, the broad shape belonging to the brush box, predominantly pale underside up.

She lay listening to the roar of her creek, taking all that water from the ridge and moving it on downstream.

———

The deck was soaked, and the table and chairs. She stood, leaning on a post with her tea, amid the mist. Every leaf dripped, vibrant green, plumped with moisture and warmth. The birds had reappeared a little after sun-up, as if not quite trusting that the rain had ceased at first, or perhaps they, too, had been washed out of their routines. Where they went when it stormed she still hadn't worked out, but they didn't look at all bedraggled, celebrating with song. Their knowledge of the seasons was passed down with a strength and certainty that belied their hollow bones and tiny hearts.

The opening had gone well, everyone said. She hadn't embarrassed herself too much – but it had left her stretched thin.

———

She reached into the shed, pulling her treeboat from its hook. And a coil of rope. She marched down past the house, past the end of the garden, into her forest. She knew the tree already – the big old bloodwood with a high crown. Her tallest. She stood at its base and placed her hands on the warm trunk. Asking permission. It was intrusive, she was sure, to have a human clambering among your limbs, ropes rubbing away at your skin. She trusted the bloodwood to help her, because it would bleed if she hurt it; it could express its pain.

She threw the lead rope over the branch she had picked out, and missed. She tried again. And missed. Craig had always refused to climb when he was angry or upset; he said that's when you made mistakes. They had fought once, on a trip, the night before they were to climb the back of Mount Buffalo. Something silly about who would cook dinner or who forgot to pack the tea. He refused to climb the next morning, so they had sat at camp and read books and played cards until they were laughing together again.

When his brother had been arrested the second time they had cancelled a trip altogether. She had thought climbing mountain ash forests would be just what he needed, but they had walked Mornington Peninsula instead.

She finally landed the rope where she wanted it on the fourth go and pulled it over the limb. She rigged the treeboat, climbed in, and hauled herself up. If only she could wheel herself in and out of the world in the same way.

Jen hung, suspended, out of sight of the house, the neighbours, any visitors: everything. She had a clear view of the mountain, the sun setting behind it. The cicadas headed into crescendo, their final orchestra for the day, competing with the birds. A treeclimber hopped up up up the trunk, piping above the din.

The sky burned orange and then red. She watched until all colour and light were gone and the stars started winking. A boobook called from down in the gully and bats chittered and squealed as they fed. The tree rocked her to sleep.

———

She woke to raindrops on her face. Not from the sky, but from the tree, passed from leaf to leaf. She should move, get down from the tree and pack up her gear before it became too damp. Instead, she lay still, swinging free. The tree was whispering.

It was a moment that approached, a shift in time. She stared up at the tree's dead heart while she listened, and at last she understood. She carried something dead inside her, too.

The rain was only mist, and the distilled drip from the leaves gentle. She struggled at the thought of letting go, as if standing on the edge of a high diving board. But she took the stone, shells and glass trinkets – the artefacts of Craig – from her pockets, and let them fall, one by one. They made a sound as they hit the ground, though not as loud as she might have imagined. The tree's rain washed any tears away.

Yellow robins perched and dived beneath her, baring their yellow rumps as they fetched their breakfast.

Wonder

From the kitchen sink, she watched a male fairy-wren performing on the deck railing, head tilted back, eyes closed, as if in wonder at its own song. The volume of trills and range of notes produced by such a tiny bundle of bones and feathers was indeed wondrous, defying physical, if not earthly, laws.

It was John Burroughs who said that you did not know a bird until you heard its song. For her, the point of knowing was when you could pick a bird out of the forest cacophony without sighting it. Jen was at that stage with many of her companions, though only through cheating: three years of observing them, singing, at her birdbaths.

Their personality was just as evident in the way they bathed. The treecreeper entered the water the same way he went about the rest of his day, in a series of furtive, jerky, vertical movements up the post, until encountering the lip of the dish. Where, caught blind, he listened to establish whether another bird was present above him. Then he had to take a leap, up to the edge of the bath, and if all was clear, would turn and back into the water, as if fearing attack.

The fairy-wrens, on the other hand, dived in headfirst, entering on one side of the dish and exiting on the other, hopping between the two dishes with a great deal of splashing and chirping, in celebration of water and life in general – as they were doing now, the extended family of husband, wife and their three children, two female and one male.

She felt guilty, sometimes, a voyeur intruding on their private space. Although they did not disrobe – or defeather – she was watching them go about their ablutions. Sometimes she thought the birds conscious of her, as a living thing, but perhaps they had grown so used to her they thought her part of the furniture.

She wiped up her cup and bowl and placed them in the cupboard. Her mother had liked birds, the more colourful the better, hanging seed-feeders out in the backyard to attract the parrots and parakeets. She had been fond of the chooks and ducks and even the turkeys they had tried to farm for a while, in another of her father's grand schemes that never quite came off. Jen had been afraid of those large, caged birds, their wrinkled feet and spurs a source of quiet horror. Even as an adult, she could not bring herself to run chooks, despite the obvious benefits, which was probably somewhat perverse for a bird woman.

She had chosen her mother's room at the nursing home for its little balcony with a low-slung blue gum, heavy with red blossom. She had hoped her mother would not only enjoy its blooms but the conversation of the lorikeets and rosellas. As it turned out, they made quite a mess on the deck – and the little table and chair Jen had put there for her to sit at – but she could hear the birds, all year round, even while in bed, which was one of the few things that seemed to give her any pleasure.

Jen had done some pieces for her mother's room, a series of king parrots in colour wash, to brighten the place, hanging one above the bed and another by her armchair. The ladies seemed to appreciate them, bringing in visitors to view the pictures of birds, rather than those outside. Her mother, although irritated by the interruption at times, was quite proud, one of the nurses had told her, talking up her 'artist daughter'.

Jen had never seen any sign of such pride herself, the only comment coming shortly after she had hung them. 'You should use colour more often, dear,' her mother had said. 'Everyone likes a bit of colour.'

———

The birds at the baths celebrated the sun's descent. Lewin's honeyeaters snapped away fantails and white-eyes; wrens and pardalotes made way for the robins; and the treecreepers preferred to bathe alone. Through sheer numbers, the robins tended to rule the roost. She took a glass of wine out onto the deck. The thing that had been worrying its way forward for weeks now, slowed by her trying to worry back at it, trying to dig it out rather than let it work its way free, was upon her.

For all their stories, Sam and Glen had not once mentioned her father's last job, the development on the edge of town. If Sam didn't get him the job, he would have at least known about it.

It was no longer the edge, but some sort of middle, overrun by housing estates, a new school and park, the outlying houses infilled as blocks were sold up and split off. A light industrial area had sprung up, with a factory that turned fruit into straps and another that put herbs in a tube. The sort of project lauded for its innovation and employment opportunities.

When her father and his team had begun clearing, it had been controversial. She remembered that much. Her parents whispering after dinner, when she was supposed to be asleep. 'We need the money, love,' he'd said. The phone would ring in the middle of the night, but after the first few times, no one answered it.

At the time she had thought the fuss was about the destruction of the forest guarding the town's edge, and perhaps for some it was. In those days, though, trees were a minority concern. The town relied on the timber-getters and the economy they created. They were the economy.

There must have been something else about the development, though: the people behind it, or the process. Not that there was much of a process in those days.

Children

She woke up tired. The neighbour's dog had barked half the night, starting a chorus of hounds all around the district. Sound carried on a clear and otherwise quiet night, and she had counted half-a-dozen different voices. They were not the voices she wished to hear. When she had first moved back, there were one or two dogs about. Now everyone seemed to have one. If she had a dog, which she would not, she would be mortified if it disturbed the peace in that way – how did their owners just sleep through it?

The brush turkeys were out and about, more ugly and bedraggled than ever. There were three of them now, which was a worrying development. One made a half-hearted attempt to chase another off. A child, blow-in or rival, she wasn't sure. They strolled the lawn with feathers flat to their bodies and showed no interest in scratching up her gardens, so she let them be.

Jen paused, hand on her cup. The fairy-wrens were cavorting below the deck and up into the birdbaths, their tails, longer than their bodies, held at a jaunty angle. They lived up to ten years, which was a long time for a bird. They tended to settle in one place, a territory of a few hectares, in an extended family arrangement – a habit returning to favour in the human world – the offspring often delaying setting out on their own in favour of the security of home territory. Although the group might have more than two adults capable of brooding, only one female laid the eggs each year. When the young wrens did finally disperse, it was usually the females who up and left.

She had always known Craig didn't want children. At first she assumed that he would change his mind when he was older, or that she could change his mind for him. Not through arguing or mounting some sort of campaign but by loving him. Demonstrating that their relationship was worth it. That she was worth it.

He was right. If she had wanted them enough, she would have raised the question – pushed the issue.

She had wanted children only in an abstract sort of way, as an extension of their relationship, but she had never felt clucky or fussed over babies the way some women did. There was something about teaching that soon drummed any idealism about child rearing out of you. She enjoyed them, their open minds and hearts, and had assumed she would get more maternal as she matured, that something would kick in. But it hadn't.

She had put Craig first, before herself, and had to nurture her art in secret. There hadn't been enough energy left over for a child.

The truth was, she hadn't found the right man. She had just left it too late to admit it. When the time came – when she could no longer keep the realisation out of her mind – she waited until Craig was at work, packed her things in three hours and hit the road. No note. Of all people, she should have had more regard for the person left behind, but it was the only way she could be sure she wouldn't change her mind.

Perhaps it was for the best that she hadn't passed on any of her defective genes: a father who left, a mother who broke down, and a child who perpetuated their patterns.

Protest

Glen found her planting out another tray of seedlings. Davidson plums, tamarinds, and a quandong. Food trees – as much for the birds as for herself. Aunt Sophie had made a Davidson plum tart one year, picking up a bucket of fruit at some market. Jen would have to wait seven years for the tree to mature, the label said. It was going to be a long time between pies.

'I didn't hear the ute,' she said.

'Parked up the top,' Glen said. 'Perfect day, isn't it.'

'It is.'

He looked about him, at the new plantings and freshly mowed lawn. 'You've got things looking good,' he said.

She tried to see it with his eyes, without all the flaws hers tended to focus on. All the things that needed doing. 'Thanks.'

'I'm going to a meeting in town. About that A-hole developer's plans,' he said. 'I wondered if you might like to come along.'

She had seen something about it in the paper, a shopping centre and units. There was a petition she should have signed. 'I don't know,' she said.

'We need to stop this guy,' he said. 'The original proposal wasn't too bad, a little shopping centre with parking underneath, a few units. But he's managed to buy up half the town on the sly, and now he's changed the development proposal. A new bank and a big supermarket. Forty-two units.'

Jen frowned, trying to picture it. 'Where?'

'The park goes, and all the original houses on Dale Street. The nice old shops opposite.'

'That would completely change the nature of the town.'

'Exactly.'

Jen looked herself over, gardening clothes, dirty hands. 'I'm not really dressed for it.'

Glen smiled. 'We could use your support, Jen. And you'll meet some good people.'

The quandong was out of its punnet but not yet in the ground, and they all needed watering in.

'I'll finish this,' he said. 'Why don't you clean up.'

It seemed she was out of excuses. 'Won't be long,' she said.

She brushed herself off and scraped out of her boots at the back door, then peeled off her jeans and shirt and dropped them in the laundry basket.

She found a clean pair of fisherman's pants in the wardrobe and pulled a fresh T-shirt from the drying rack. Tied her hair back into a ponytail. In answer to her stomach's grumble, she took two Granny Smiths from the bowl on the dining table. Her slides were at the front door; she'd have to go round.

Glen was washing his hands under the tap. He had finished the planting, watered in the seedlings and stacked the empty punnets next to the watering can.

'Ready?' he said.

'Ready.' She threw him an apple.

He caught it in his left hand, smiled. 'Thanks.'

They walked up to the ute, crunching. Sun on their faces. Glen wiped his mouth on his sleeve. Opened the door for her and cleared off the seat. Bills and soft drink bottles spilled out. He couldn't have counted on her coming along, which was good to know.

He held the apple in his mouth while he reversed out of the drive and then drove one-handed towards town.

'How's Karen?'

'Good, good,' he said. 'Having a few problems with Sarah, at the moment. She wants her freedom and independence. And we want to know where she is – At All Times.'

'It's hard not to worry. Especially now.'

'I know the Jones girl and Michael were probably one-offs, but —'

Jen looked at her apple.

'Sorry,' he said.

They had stopped eating. 'We don't know that,' she said. 'There's plenty to worry about.'

He crunched his apple.

They passed the lagoon, empty of birds today.

'Didn't some of the land you're talking about belong to the council?'

Glen nodded. 'They sold it to him.'

'Can they do that? Without putting it on the market?'

'Apparently.' He took one last bite of the apple and threw the core out the open window. 'The guy's a real sneak. He came along to a community meeting years ago. We were trying to come up with ways to bring the town together, give it a heart. He already owned a lot of property then but pretended he was on the same page. That's where we came up with the idea for the market space and the walkway.'

'He was planning a development all along?'

'Exactly,' he said. 'He got all the information he needed at the meetings, all of the property owners' details. And approached them, one by one. Somehow, he stopped them talking to each other. A year or so later – boom – he owns the centre of town.'

Jen picked a piece of apple skin from between her teeth. 'What a bastard.'

'You got that right.'

A semitrailer laden with mangoes pulled in to the fruit strap factory. 'Has Sam ever mentioned that development that went bust here when we were kids?'

'Only that it was a rotten business,' Glen said.

Jen turned. 'Was he involved?'

'I don't think so,' he said. 'Why do you ask?'

'I only remembered it the other day,' she said. 'I guess there was so much else going on.'

Glen pulled a face. 'Over our heads then, that sort of stuff.'

'I guess it's our turn, now,' Jen said. 'To do something. So – where's this meeting?'

Storm

The irises, for once, hadn't seen it coming. By the time their flowers began to open, it was already raining. Cyclone Haydos must have been heading somewhere else, changed course at the last minute and fooled nature herself. It was encouraging, especially for the Bureau of Meteorology, that even irises could be wrong.

Above the rain and the wind, the roaring in the treetops, she heard the piping call of a lone treecreeper, optimistic as ever.

The trees were lathering themselves, soapy suds running down their trunks and foaming at the base. Their tannins doubled as a washing agent; the trees were taking the opportunity to bathe.

She watched as the wind picked up, bending the treetops over. Water rushed over the gutter outside the kitchen window. The rain was about as heavy as she had ever seen but the downpipe must have blocked, or the strainer the plumber had talked her into installing, not realising the volume of leaves and rain it would have to deal with. She had meant to clean the gutters properly again by now – but had put it off one day too long.

Jen pulled her singlet over her head and stepped out of her fisherman's pants, leaving them in a pile on the floor, like a slipped skin. She shut the back door behind her and ran out into the rain. It was coming down in slap-like drops. Slops. The roar was disorienting and her hair was soon plastered to her head. She had to stand on the edge of the deck to reach the box downpipe. Water washed over her, forcing her to work blind, unclipping the cover, removing the filter and plunging her arm in to the elbow. She removed a plug of leaves and muck from the bend and threw it over her shoulder, then another.

The waterfall ceased, rushing down the gutter again instead, beneath the house and into her underground tank. She tapped out the sieve and put it back in place, then the mesh cover, before stepping back down to the ground. The force of the water had washed a great hole in her garden bed, sending her plants sailing out onto the lawn, each its own island.

She ran back to the cover of the deck and stood dripping on the boards, the rain deafening on the iron. No sign of the birds today.

She slipped and slid to the bathroom for a towel.

———

Still it came down. Seven hundred millimetres in twenty-four hours alone and eighteen hundred for the week. The underground tank had been overflowing for days. The rain was so loud on the roof overnight she had not been able to sleep. That and worrying about the water getting in around the fireplace and the corner of her studio.

All she could smell was damp wood. She had lit the fire to try to dry things out, turned on all of the fans. Burned incense to cover it over.

She had been cut off since the morning before. No phone, no internet, no mobile reception, and the road out flooded in both directions. Her own driveway was a stream, and the steps down to the house a cascade.

The power had been out for eighteen hours, and then returned after breakfast. On one side of the house, anyway. The other was still dead, probably just a circuit shorted out. She had hooked up an extension cord, running yellow across the dining room, to keep the fridge going.

Jen watched the clock. The second hand, she was sure, had just moved backwards: stealing time. There, it did it again. One back, three forward. How long had it been doing that? She marched into her studio and turned on her laptop, waiting for it to wake up and tell her it was ten past twelve. The clock said twenty-five past nine. No wonder she had felt out of whack. How long had she been operating in her own private time zone? There was a new battery, at the back of the kitchen drawer, still in its packet. She pulled the clock down and changed the battery over, reset the time, and hung the clock back on the screw in the wall, adjusting it until it was straight. It didn't move. It had stopped altogether. Swiss it might be, but her clock could not keep time in the tropics. It probably dreamt of snow and dry air, the alps of home.

There was a line of condensation spreading outwards on the freezer door. Its seals were on the way out, although only a few years old. Fridges were apparently not designed for high humidity. The complaints representative had explained that the problem was that she was failing to moderate the indoor temperature with air-conditioning – a larger fridge – so that the smaller fridge could work in comfort.

Only the television worked fine, beaming in calamitous images that had become addictive. The coast had been declared a disaster area, whole towns cut off, roads caved in and washed away. Every river, stream and seasonal creek had broken its banks, and still the rain came down and water rushed off the land; there were flood warnings across most of the state. The worst in a hundred years, they said.

A whole town had been washed away west of Brisbane, and now, water had to be released from the dam housing the city's water supply, worsening the flooding downstream.

———

As the floodwaters began their advance on the city – river levels rising by the hour, residents sandbagging their homes and moving their valuables to higher ground, and authorities evacuating the central business district – the media spotlight finally shifted away from the disaster-declared coast.

Only then did all that water finally flush out the very thing everyone had been looking for, but no one had wanted to find.

Jen heard the helicopters throughout the afternoon and had to stop working, she felt so unsettled. Now it was all over the news.

A woman walking her dog for the first time in ten days, after the rain had eased overnight, had found a muddy pink schoolbag snagged among paperbarks, in the national park. By nightfall, the area had been taped off, declared a crime scene. The police had found human remains.

Long held beneath root and soil, gestating in decomposing plant matter, the hinterland delivered up its lost children, and the lost child in them all.

Flotsam

Jen turned off the television. She was wrung out for all those who had lost their homes and businesses and family members. Thankful for her own life untouched, unchanged. Almost.

For Caitlin's parents, it was finally over. A loss of hope in exchange for knowing. The beginning of getting on with their lives.

She no longer knew how many days had gone by. It had stopped raining, though humidity was still at a hundred per cent. She had all the fans on but everything was damp. The book covers on the coffee table had curled back like leaves. Above the mosquito coil, and the bergamot, lavender and cedar combination in her oil burner, she could not escape the nose-tickling smell of mould.

She had put it off as long as she could. The fridge was empty but for condiments and there was nothing in the cupboard but dry pasta and lentils. The Hilux smelt damp. It was damp, the seat sticking to the back of her arms. She urged it up the drive, slipping on loose gravel. There was still detritus all over the road, and potholes deep enough to swim in.

The post office was shut, the co-op too. NO POWER! their signs said. The road was still littered with leaves and branches. Palm fronds. Her forest had sheltered her from the worst of it, it seemed. After all this time without power, the shops would have lost all their stock. Terrible. Still, she couldn't help feeling put out. It had been almost a week since she had left the property, and she needed food, fuel and mail. Human contact.

She kept on driving down the coast. Things would have to be more operational down there. She steered round the 'road closed' sign beneath the railway bridge, driving up onto the raised footpath to get through. There were a few other cars on the road in front of her and they all slowed to pass through the water over the highway, sending great jets up into the air.

There were more cars closer to the coast, and McDonald's was doing a roaring trade. Jen sped past, to the river.

The river was fat, swollen and brown, pocked with flotsam and jetsam, the streets covered with scum the retreating waters had left behind. The shops were all closed, bar the tavern and corner store.

The rain had flushed out the river, and now wild surf washed it all back up onto the beach. Logs, esky lids, thongs, milk bottle tops, mangrove leaves and orange mangrove flowers, still on their cigar-shaped stands. A whole tree had been beached. The surf produced a great brown foam, like a dirty cappuccino, which had built up on the beach in fluffy mountains, blowing back over the car park and road.

The beach was closed and lifesavers were on hand enforcing the decision. With sets coming in at up to twenty foot, and the water rich with debris, it was fair enough. Children played in the foam, running through it and throwing gobs at each other. Jen considered pointing out that it was toxins and effluent that made the water froth like that, but who was she to spoil their fun?

Blue

They had been asked to wear blue, like wrens or bowerbirds. Jen had washed and ironed a silk shirt that was just the right shade.

She parked the Hilux around the corner and walked back. People were already beginning to move inside, heads down. Half the town had turned up, maybe more, most in dark colours with blue touches, which made standing in the bright sunshine unpleasant, even at this hour of the morning.

Her own suit, bought for her mother's service, had grown patches of pale mould in the cupboard, especially around the crotch and armpits. There was nothing like humidity to remind you of your humanity. She had known about the service for a week, plenty of time to have it dry-cleaned, but had not managed to think in such an organised fashion. She had aired it out and sponged it off as best she could, and sprayed on a little extra perfume, but the spores tickled her nose.

She needn't have worried. The whole church smelt mouldy – whether from the formal clothes of the attendees or the structure itself, it was hard to tell. There was more than a hint of mothball, too. Instead of the sombre organ music she had expected, a CD was playing: young people's songs. Reminding them that they were farewelling someone whose life had only been beginning.

The police hadn't released Caitlin's remains, so it was not a full funeral, more of a ceremony.

Jen took a seat at the back, on the outside of the pew. Ready for a quick getaway, her father used to say, preferring the rear of the room and seats near the door. That should have been a clue.

She was a little close to the speaker, which was blaring a song she had heard before, from incidental radio play in stores and service stations, something about a young woman coming into her own, which Caitlin would never get to do.

Jen picked out Henry's back. His class were sitting together, three pews of them, all in school uniform with a blue armband, which was a nice touch.

Henry turned, as if he had known exactly where she would sit. She tried to smile, and send him 'be brave' vibes, but her face was uncooperative. She would have made an awful parent.

Kay and Montana sat in the row behind him. His father did not seem to be present; interstate and underground, perhaps. Caitlin's family were up front, everyone's eyes on them. She wouldn't dare say it out loud, but it was the best they had looked since their daughter went missing. Their faces were sad but human, which was proof that even knowing the worst was better than not knowing.

Lil slid in next to her and half-smiled. Patted Jen's shoulder. Jen watched a palm tree, the tine of one frond quivering in what was barely a breeze, while the minister droned. A schoolfriend read a poem and did a good job, while her classmates stood with their small, soft hands folded in front of them. The friend ended with a funny story about Caitlin, which was smart, and she was rewarded with laughter.

'Did Michael have a funeral?' Henry had asked the week before.

She had struggled to explain that they couldn't really have one without knowing for sure he was dead. Time had passed, and his parents separated and moved away, one to New Zealand and one to Tasmania – as if by leaving the continent, and each other, they could escape their loss.

Jen watched the class up front: upset, but together and dealing with their grief. They would be able to move on now. That's what funerals were really about, after all: closure for the living.

Gone

She wandered the back garden as if without purpose, gathering up clutches of leaves and sticks although it was far too warm for a fire. The lawn needed mowing, straggly lengths brushing her legs. She followed the line of lomandra around and down, touching her hand to the strappy leaves. They were growing high and wide, boosted by the summer's record rainfall.

She stopped beneath her climbing tree, bent to gather up a perfect stick, in between kindling and wood, and well seasoned. All the while she scanned the ground.

Craig and his new partner, a younger sports teacher from his school, had apparently had a child: a daughter. A former colleague had called to tell her before she heard it on the teachers' gossip line. Two years after she had left. Jen had still been teaching, then, at the little school on the south coast. The colleague said that they had fallen pregnant by accident and decided to keep the baby. It had been that simple.

They were gone. Her Craig objects were all gone. Washed away by the rains, or carried off by an animal to decorate its house. There was a little lurch in her chest before she caught herself. She had cast them off, even telling the shrink about it – eliciting a rare smile of approval – and she couldn't expect to fetch them back again.

———

Jen watched a brown tree snake making its way along the deck railing, towards the birdbath. In the light from the house windows, he was gleaming pink. It explained why her candle holders kept disappearing, falling onto the ground below. Dislodged by a slithering drinker. He extended his head over the edge of the bath. She hadn't seen a snake drink before, or even imagined them doing so.

The frogs had fallen silent. Could they sense the movement of scales on wood? Or smell him there in the dark?

The discarded skin of a gecko floated down, whole, from the rafter above, like a ghostly suit, and landed on the table. Tiny white gloves, a hood for a tail, an all-of-body fingerprint.

Jen sipped her wine and looked out into the night. She had grown fond of her companions. Comfortable. And there was never a dull moment.

Glider

Jen sat up in the window with her sketchbook and pencils. She erased and retraced some of her lines, to suggest movement. Outside she could sense the maroon blur of schoolchildren, released already. She had lingered too long.

Elena appeared at her elbow to remove her cup and crumb-strewn plate. 'Another chai latte, Jen?'

She should really get moving – she had promised Glen she'd write their letter to the local member about the development in town, which looked like being approved – but she hadn't quite finished her drawing, and the air-conditioned cafe was far more pleasant than her own place would be. 'Yes, please.'

'Coming right up.' Elena spun on her heel, or rather, the flat sole of her sensible clog. The music was good today, too, some local indie band. It disappeared for a while, under the frothing of milk, and then Elena was back.

'Thanks.' The door opened, tinkling the bells. She slid her coffee closer, but managed to elbow her sketchbook off the bench. 'Bugger.'

She turned to face a child version of herself, or so it seemed. Jen blinked. It was Caitlin's sister. Holding out her sketchbook.

'Thank you.'

'Is it a possum?'

'Sugar glider,' Jen said. 'I saw her last night. Swooping into the mango tree.'

'They can fly?'

'A little. From tree to tree,' Jen said. 'They have extra skin here, between their arms. Like a built-in parachute.'

Briony smiled. 'She's cute.'

'Thanks,' Jen said. 'Getting some afternoon tea?'

'A coffee, for Mum. She's having her hair cut next door.'

'Cappuccino, love?' Elena said.

Briony nodded.

Elena waved her arm over her cakes and slices. 'Anything for you?'

Briony stared into the drinks fridge, everything subdued colours, organic and healthy. A child's nightmare. She opened the door and reached for a pink bottle – fizzy lychee – and took it to the counter.

Jen sketched in mango leaves, the base of a fruit hanging down, brightened the glider's eye and fluffed up her tail, added veins to her delicate ears. She heard the coffee land on the counter, the lid go on. Jen signed her name and tore the page from her sketchbook.

The girl put the change in her pocket and took the drinks from the counter.

Jen held out the glider. 'Got room for a friend?'

'Really?'

'A gift,' Jen said. 'If you'd like her?'

Briony grinned. She tucked the bottle under her arm and took the drawing. 'Thank you.'

Charge

A fine day and cooler morning presented an opportunity to arrest the lawn's growth. She found a hat, rolled down her sleeves, and sat on the ride-on. She turned the key in the ignition. Nothing. Flat battery. She rummaged around in the shed for the shifter, and propped up the mower's bonnet. The bolts were stiff, and removing the battery awkward; it was heavy and wedged in tight. She managed, but not without a skinned knuckle.

She watched a pair of spotted pardalotes, with their stubby tails and yellow throats, almost hovering, pinching pieces of straw from a hanging basket with a right to left movement, one strand at a time. All of her baskets ended up with the bottoms falling out, but the pardalotes and finches for miles around had lovely woven nests. She had seen them, hanging in the understorey, where it was thick: grassy domes with a side entrance, nursing a clutch of white eggs. Very appealing residences, indeed, and much more snug and secure than an open nest.

She dropped the dead battery in the back of the ute. After searching the house and studio, she found her wallet and sunglasses still on the passenger seat from last time.

She let the Hilux speed up downhill. It was that or ride the brake. A long-tailed brown blur flew out from the tangle of lantana, barely making it in front of her grille to the other side of the road. She had flushed a pheasant. Though a vehicle was not the ideal way to do it. And there would be no roast for dinner.

She pulled up in front of the mower shop. Closed. It was hot, but not yet two in the afternoon. 'Great.'

The steering wheel was hot under her hands. She turned the Hilux around and headed back to the main street. The garage was one of the few things unchanged about the town. The same faded red bowser still stood out the front.

Jen tucked the battery under her arm, attempting to make it look effortless, and stepped into the sudden dark. 'Still doing mechanics?' she said.

The girl blinked. 'Some,' she said. 'What were you after?'

'Just need a battery charged.'

'Go on through.'

'Thanks.' The door opened out onto steep steps. She made her way down to the cement floor, among three cars in various states of undress. She felt herself wilting; the workshop copped the full force of the afternoon sun. 'Hello?'

A fellow looked out from beneath the hood of an oversized ute. 'Hey.'

'Will you charge a battery for me? The mower place is shut.'

He made his way over, his pace and enthusiasm slowed by the heat. 'No problem.' He squatted, attached the chargers. 'Mower shop's closed down,' he said.

'What?' she said. 'When?'

'Few months ago.'

Surely it wasn't that long since she'd been in there with the chainsaw. 'Why?'

'Sold it,' he said. 'Some bloke took it over but then he was electrocuted. Building's not safe. Condemned.'

'Goodness.'

He stood. 'Not good, eh?'

'How long will it need?'

'Three or four hours,' he said.

'I'll come back in the morning,' she said. 'Thanks.'

———

Jen dropped one side of the ute's tray, hopped up and rolled the round metal frame to the edge. It was not heavy but unwieldy. She had popped into the second-hand store looking for something she could use as a bench seat or stool in the garden, but the hanging ball had caught her eye from the car park. It had been some sort of child's hammock, more like a cocoon – homemade. Hung beneath a big old tree, no doubt. She lowered it onto the wheelbarrow, a bit like a giant egg in a teacup, and jumped down.

She used her Stanley knife to cut away the faded, mouldy canvas, looped on with nylon rope, dropping it all in a pale green pile on the driveway. What was left, when she had finished, was a black metal frame. There was a little rust but it was perfect for her purposes.

She gripped the barrow's edge and the frame in one hand and lifted the barrow handle with the other. It was precarious, but easier than taking all the weight of the ball. She eased forward and lurched down the path.

Nest

Jen piled bamboo cuttings high in the wheelbarrow, slipped the secateurs in one pocket and wire in the other, and set off down to the bottom of the garden. Those pardalotes had given her an idea.

It was Karen who had harvested the bamboo, Glen said, from a screen planting gone feral by their pool. It wasn't Jen's first choice – not being native to the area – but the canes were green and flexible, which was what she needed for the first stage. Jen followed the path, kept in use as much by the wallabies and turkeys as her own feet, as far as she could along the slope.

She sorted the bamboo into piles of short, medium and long, and set herself up next to the round frame, already hanging from her tree, just above the ground, so that she could work. At the moment, it looked more like a cage, but she meant to change that. She began with the entrance, choosing a thin, flattish cane to form a circle, and attaching it to the frame with copper wire lengths. From there, she worked back, still in a circular fashion, weaving the canes in and out of the frame like a giant basket.

Birdsong filled the clearing, the perfect accompaniment to her work. She experimented with splitting some of the canes, starting a cut with the secateurs and pulling the bamboo apart. These lengths were more flexible, easier to weave around the tighter ends of the ball.

She sat on a stump to drink from her water bottle and rest her arms. This was just the sort of project Craig would have been bored by, which was all the more reason to enjoy it. A young goanna skittered down the tree trunk beside her, all tail and enthusiasm. He leapt the final five feet to the ground, giving himself a fright as he came face to face with the basket.

He scuttled away, loud through leaves, and ascended the rear of a tallowwood, sending bark particles flying; he had a bit to learn about stealth if he wanted to pinch anybody's eggs.

Jen turned the basket, resting it on its front. She continued weaving the canes, having to stretch over the belly of the ball in a kind of hug. The pile of bamboo was disappearing fast, but there would be enough to complete this layer. She stretched her neck and flexed her hands. Dappled light danced over leaves. Robins and fantails fussed about nearby, as if recognising what was beginning to take shape.

———

She set off with her water bottle straight after breakfast. The nest was lying where she had left it, on its side among grasses. It was still cool in the shade, the sun yet to reach through the canopy. She started the day's work gathering long slender sticks, preferably with a bit of bend left in them. When she had an armload she wandered back and began weaving them into the spaces around the bamboo.

Her hands and forearms were sore this morning, their muscles unaccustomed to nest building. She alternated gathering and weaving, all punctuated with watching birds. She had heard a new call, in the canopy, and was determined to identify it. It was parrot-like, igniting her fantasy of discovering the Coxen's fig parrot in her forest.

Sometimes a stick would snap as she was weaving and she would fall forward with the sudden loss of tension, but she was making good progress. The smooth green of the bamboo was disappearing, dropping into the background, replaced by rough browns.

She lay back to rest, arms above her head, watching the light sifting in: magic beams in her enchanted forest. A pair of robins gripped the fibrous trunk of a tallowwood and peered down, their yellow chests aglow.

She sat up and sipped her water. On its side the basket looked a little like a bloated fish trap. All that had been caught inside were a few flies, buzzing against the canes. It was warmer now, and she slipped out of her shirt to work in her singlet. She had to go further afield for the last round of sticks, one eye on the canopy for the owner of the new voice. A rose gum offered up a handful of long slender twigs ideal for trimming around the opening, and she could begin to imagine finishing. Perhaps that explained the nervous feeling she had been carrying all morning, as if something was about to happen. As if enough hadn't happened already.

———

She had already gathered a wheelbarrow load of bark, and was now hunting for vines – at last, a good use for velcro creeper. She cut them off at the base and poisoned the root while she was at it: creative gardening.

She alternated bark and vine where she could, threading and poking through any remaining gaps to build texture and colour, as much for camouflage as aesthetics. A good nest should not be visible from the ground.

The birds had grown used to her, and the monster nest, sing-songing all around and darting down to take insects she disturbed. The rope had bothered them for a while, resembling a super-long snake. She gathered it up now, and fed one end through the great steel ring at the top of the nest, knotting it off according to the instructions she had written out. She ran the other end through the pulley, and tossed it over the branch. She raised the nest, hand over hand. The nest's shape was almost as she had imagined, drawn and planned. She looped the end of the rope around her log, as if securing a horse.

Her stomach was complaining about lunch but all she grabbed from the house was the camera. She forced herself to walk on the way back, lest she trip and damage the gear. Her first decent camera had gone missing in the Nymboida National Park when she had become distracted, following a bowerbird to its nest. When she returned to her lunch spot, the camera and case were gone. It had glinted blue-black in the sun and she had always suspected the bird, and his less showy mate, of tricking her for the prize. Ten years later she had learned little, dropping a thousand-dollar telephoto lens from a tree when she saw her first lyrebird.

Today she had both feet on the ground and her wits about her. She photographed the nest from all angles. Warm and round, a little rough, and already almost at home in its environment.

She took the camera back up to the house and sat it next to her laptop for later, put an apple in her pocket, and carried down an old feather doona and pillow to line the nest with for now, until she came up with something more durable. She pushed the bedding through the hole and climbed after it, nestling in.

She raised herself with the rope. It was just like the treeboat – only vertical and roomy. No synthetics in sight. The nest swung, and she swung free inside. Weightless as a bird.

The view was, as she had hoped, perfect. A glimpse through leaves out to the coast.

She snuggled deeper into her feathers, hummed a tune, all the while listening to the song around her, the wind in the leaves, birds gossiping about the installation of a giant nest in their woods. That's what it was, she supposed: an installation. A hide.

Michael

The phone was ringing. She had forgotten to unplug it while she was sketching a better design for her knots and pulleys. Today something made her put down her pencil and answer it.

'Um, it's Henry.'

'Hi, Henry.' His mother said something in the background and the radio was on at their place, making it difficult for Jen to focus on his voice.

'You need to listen to the news today.'

'I do?'

'Yeah,' he said. 'They . . . they've identified those bones. It's Michael.'

She let out a breath.

'I'm sorry.'

'No. It was very thoughtful of you to tell me.'

'Okay. Well, I'd better go.'

'Okay,' she said. 'And Henry . . .'

'Yes?'

'Thank you.'

She put the phone down. The sun was out, and scrubwrens chirruped in the grevilleas by the side of the house. A gumnut plonked on the roof and rattled down the slope and off the edge. Into the abyss.

She stood, filled the kettle, and fired up the gas. Waited for it to boil. She rinsed out a mug, a gift from her mother with a botanical print. Quite pretty, really. She took her time drying it, watching a cuckoo dove trying to land on the edge of the birdbath.

The kettle boiled. She turned off the gas, poured water over the infuser. Inhaled the gingery steam.

It was almost nine. Jen picked up the remote, pointed it at the stereo. The ABC news theme music was already playing. She sat on the arm of the lounge, holding her tea against her chest. It was the lead story. DNA testing had identified the remains found with those of Caitlin Jones as twelve-year-old Michael Wade, missing since June 1977. Police forensics had been able to match samples to those taken from a Wade family member.

There was an interview with Michael's father, an old man now. He said he had been relieved to finally get the call, but not surprised. The family had been cooperating with the police for several weeks.

The next story was more on the blame game about the floods, as if any of it could have been predicted. Jen turned off the radio and took her tea outside.

Arrest

The day summer finally ended, police arrested a man in his twenties and charged him with the abduction, sexual assault and murder of Caitlin Jones. Another man, believed to be related, had been charged as an accessory. Jen had been supposed to go to a meeting about the proposed new development, but town was the last place she wanted to be.

Jen switched off the radio. She sliced an onion and cubed leftover vegetables for a curry, fried them off in the spices and added tomato and yoghurt. She turned down the heat, and left it to simmer.

The sky was burning red over the mountain, her forest in silhouette. She opened a bottle of wine, which she didn't often allow herself during the week, and sat out the back with the birds. The arrests didn't explain what had happened to Michael or quite let her father off the hook, but surely it couldn't be coincidence that the children's bodies had been found in the same place.

———

Jen spooned curry over rice and took her bowl in to watch the
news. Another glass of red, too, which she needed. She turned
on the television and flicked through trying to find the ABC.
The channel seemed to have dropped off somehow, as if insulted
by the scarcity of use. Perhaps it had been taken off the air
due to a lack of funding. She fiddled with the buttons on the
remote, bringing up every menu on screen except the one for
tuning in channels. It was almost seven, and it was bound to
be the lead story.

She found it. Three layers down; she had to select digital.
Now it tuned itself, with a low hum, running through the whole
frequency range. It was taking its time.

The ABC was back. She sat on the floor, cross-legged in
front of the screen, as the lead-in music ended.

Mathew Fergusson was twenty-two and had lived in the
neighbouring town with his uncle, Callum Fergusson, fifty-nine.
Mathew had left the area shortly after Caitlin disappeared. That
should have been a red flag. The presenter cut to a journalist
outside the courtroom, with the news that the uncle had not
only been charged as an accessory to Caitlin's murder but for the
murder of Michael Wade. The picture they showed on screen
was Michael's last school photo, his grin almost as silly as her
own that year. Michael had always been able to make her laugh,
but not now. She wiped her face on her napkin. Of course he
was dead, she had known that for most of her life – but now
something else filled the space once occupied by hope. Grey
over yellow.

Jen sipped her wine. She muted the sound for the rest of the
news, staring at the blur of faces and places going by.

The more in-depth coverage on the *7.30 Report* said the
Fergussons had been attached, for a time, to one of the Brethren

communities in the hills. The uncle had had a relationship with a woman there, with whom he had a child, and dropped off the grid for several years after Michael's disappearance. Another red flag. He had later left the community, raising his nephew after his sister had died, while his own son had stayed on with his mother and the Brethren. None of it made any sense. There was no mention of previous convictions, police suspicions. Would the nephew have gone down the same path if he had chosen to stay with his own father?

She switched the television off. It would be months, at least, before all those questions were answered. She sat for a moment staring at the blank screen, feeling the sudden quiet. Emptiness. A boobook called, so loud it must have been perched on the gutter.

She padded out to the kitchen, filled the kettle, returned it to the hob and flicked the gas. Insects threw themselves at the light. She must have left a window ajar somewhere. She leaned on the kitchen bench, watching the undersides of moths, and bumping beetles, waiting for the water to boil. She considered, for a moment, calling Henry, but decided against it.

It was still outside, as if a blanket of relief had been thrown over her forest. She chose a Sleepytime Tea from the box, removed its paper seal, and hung the little sack over the edge of the mug. She was tired enough, but her mind was turning circles all the same.

Memorial

Glen had offered to pick her up and she had accepted. He was bringing Phil, too, who was up from Sydney. There was to be a bit of a gathering, Glen said. They wanted Jen to go, but she wasn't sure about the idea of an impromptu school reunion tacked onto the memorial.

Michael's father's family was to fly in from Tasmania, but she hadn't heard anything about his mother.

A thrush sang for her from the rose gum outside the bathroom, an aria of notes and intonations delivered with some volume. She wiped away a tear at the joy the bird delivered through song. Tears would not do if she was to wear the make-up she had dug out. She patted her eyes with a tissue.

She had washed her hair, and forced a comb through it, delivering a handful of grey and brown to the bin. She pulled it back, off her head, and tied it up with a band almost out of stretch.

It was going to turn out a nice day, the cloud drifting off and sun slanting in. She tried to think of Michael as she had known him, without sadness.

———

The service lacked the immediate grief of a funeral. There was not much black; it was a warm day, after all. Nor was there the organised colour coding of Caitlin's memorial. Jen hadn't recognised many of her classmates at first, and those she did she thought much changed. Time was unkind; most of them grey and heavy. But as they came up one by one and spoke to her, the years seemed to drop away, and they were the people she had always known. Older, sure, and with adult children and second marriages and jobs she may not necessarily have anticipated, but the same people. By this age, life had thrown most people a curve ball or two, so there was not the jostling for most successful or best preserved.

In some ways, they knew each other better than anyone, growing up together in this place. They had all been through this thing, this defining thing, together.

She had recognised Glen's wife, Karen, straightaway, and his daughter. Sarah looked exactly as Karen had at her age. Glen's genes hadn't had much of a look-in.

The big surprise was Phil. He had never been anything special, looks-wise, and had cruised along doing the minimum. Until she had left in grade nine, anyway. In maths, he had always sat behind her, his long legs reaching under her chair. Always chatting and joking. In the end he had become a bit annoying, or she had thought so at the time. All he really did was stay steady, while she was intent on her own private shipwreck.

He had matured into a handsome older man, tall and still slim. He had a way of looking right at you, while you spoke, though he had to bend his head down a little to do so. His eyes, behind round glasses, reminded her of those of a robin – much larger, of course. But perhaps it was just the yellow in his checked shirt, and the neat grey of his jacket.

Henry was there, too, with Kay. Wearing his suit. He made his way through the crowd. 'Hey.'

'Henry, this is Phil,' she said. 'We went to school together.'

Henry shook Phil's hand, nodded.

'Pleased to meet you, Henry,' Phil said. 'I hear it's been a tough year.'

Henry shrugged.

Jen put her hand on his shoulder. 'Henry's going to St Albans next year, to do their arts program,' she said.

'That's quite hard to get into,' Phil said.

Henry grinned. 'Jen helped me,' he said. 'She's helped me a lot.'

The music from inside the church swelled, the doors opened and people began to file in.

'Should we?' Phil said, and offered her his arm.

Jen smiled. He hadn't learned those manners around town. Glen had said he was a widower now, but she hadn't wanted to ask any questions. She sat in the second row, behind Michael's family, and between Phil and Glen. They each gave her plenty of space on the pew, not moving even when people started pushing up along the rows. Michael's mother turned and smiled. Jen did her best to smile back.

Aunt Sophie turned up just in time, on Maeve's arm. They tottered to seats on the other side of the church.

The minister had a pleasant voice, for which she was thankful, because he spoke a lot. Michael's father, in a suit rather tight about the middle, acknowledged the community for its support, the police, his family. Someone read a poem by

Wilfred Owen, the war poet. No one had approached her to see if she would like to speak. Although she would probably have refused, it would have been nice to have been asked. Perhaps she could have recited a few quotes from *Rocky*, and made people laugh, but more likely it would all have fallen flat. Or she would have fallen flat herself.

The light came in all colours through the stained glass. At the end they stood, as one, to say a prayer for Michael and missing children everywhere. All down the rows, they held hands, schoolchildren again. The words, and the warmth of the men beside her, were too much and she cried. For Michael.

———

Aunt Sophie found Jen afterwards and wrapped her in a parent's embrace.

'Thanks for coming,' Jen said.

'I wouldn't have missed it,' Aunt Sophie said. 'It was a lovely service, don't you think?'

'It was,' Jen said.

Glen made his way through the crowd. 'We're going up to the hotel for a drink,' he said. 'Maybe a meal. Would you like to join us?'

Jen looked at Aunt Sophie.

'Karen can drop you both home if you prefer,' Glen said.

'You should go, Jenny,' Aunt Sophie said. 'Maeve's cooked us something, and she and I have some catching up to do.'

'Okay,' Jen said.

Glen smiled. 'That's sorted then.'

Aunt Sophie leaned in to kiss Jen's cheek. 'I might drop in on my way home tomorrow?'

'Do,' Jen said. 'I'll bake something.'

The sun was shining, scrubwrens chirruping in the church hedges. Mowers hummed all over town, reining in the summer's growth now that it had slowed.

Phil was leaning on the open door of the ute, watching a flight of black cockatoos lope past. He turned and smiled. 'I've missed those,' he said.

She slid onto the bench seat, between the two of them again.

'Whoa,' Phil said, at first sight of the pub. 'That's quite an upgrade.'

'Three mill,' Glen said, and reversed into a shady park. 'They have proper bands there now and everything.'

She let the men lead the way into the bar, where ten or fifteen of their classmates were already clumped together.

Phil turned. 'Can I get you a drink, Jen?'

'Schooner of Gold, please.'

A slight shift of his eyebrows suggested surprise. What should she have ordered? A glass of white wine?

'Glen?'

'Schooner,' he said.

Jen scanned the crowd. 'Karen's not coming up?'

Glen shook his head. 'Taking Sarah home. She'll come and get us later.'

'What did you think of the service?' she said.

'Good,' he said. His eyes were a little red. 'Great to have so many of us there.'

'Yes,' Jen said. 'He would have liked that.'

Phil returned with their beers. A middy for himself.

'Cheers.' They clinked glasses.

'To Michael,' Phil said.

'To Michael.'

'You're a brave man ordering a New in this town,' Glen said.

Phil held the beer up. 'You can tell by looking at it?'

'Saw the barman's face,' Glen said. 'And his hand on the tap.'

'They wouldn't have it if they weren't prepared to serve it.'

Glen turned away to talk with his football pals, more gut than muscle these days.

'Glen said you live in Sydney?' Jen said.

Phil nodded. 'Have done since I left, except for a stint in the Blue Mountains.'

'Do you like it?'

He sipped from his beer. 'Not much. But my work has been there. And my daughter's in her final year of school. I felt like I had to stay put when her mother died. Keep as much as I could the same.'

'She'll appreciate that. Later, I mean.'

'Do you get down to Sydney at all?'

'No.'

His eyes crinkled at the corners. Amused at her country ways, perhaps. 'My daughter wants to go to uni in Brisbane,' he said. 'To do astrophysics of all things.' He smiled. 'So I'm looking at moving back this way.' He watched her over his glasses.

'And what's your work?' she said.

Glen turned, as if to catch the answer, though surely he already knew.

'I lecture at Sydney Uni now. But I'm an ornithologist by training,' Phil said.

Jen had to concentrate on keeping her face blank and her hand tight around the slippery glass. 'Really?'

He grinned. 'I gather you're still quite fond of birds yourself.'

Glen manoeuvred back between them. 'Phil here paid a visit to the gallery yesterday,' he said.

Phil had gone quite pink about the cheeks.

'Oh?'

'I went to your exhibition,' he said. 'It was wonderful to see so many pieces, and the sense of development over time.'

She smiled. 'Including one of yours on loan, I understand. Thank you.'

'Another beer?' Glen held up his empty glass.

'Sure,' Phil said.

'Jen?'

'Please.'

They watched Glen's back as he threaded his way to the bar.

Phil cleared his throat. 'Jen, I'm sorry I wasn't a better friend back then.'

Jen filled her mouth with beer, swallowed it. 'But you were.'

Notebook

Jen heard the car turn in and for a moment thought she had forgotten Henry's visit. She put down her pencil and focused on the world. It was Monday, and Henry didn't come for classes anymore. She pushed her chair back from the desk and stood. A policeman was walking down the path, hat under his arm, a yellow package in the other hand.

Jen shut her studio door, checked herself over. Her drawing shirt was worn and stained but covered her sufficiently. Her shorts were cleanish. Her hair not too greasy. She greeted him through the screen door. 'Morning.'

'Morning, Ms Anderson. Sergeant Evans, we met at the station a few months ago.'

She could hear her blood rushing in her ears. Feel her breath shortening. 'Of course, come in.'

He wiped his feet and followed her into the kitchen. 'Nice and cool in here,' he said.

'Tea, water?'

'Water would be good.'

She poured them both a glass from the jug in the fridge.

'Thanks,' he said. 'I saw something in the paper about you doing some work for the mayor?'

'A commission, yes. Something for the council chambers and the new library foyer.'

'Well, that's one decision people will be happy with.'

'I hope so.' Jen sat, perched on the edge of the chair, hands folded in her lap.

'As you probably already know, Mathew Fergusson has now been charged with the murder of Caitlin Jones, and his uncle, Callum Fergusson, for the murder of Michael Wade.'

'Yes.'

'In the course of our enquiries, we did find some information about your father and I see no reason why we can't now share that information with you.'

Jen's throat constricted, to the point where she could only get out a squeak.

The sergeant lowered his voice. 'First. He does not appear to have had any involvement with the murders of either child.'

She breathed in, eased the air out.

The sergeant sipped his water and set the glass down on the table. 'As you know, your father would now have been in his seventies.'

Past tense. A tear escaped, despite her best attempts to sniff it back in. Ridiculous. To have hoped. Still. She was a slow learner.

'In June 1977, your father relocated to Perth. He appears to have begun a new life.'

Jen looked up.

'He worked in the forest industry over there for a time, under the name of David Jenner. And in 1988 he remarried and had another family. Two boys.'

Jen stood and reached for the tissues on top of the fridge. 'Sorry.'

He waited for her to compose herself. 'He retired in 2004, moved down to Albany.'

She blew her nose. The cicadas quietened outside.

'Unfortunately, he passed away last year,' he said.

'Last year?'

'In April. I'm sorry.'

She blubbered now and couldn't rein it in.

He sipped his water and set the glass back down on the table. 'We have no firm evidence of this, but there were some problems around a development site in town at that time,' he said. 'Some work your father was doing?'

Jen blew her nose. 'Yes?'

'There were some questions about the site. It had been an old depot, and the soil was never tested. The men clearing it knew it wasn't safe.'

'Okay.'

'Someone called the press. There was an investigation, and the thing never went ahead. Some people around here lost a lot of money.'

How had she missed all that? It must have been in the papers.

He opened his hands. 'I'm really just guessing here, but I think it might have been your father. The timing. The name change. And he was a bit of a greenie?'

'Yeah.'

'It would have been difficult for him to come back,' he said. 'He pissed off some pretty serious people. It might have brought trouble for you and your mother, too.'

'Maybe.'

'Some of those people are still around.' He pushed the package across the table. 'There are a few things here his family thought you might like to have.'

Jen touched the stapled yellow edge. Another envelope. She was the curator of her father's life. Lives.

'The family would like it if you got in touch. There's a number in the parcel,' he said. 'One of the sons lives on the east coast.'

Jen blinked.

'If and when you want to.'

'Okay.'

He looked at the clock behind her. 'Will you be all right? Is there someone you can call?'

'I'm fine,' she said.

He hesitated but stood. Required elsewhere, no doubt. 'I'm sorry it wasn't better news.'

'I've waited a long time with no information at all.' A lifetime. 'Thank you.'

———

She sat staring at the package. Held hostage once again by the possibilities of the contents. The day had escaped her now, she was outside its rhythms. She put on the kettle for tea, made it strong and sweet. Half a capful of brandy for good measure. 'For shock,' as her mother used to say.

She slit the end with the kitchen scissors. Tipped it all out on the table. She placed a finger on one item at a time, dragged it closer. Two photographs of her, one as a child, the other her individual school photograph the year before he left. The one with the stupid grin.

A notebook containing a handwritten list of J. Vogels: phone numbers and addresses, with lines ruled through them. Dates. Fuck. He had begun looking after she had changed her name.

And there was his old watch, with the pale blue face, the glass dull with scratches and chips – but still ticking.

——

She snuggled into the doona, curled around her pillow. The sun was up but hidden by light cloud, giving the world a gloomy feel. Mist ribbons clung in the valley, water dripped from leaf to leaf. Her bedding was damp – her nest water-resistant rather than waterproof – but gaps in the weave allowed air and light to filter in. She was a nesting bird.

Perhaps, from here, she could take flight and leave the land altogether. Leave this life. She swung a little, and turned.

A robin landed on the opening, head cocked, feet hooked over a stick within the nest she had woven. That cheery splash of yellow.

'Morning,' she said.

The bird stayed, looking right at her, and chirruped.

Release

Jen walked around the garden, admiring all of the new growth and noting new invasions to be tackled. It was pretty good, being here. Being back here. Birds, after all, leave and return, build new homes in old places, their lives defined, in the end, by a relatively small patch of territory. Their patterns, flight paths and habits were their own, though driven by something larger, and shaped by the seasons, the forest, the rain, the earth.

She stopped beneath her nest. The colours had already dulled, such that it would soon be almost invisible to anyone else. It swung in the breeze, tempting her to climb up with a book and pillow.

'Ha.' She found the leaf she had been looking for. Dry but undamaged, and large enough to write on. From a brush box. She carried it up to the house, bird and cicada song building to full-pitch. How had she ever thought her forest a place of quiet?

She wrapped *Robins Bathing* in newspaper and found some green hemp ribbon to tie around it, and sat down at the table to write on the leaf-card.

She had been up at five to bake chocolate cake while the air was still cool, all the fans on to keep the humidity down. She iced it now using a palette knife; melted chocolate was somewhat easier to work than oils. Her veins were raised across her wrist. Cicada song rose to a shriek then fell away, like a pulse.

Scrubwrens chittered about the lomandra by the deck, a new generation or two swelling the numbers.

————

She fetched the drill box from the shed, wanting to hang *Flightless Bird* before she tripped over it again. The drill battery was flat, and she had to grip the machine between her legs to pull it free. Like most tools, it was not designed for a woman's hands. Although hers were not particularly small or fragile, she could not reach around the battery to push both lugs and release it one-handed. She could have bought a smaller one but it lacked the power for drilling into brick and hardwood. And the spare battery only came with the larger 'tradesman's' models.

Craig had once said women weren't suited for power tools. He had been in a bad mood at the time. She had left the drill bit in the chuck, instead of returning it to its little stand, though she suspected it was more to do with her finishing off the bird feeder that he had left in pieces in the carport for five weekends.

Jen exchanged the battery for the spare, jamming the other on its roost to charge. Any woman could operate a drill or a sander. The real problem was that men didn't bother building tools to suit women, thereby enforcing their own rules.

The bit struck some sort of knot or burl and complained. She had to finish driving in the screws by hand, sweating even in her singlet. She hung the frame, adjusted it and stood back. Polished the glass with a soft cloth. It wasn't the perfect spot, the afternoon light glaring a little on one side, and she worried about hanging what was essentially a self-portrait in the dining room, but it would have to do. She returned the drill to its box, the bit to its roost, and packed away the battery and charger.

Aunt Sophie had pronounced the painting her best work. It wasn't true, but most people responded better to portraits than trees and birds. And oils were always so much more definite.

Aunt Sophie had left a book about Stan. He was a painter, too. Abstract. Large scale. Not her thing – but quite big in the States in his day. Apparently he didn't paint much anymore, which was curious. As if you could stop what you do. Who you are. Soph had given her his email address, too. 'For when you're ready,' she'd said.

Henry was running down the steps, thongs flip-flopping, although there had been no car in the drive. He was in the door before she had even filled the kettle. 'Hey, Henry.'

'Hey.'

'Your mum didn't drop you off today?'

'She said now that I'm going into high school I can walk. And Dad bought me an iPhone! So I can call if I'm running late or whatever.'

Jen wiped her hands on her shirt front and leaned over his shoulder to peer at the bright screen. 'Wow.'

'We've been buying all my things for next year,' he said. 'This year.'

'That sounds like fun.'

'We got the stuff you said, plus everything on the school list,' he said. 'I wanted to bring it all, but there was too much to carry. I took pictures, though.' He held up an off-centre shot of brushes and inks and paints and blades and pencils all laid out on a table.

She smiled. His parents were really getting behind him now. 'It will be nice to have all your own gear,' she said. 'How long till you start?'

'Week after next,' he said.

'The holidays have gone fast.' She hadn't done anything about looking for another student. She wasn't sure she wanted to. Maybe if she had a couple at once, she wouldn't get so attached to them. Though, with the commission, she could probably manage for a while

'Reckon,' he said.

'So, let's have some afternoon tea.'

She walked to the stove and clicked on the gas. 'I baked chocolate cake.' She cut two large slices. If there was an upside to the end of the lessons it was that she would eat less sugar, without the baking. But then, she had become fond of a few slices of cake each week. Her elbow poked a hole in her worn shirt, inviting mosquito attack.

'What about your other subjects?'

'I got into the Summit program, too. So I'm in the top English and maths, and I'm going to do Japanese.'

'Hey, that's great. Your mum must be pleased.'

'We didn't really think I'd get into both.'

'It's fantastic, Henry.'

He shoved cake in his mouth and washed it down with milky sweet tea.

She touched the sketchbook he had brought with him. 'Have you been doing some drawing?'

'A comic strip,' he said, his mouth still gluggy with cake.

'Let's see it, then.'

He flipped the cover open. The title page featured a boy and girl either side of a gnarly tree. *The Black Forest*.

'The title was Dad's idea,' he said. 'There's a fire, but they save the town.'

Jen turned the book around to flip through the pages. 'This is really good, you know. Your ink work is great. And I like the trees here,' she said. The girl's face was a little like Caitlin's, though more elfin. And the boy a taller, squarer-jawed version of Henry.

'I haven't quite finished it,' he said. 'I'm not sure about the ending.'

'It will come,' she said. 'More cake?' She stood.

Henry pointed at the portrait behind her. 'She looks good there,' he said.

'It's the only wall long enough.' She placed the cake in front of him. 'Tuck in,' she said. 'I have something for you.' She fetched the parcel from behind the laundry door. 'A good luck present for high school,' she said.

'Thanks!' He ripped off the paper but stopped when he caught a glimpse of the robins. 'No one bought it?'

She laughed. 'It was never for sale. It's yours.'

'Thank you.' He stood and leaned towards her for an awkward hug. 'But it had a sold sticker on it, at the gallery.'

'I put that there,' she said. 'When you weren't looking.'

'Sneaky.'

Maureen had said several people had asked about the piece, and *Flightless Bird*, including the city fellow who had bought *Bird Man*, hoping she would change her mind and let him have the pair.

'Good cake.'

'Thanks.'

Henry nodded at the birdbaths. A king parrot pair; one bath each. For a moment, it looked as if the female was going to step into the water, but then she dipped her beak and drank. And dipped again.

'Nearly,' Henry said.

Kay pulled into the drive. Henry's shoulders dropped, and Jen had to subdue a fluttering in her chest.

She followed him up to the car, focusing on the sun on her face, the breeze shifting her hair. He threw his bag in the back and climbed in next to his mother, still holding the robins.

'Look,' he said, holding up the picture.

'That's very generous of you, Jen.'

'Great news about school,' Jen said, through the open window.

Kay smiled. 'It is, isn't it?' She patted Henry on the back. 'He's done well,' she said. 'You've been a great influence on him, Jen. Thank you.'

'Henry is very talented. And a good worker.'

Henry raised his hand in a peace sign. 'Later.'

'Good luck, Henry,' she said. 'Drop in sometime and tell me how you're going.'

She turned her back on the car reversing out of the drive and away onto the road, the crunch as it hit tar and then faded away.

The afternoon light was softening, the sun slipping behind the mountain. She stopped at the top of the steps. A pair of black cockatoos swooped low and close, right across the clearing. The slim trunks gathered in a little closer. Her robins chirped and piped their evening song.

Waterways

Jen took another tray of sedges from the back of the ute and headed down to the creek bed. They were replanting along the banks, where they had removed lantana over the last year.

Within her section, she worked her way downhill, leaving the softer soil for last. It was a process: removing a trowelful of soil, squeezing the punnet and freeing the sedge upside down, fingers either side of the plant stem, before righting it and burying it again.

Something flew overhead, and green-thighed frogs quacked, like little ducks.

Lil came around with her backpack-mounted reservoir, watering in the new plants. 'Nice job there, Jen.'

Jen smiled. 'Thanks.'

'Not sure why I'm bothering,' Lil said. 'It's going to rain.'

Jen looked up at the sky. 'Really?'

'It's a world unto its own in here.' It was true. They were in a kind of hollow, the water and undergrowth absorbing sound, and the canopy shutting out the sky. The creek deepened and widened to cup a pretty waterhole, reflecting green.

'I love it,' Jen said. 'Best project we've done. Well, I've done, anyway.'

Lil tucked her white hair behind her ears. 'Waterways are the most satisfying, I reckon. This one was small enough to get perfect.'

'How's your mother?'

'Crazy as ever,' she said. 'But you were right. Putting her in the home was the best thing I ever did. For the both of us.'

The others were starting to pack up, whacking the soil from their trays and stacking them on the back of the ute.

'I'm glad it's working out,' Jen said. She could feel, now, that the air temperature had dropped, and the low cloud cover had brought down a kind of hush – a feeling of expectation. 'I'd better get these last ones in.'

'I'll fetch the mulch,' Lil said.

The soil was loose and dark, perfect for receiving new seedlings. Jen alternated tussock rush and tall flat sedge, edging back towards the water.

'How's your place going?' Lil said.

'Slowly,' Jen said. 'I'm considering dedicating my life to lantana.'

'Are we helping you with the replanting?'

'Some. And I got the grant. Three hundred seedlings.'

'That's great!'

Jen smiled. 'Well, I have you to thank. I wouldn't have found the right words.' She patted down the last rush, waited while Lil watered it in, and then began piling up the mulch around it.

'Give me a yell when you're ready to start planting.'

'I will.' Lil would have clever ideas about where to place things – and Jen could use the help.

It started to rain, big drops far apart spotting Lil's shirt. Jen got to her feet, stiff from so much up and down, particularly the down.

Lil grinned. 'Told you.'

They watched the rain pocking the pool's surface, sending up silver teats. For once, the weather's sense of timing was spot on. It was all Lil, she was the regeneration guru; even the rain fell in line.

'You coming, Lil?' Mitch said. 'It's going to bucket down.' Dan, in the back of the dual-cab, was winding up the windows.

'I can give you a lift home if you'd like,' Jen said.

'Thanks.' Lil waved the men off and Mitch reversed up the lane, leaving them alone with the slap and splash of the water.

'Beautiful, isn't it?' Lil said. The waterhole was rimmed with rushes and sedges, not a weed in sight. The creek swelled upstream.

Their hair was plastered to their heads, their shirts already wet through.

'Let's swim,' Lil said. 'We're soaked anyway.' She slipped out of her clogs, peeled off her shorts, shirt and skin-tone undies and bra, and ran down the bank naked, throwing herself in the water with a shriek.

Jen stood in the rain, beside the pile of discarded clothes. She pulled off her boots and socks, struggled out of her jeans and unbuttoned her top.

'Come on! It's gorgeous,' Lil said.

Jen slipped and slid down the slope into the water, laughing and splashing.

Acknowledgements

Thanks to Bernadette Foley, Kate Stevens and Elizabeth Cowell for nurturing the best-shaped *Nest* from my manuscript; Emma Kelly, for the gorgeous illustration and Christa Moffitt for the cover design; Anna Egelstaff and my extended Hachette family, for giving my books (and me) the support an author dreams of; Nike Sulway, who knows more than anyone where this story came from, for valuable first draft feedback; Barbara Simpson, whose support makes it possible for me to continue to write; Ellen van Neerven, for the line on page 142, and the conversation that flowed from it.

Jen's 'treebed' and accompanying wilderness memory is taken from true accounts of wild tree climbing as described in Richard Preston's *The Wild Trees*.

Inga Simpson began her career as a professional writer for government before gaining a PhD in creative writing. In 2011, she took part in the Queensland Writers Centre Manuscript Development Program and, as a result, Hachette Australia published her first novel, *Mr Wigg*, in 2013. *Nest*, Inga's second novel, was published in 2014, before being longlisted for the Miles Franklin Literary Award and the Stella Prize, and shortlisted for the ALS Gold Medal. Inga's third novel, the acclaimed *Where the Trees Were*, was published in 2016. Inga won the final Eric Rolls Prize for her nature writing and recently completed a second PhD, exploring the history of Australian nature writers. Inga's memoir about her love of Australian nature and life with trees, *Understory*, will be published in June 2017.

www.ingasimpson.com.au